Sunset Across The Rockies

To complete Pamela's circle of Morgans,
this last India volume is for:
Alece
Antoinette
and
Melissa

AUTHOR'S NOTE

The opportunity to take Lottie on a journey of three volumes, rather than the customary one, has proven most rewarding and exciting to me. The fabric of her life has been woven more intricately and richly, with vital threads interlaced and lovely designs more nearly completed, so that a sense of the whole can be grasped.

I would like to express appreciation to my dear friend Mark Killgore. Volume 3 could not have become a reality without his generous, patient assistance as I attempted to master the mysteries of the computer through whose voice, for the very first time, one of my books has been told! I also appreciate the willing assistance of Adam Morgan who provided me with insights and expressions representative of the Italian Saints I wished to include in this story.

I am particularly grateful for the interest and support—even the prodding insistence—of my readers and fans who waited impatiently for each new installment of Lottie's life and adventures. Many of their insights and observations—even their requests—were invaluable to me. The spirits of sensitive and discerning readers, mingled with the spirits of the characters, make the books come to life. This I know, and this I acknowledge with gratitude!

SUSAN EVANS MCCLOUD
Provo, Utah
May 1997

CHAPTER ONE

Life is a journey of growth and discovery. Sometimes we walk with our eyes closed, in fear; sometimes with heads bowed, in weariness and anguish of heart; sometimes we laugh our way lightly through, scarcely noticing the ruts and rocks that would hamper our way. Sometimes we learn, and sometimes we choose blindness—feigned ignorance our only defense against the pain of growth and unwanted knowledge. Some men never think or reason, question or wonder, but wander aimlessly through life, putting their time in because they have to, then at length fade away, never having tasted, never having anguished, failed, or overcome—empty vessels, like whited sepulchres.

For ages, great thinkers of great moral fibre have attempted to explain mankind to itself. Sometimes they stumble upon truths, or their spirits are pure enough to be touched and enlightened. But we still know so little of what we are—and what we yet may become. Our Father in Heaven has told us: "my thoughts are not your thoughts, neither are your ways my ways." So it seems to me there is only one answer for us: to learn his ways as much as we are able, to walk them as well as we can, imperfect though we may be. I have not found this easy during the years of life I have passed through. It requires concentration of will and energy of soul. It requires faith in him and dedication to the highest within ourselves. But what other way is preferable to this—to the freedom and light and eventual joy of this way?

I will begin with September of 1855, seven years after we entered the Valley of the Great Salt Lake—nearly fourteen years since a ship leaving Liverpool brought Seth and myself to America with our hodgepodge family: Winston, who was not the natural child of either of us; Sarah Elizabeth, who was only mine; Grace, born shortly before

1

we left England, who indeed was the child of our love; and Emma, erstwhile friend and companion, who one could say, in an odd way, simply came along for the ride.

England. I remember my terror at leaving my home in India to go there. My experiences in that place all seemed tinged with the shadow of suffering; yet, all I am now, all I ever hope to become was brought to life on that cold northern island I came to love.

The fact that my best friend, Merin, was marrying my brother Arthur proved to me how inexplicable the ways of God are. *Arthur here? And a convert to Mormonism?* Both of his parents would turn over in their graves at the thought. I smiled to myself: *Arthur is no more my real brother than is Winston my son.* We were raised together by his parents, Ralph and Constance Reid, in the British station at Barrackpore, and since his sister, Roselyn, died when we were but girls, I became the only sister he had. He and Hugh, two years his junior. And, for all intents and purposes, they *were* my brothers. Yet, when life so cruelly separated us, I would never have dreamed to one day be united with him in a cause so inexorable and intimate as the gospel of Jesus Christ.

On this September day the desert had been refreshed by an early-morning shower that left a crispness to the air which the hot sun could not quite dispel. Autumn flowers still bloomed in profusion—hollyhock and asters, sunflowers and sweet honeysuckle, defying the inhospitable desert soil. From our own garden we picked armfuls of English lavender and selected the most fragrant from among our roses to weave into a garland to grace the bride's luxuriant auburn hair. Thanks to Julian Winters's generosity and taste, Merin had lace mittens for her hands, a fan made of ivory and silk, a shawl of the most exquisite Brussels lace, and flowers of silk ribbon to adorn the pale modesty of her plain satin gown. I thought she looked as fresh as any of her daughters or mine, who were half her age. Arthur was a bit somber. He has always been of a serious, reflective bent, like his father. Only the tender light in his brown eyes betrayed him. And, oh, he did look the gentleman that he was, with his gray-striped trousers and swallowtailed jacket. A gentleman. An English landowner of means and refinement. I wondered what place there might prove to be for such creatures here.

Everyone I cared about was there at the wedding, which we had meant to be rather a modest family affair. But Emma came all the way from San Francisco and got together with Susie, both of whom have more money than they could possibly need. Together they stirred up more magic than I have seen since the gala officers' affairs when I was a girl at Simla.

But that was all well and good. Merin had waited long enough for happiness, and I do not believe Arthur knew what the taste of it was. I enjoyed watching the two of them move among their guests, his arm round her waist, her face lifted to his whenever propriety would allow it. If the pure joy in her eyes cut my heart with the sharpness of a razor, it was a clean wound I could understand and accept. Emma was a different matter altogether.

"Could have been you," she chirped, coming up behind me, her cockney accent only slightly softened by the passage of years.

"It could not have been," I countered. "Merin is in love, quite obviously so, and I never was."

"You never let yourself be." She poked me gently in the ribs. "That was a decision, missy, which you made for yourself up here." She tapped her forehead with a plump finger. "If your heart had anything to say in the matter, you did not give it a chance to be heard."

What do you know of my heart? I thought, a little bitterly, recalling her eagerness to interfere, to use her money and worldly influence to bear upon my own daughter's decisions and eventual course of life.

"You be too pretty a woman, Lottie," she continued to blare out. "You always were. Too pretty to be wasted."

I wondered, a little uneasily, how many swigs Emma had taken from the little flask she carried inside her deep pocket. "Leave it alone, love!" I hissed under my breath. Then, hoping to turn the subject even a little, I added, "I don't see you with a husband right now."

Emma laughed heartily. "Give me a six-month," she cried. "I just can't make my mind up about which one to accept."

It was true. Despite the breadth and size of her loud demeanor and florid appearance, she attracted men to her. She always had. She had married three times since reaching America, not to mention the husband left behind in England. "It is her tender heart, bigger than anything else about her," Seth used to say. But, nowadays, I did not feel so certain of that.

Of course, Emma's lavish gift was the highlight of the day. I should have guessed what she would do. Money was not an object with her, and the last time she came to Zion she had been vexed to learn what Merin and I had done.

She led bride and bridegroom, blindfolded, into Susie's large parlor, the rest of the assemblage following noisily along. It was gratifying to see Merin's expression when Emma pulled off the cover and unveiled a lovely rosewood piano much like the one she had sent to Nauvoo for us, but on a grander scale. Merin had not expected it; I could see that, and her delight was contagious. She ran to hug Emma, her eyes brimming with tears. Then she turned to me.

"Where would I be," she whispered, "if I had not run into you that day in Nauvoo? All the joy in my life, all the purpose—"

I shook my head. "Merin, Merin," I protested, "you bring beauty and goodness with you wherever you go."

Our eyes met, and that moment, for me, was the most perfect part of the day.

It grieved me that Winston was not with us—the one person, outside of Seth, I most wanted there. He had been in Italy on a mission since Christmas, and Abbey had carried on gallantly while he was gone, not even telling him she was expecting their second child until weeks before it was due. Her mother, whose skills have pulled me through many a tight spot, was there at the delivery, and so was I— there to see Winston Seth come into the world.

"Winston, yes," I told Abbey. "But Seth? What of your own father?"

"Seth," she answered, with amazing firmness. "You know how Winston feels."

I bit my tongue and nodded. Then, on impulse, I bent close to her. "It's a bit one-sided, don't you think?"

Abbey only smiled at me. "My mother understands," she said. "With me and herself there are already two Abigails; both Seth and I wanted Charlotte." Her eyes grew thoughtful. "Perhaps he loves you even more, Lottie, *because* you are not his real mother, and it is very much the same thing with Seth." She sighed. "There will be other babies. The next son for my father, I promise."

I could never tell her in a million years how painful it would be for me if they chose to call this child Seth rather than Winston or some other derivative. Thoughts of my dead husband were still painful, and I believed it would be a haunting feeling to call a growing child Seth, when every time I spoke the word it would conjure up visions and memories of *him*. Others might find it a comfort, but to me it would be placing the little one at a disadvantage. Oh well, it was petty to concern myself with such matters. When I gazed upon the child I was stricken by his resemblance to his father, especially in the line of his chin and around his eyes. I wondered if Winston's real mother was looking down, sharing this moment—the frail, pretty creature who lacked the tenacity to endure the harsh elements of India and the even harsher elements of her marriage.

Now Abbey was here, with her new son and her three-year-old daughter, her brown eyes glowing in the warmth of her freckled face, her waist looking nearly as slender as when Winston had married her. *I wish Winston could see her,* I thought, *and drink in the beauty of her presence when that halo of new motherhood yet envelops her.* I put my arms around the girl and drew her close for a moment. "Are you all right, sweetie?" I asked.

She did not give me a cursory or insincere answer; we were too intimate with one another for that. "Right now. Because the joy here is enough to uplift me and make everything else go away." She glanced down at her sleeping infant. "It will come later, when I am alone, nursing the baby, wishing Winston could see his little face nestled against me, touch the softness of his new skin."

I nodded. "I wish you were closer, so I could run over more often."

She looked a bit wistful. "So do I. Mother comes when she can, but nursing keeps her very busy. And, besides, I miss *you*. One person cannot compensate for another."

"We shall work out something," I promised. Davis County was up north, above Salt Lake City, and the small community where they lived was perhaps twenty miles away. But now, with Merin gone, I would certainly have extra time on my hands.

"The day has been perfect for a wedding, anyway," Abbey sighed. "Aren't you grateful for that?"

"I am," said a man's voice. "If the weather had been stormy, I could not have made it, and would have missed the chance to see the bride, and Emma . . . and you, Lottie."

I turned round to respond to the speaker, and, with a kindly wink, Abbey melted away.

"Maurice." I took in the sight of him. He was, by any measure, a handsome figure of a man. His dark hair, where it curled at his temples, was going gray. But the jut of his chin was just as firm as ever, and he gave the impression of strength that was solid, unbendable. "I am glad you did come," I said, meaning it. "But your wife—"

He shook his head. "Her child is due in less than a month, and she did not wish to travel." He paused for a moment, then began again. "Lottie?"

I looked up. The now serious brown eyes were watching me closely.

"Are you all right? I think of you often, I fear, and I worry about you."

I reached for his hand and squeezed it gently. "Bless you, Maurice. But do not worry. I am fine. I am where the Lord wants me; I feel certain of that."

He raised my hand to his lips with a sigh, then let it go with reluctance.

"You are now a grandfather," I said, "and soon to become a father."

He laughed with me at the absurdity of it. If his wife had lived, if his children had survived, he would not be starting this new family. But in these times and in this place regular patterns were altered. And, though much was sacrificed, the gain to each suffering soul was immeasurable: glory in the celestial kingdom of God and eternal life.

The bridal couple were ready to leave. I joined the bright group surrounding them and threw Merin a kiss. "Take good care of her, now," I told Arthur as I hugged him. But he needed no admonition. All that was tender and good in him had been waiting for this. He had seen the bitter unhappiness that selfishness can cause in a marriage. He had seen his own parents divided by weakness and fear and greed. He had seen, and he had also learned; he would make a good husband, indeed.

How deflated is the aftermath of such occasions, like a stale taste in the mouth and a bit of a fog in the head. I stayed to help Susie for a while, but then she shooed me home.

"You have children awaiting you," she scolded, "and I can pay to have this sort of work done."

I wondered if she had been terribly lonely since Aaron's death. She kept herself busy, with her finger in a dozen pies, all of them profitable, but she had no one, no parent or child or husband. The thought of that kind of aloneness devastated me. I kissed her plump, sweet-smelling cheek and departed. Emma had gone up to Farmington with Abigail and Abbey for a couple of days. She had already spent time with me. We had already talked about everything, save the subject of Sita, which we lately avoided. She would be anxious to get back to the bustle and glamour of San Francisco. Salt Lake and the Mormons moved at a pace she could neither understand nor countenance. *To each his own*, they say. But I love Emma, and it was difficult to go my way, and let her go hers.

Three days following the wedding a letter arrived from Sarah Elizabeth. A letter postmarked Bombay. I held it tightly in my grasp and realized I was trembling. My first thoughts were not of Sita. A flood of memories had begun to push against the walls of my heart, threatening nearly twenty years of intentional forgetting. Now Constance and the Major, gentle Dr. Fielding, Barrackpore with the scent of jasmine and the swishing sound of the tatties as they cooled the rooms; my horse, Cinnamon, and the monkey, Mischief; the child Winston, and Major Hillard, the first time I danced with him—all came flooding back, too much to bear at once! And, through it all, *him!* Karan, like a melody, like a haunting poem whispered on the wind, rising up now to torment me.

At last I sat and tore the letter open. It was longer than I had hoped for. I read it through quickly, hungrily, then once again slowly, savoring every word.

We have arrived safely, Mother dear, and before we head inland I knew I must write to let you know. There is so much I would like to share with you, and watch your face as I tell it!

7

The tender enthusiasm of that beginning amazed me; this was not the unhappy, resentful Sarah Elizabeth who had left. Could her own experiences be lending her, already, a measure of understanding?

The journey aboard ship was long, but uneventful. There were dances every evening, marvelous suppers, and several good-looking men to flirt with. But all I could think of, Mother, was you. You coming from India to England—you coming from England to America—you bearing a child in the middle of the waste of water, and that child being me! I felt I could almost see you, when I turned around of a sudden I would find you there—the young Lottie, with whom I suddenly feel much in common.

And now, in this place, I try to see it as it would have appeared to you: knowing it intimately, both loving and hating it; the smells and sounds familiar to you.

Aunt Marion promises we shall see Barrackpore, but probably not go as far as Simla. You are right; the food here is ambrosial compared to English food. I cannot get accustomed to the harsh class lines here, to see servants moving everywhere, with that slow, quiet dignity. To think of you in this setting, Mother, with a huge household and a dozen servants of your own to manage! It strains my mind, and it stretches my imagination.

So. We shall have a wonderful time. Do not worry. Marion takes good care of me, and has money enough that we live here as kings. But then, you know that—you know so much that I shall be learning and discovering.

Give all the girls a kiss for me. I miss everyone more than I thought I would. But I am well—truly. I am much better, as to inner matters, and my health has not suffered from the strains of travel nor the changes in diet and climate. You are with me, Mother, in a very real sense. I intend to record a diary of all that happens to bring home to you, and we can discuss it together. I hope you like that idea. Take care of yourself—not just everyone else.

Love, Sita

You must not hope for too much, I warned myself. This was already more than I had prayed for. She had been so determined to hate and punish when she went to England. Perhaps India had been a good idea, after all. But time! She had been gone for over a year already, and India was certainly prolonging that separation. At least I wanted to believe in my heart that it was. I could not accept the cruel, nagging chance that Sarah would never return to me, that she would prefer England and Marion and the ways of the world above home and family and the gospel. I could not face that as a real possibility, at least not yet.

CHAPTER TWO

It seemed good weather held through the wedding as an act of kindness. By the end of September we were having cold rains and high winds, which churned the ever-present dust into mud and tore the last blossoms from their stems. By the time of the general Church conference in early October, the rain had turned to wet snow, and by my birthday, when the dismal month ended, the colors on the mountains were fading and the air, pouring down from the canyons, bit with a winter sharpness.

As things turned out, I was all alone on my birthday. Seth's father, Kenneth, was ailing and I had sent Grace and Emma to help Phyllis, who normally had her hands full trying to care for him but was now ill with a cold. Merin and Arthur, newly returned from their honeymoon, were busy moving into their new house, which stood near the top of the hill close to Susie's. I knew Merin had not meant to forget me; at such times the days are difficult to keep track of. Besides, Susie's patronage, as one might call it, was proving a blessing to them. She had no children of her own, and she had taken a liking to Arthur, hiring him to help manage her several businesses, with the thinly veiled promise of a partnership if all between them went well. He deserved the security of such a situation, and he would do well with the challenges of organization and responsibility, being, in all of the good ways, his father's son.

I spent the quiet day doing things I did not usually find time for: putting the garden to bed for the winter, darning Emma's socks, cleaning the cupboards, which had become an untidy jumble with Merin's moving. There was a little more room now; that was the only advantage to having her gone. I would miss her help, the calming influence of her presence, the intimate conversations we shared. But I would miss most of all her music. Even without a piano she contrived a way to make song and laughter a daily part of our lives. I was sober beside her. I took life far too seriously, but then, I always had. *Thirty-seven. I could not be thirty-seven.* The numbers meant nothing to me. I was myself. And that self, though torn and battered by life, though at times bone-weary, had not really altered since the days in Barrackpore when I was eighteen and rode Cinnamon to the English cemetery and walked to Roselyn's grave . . . and met a young Indian officer as darkly handsome as any man I had ever looked upon.

All day I chided myself for letting such memories possess me. *It is this India thing,* I reasoned. *Knowing that Sita is there, wondering what is happening to her, I cannot help thinking, and then remembering.*

But I had made my inexorable choices long ago. No good came from this kind of remembering, which let in the uselessness of regret, of longing.

So the days passed, one after another. Both Grace and Emma Roselyn had begun a new session at Sister Shumway's common school; actually, Grace at fifteen would be assisting in instructing the little ones this year. I kept house and looked after them, and worked more and more hours for Julian as he pressed me. His business in ladies' goods and fancy apparel was not thriving as it had when we first came here, but it was holding its own, despite the pinch of the last few difficult years. He was loyal by nature, and he still placed a great deal of trust in what he called my "judgment and charm." "Worth paying for," he would say. "You're part of the spirit of the place. I do not wish sales clerks; they're a dime a dozen. I want a compatriot"—then, with a wink, "a partner in crime, as it were." He had made me a partner of sorts, signing over a small percentage of the business to me, "in lieu of the wages you deserve and are not getting," as he put it. His generosity at first made me feel uneasy until Winston, with his acumen, talked me out of it.

"He knows what you are worth, Mother, and that is much more than wages. You have enhanced his business as well as increased it. Besides, he wishes to keep you."

"Keep me?" I had asked, a bit puzzled.

"Yes. His generosity, as you choose to view it, obligates you to him. In other words, you will not walk away when the going gets rough, or you become bored or simply tired."

"The old tyrant."

Winston laughed with me. "Yes, in his way he is that. But a benign one, certainly."

I was fortunate, and I knew it. But how mundane my life was! I chafed against something I could not put a name to; I longed for impossibilities which could not be put into words.

Emma wrote soon after her return to San Francisco, requesting—nay, demanding in her blustery way—that I send the girls there for a visit. "That is impossible," I had responded. "They have their studies to attend to, and cold weather is about to set in."

That was in early October, and my prophecy proved correct; but it was only an excuse, really, and Emma saw through it. "Such a trip would be an education in itself, Lottie," she replied, "and you know it. Worth more than the bit of school learning they would miss."

But by the time her second letter arrived we were well into November and I could respond demurely and innocently something to the effect of "we must now wait till spring." Perhaps Emma did not truly recognize, much less admit, what she was doing. She had already influenced my eldest daughter away from me, even financing her headstrong foray into the world. Did she really believe she had some right to do this? I knew, despite her bravado, that she was lonely inside. She had no children of her own to fuss over; even back in England I had been aware of her disappointment in that regard. I remembered well how she worked to please and spoil her nieces and nephews, how liberally she had bestowed her affection on Winston and Sita when we needed it most. I owed her something for that, I supposed. But I did not owe her my children. I felt at times she was purposefully, if unintentionally, attempting to woo them away from me, away from a life she thought odd, unrealistic, and stifling, to say the least. Perhaps she did not realize how deeply her behavior wounded me, or perhaps she simply chose not to see.

As soon as she was settled, Merin proudly invited us over for a dinner in her new home, which boasted a real dining room, as well as a parlor, a marvelous kitchen, and three upstairs bedrooms.

"Susie insisted," Arthur explained. "Though it was beyond our means at present, she made the down payment a wedding gift."

"That was most like Susie," I responded, aware that Merin was watching me closely. She knew the pain her altered circumstances might cause me. We had been brave together for so long, suffering through the nightmarish days of Nauvoo, crossing the plains together, living in tents with the sagebrush and snakes for bedfellows. Indeed, in the beginning it was I who shared my fine Nauvoo house with her, rescuing her and her young daughters from the gloom of Widows' Row. Perhaps she felt guilty—sudden good fortune can do that to one. Although I felt a pinch of desire for the beauty and security she had achieved, I did not envy her the prosperity and happiness which had come to her; I loved her too much for that.

Of course, Gracie and Emma were much impressed. They were of an age to be delighted with the lovely things that their own lives lacked, with the romance which had come into Merin's rather drab existence in the shape of the handsome young uncle they had never known. Arthur was good with them, charming in his reserved English way and sincerely affectionate.

"I shall work hard," he announced, catching me alone for a moment. "Please do not think me foolish to take advantage of Susie's munificence. I truly attempted to refuse her, but she would have none of it. 'Let me do this,' she said, 'let something good come of my abundance.' Those were her words."

I smoothed his dark hair back from his worried brow; I could not help myself. "I have not censured you in my mind, Arthur," I assured him. "I know the extent of your integrity. I know the fine heritage you come from."

The darkness that flickered over his gaze for a moment saddened me. We shared many nightmares of shame and suffering, he and I. But his part in it was worse than mine, and my heart ached for him now. "You know I mean it," I pressed. "Arthur, my dearest, you steel yourself against the good and open your arms to the bad where your parents are concerned. Can you not yet reverse that process?"

He smiled a bit ruefully. "I believe with Merin's help I just might be able to."

"Yes," I sighed. "She has her own share of darkness to deal with." I thought of her daughter's stark grave on the prairie, of the two sons her husband had wrested from her when she joined the Mormon Church, entirely lost to her, for this life at least.

"Merin, my dear," I whispered as she said good-bye to us. "You must know how happy I am for you. Put your mind at rest and enjoy your hard-won joy." I hugged her to me for a moment and felt her relax in my arms.

"I'll come over next week," she called after us, "and we'll put up the last of the tomatoes."

I nodded in reply. But she did not come. The demands of her new life were too prohibitive. Instead, my twelve-year-old Emma Roselyn began going there. The piano drew her. Love of music had been bred in her since her baby days. Merin was only too glad to sit and work with her. She was perhaps not the best of teachers, but she knew how to inspire and enthuse. It was good for Emma to achieve, to begin to excel at something. She was the baby, and pampered as last children are. But, by the same token, she stood in everyone's shadow and had not yet found a place of her own. *This will be good for her,* I reasoned. So I picked up the slack when she left her chores undone and tried not to scold when she neglected her schoolwork in favor of practice and more practice.

But as the old year muddled to its close, I felt bereft in many ways. Winston was still gone; I had never spent a Christmas without him since I was nineteen. Abbey and the children were up in the north where I seldom saw them. Emma and I stood, for all intents and purposes, estranged. My oldest daughter was on the other side of the world doing heaven knew what. Merin, who was like a sister to me, was immersed in a new life of her own. My youngest was starry-eyed and preoccupied— and yes, if I would admit it, selfish, as Grace fully claimed.

Early in December Merin and I did manage to get together for a morning to make our famous mincemeat pies. At first it seemed a bit awkward, especially since she had talked me into coming to her house where we had much more elbow space and a large oaken table on which to roll out the dough. I was just relaxing, falling into the old intimate pattern, when fate contrived to try me again.

Of a sudden Merin's face turned white, and she groped her way to a chair. I was beside her immediately, but she waved a limp hand at me. "It is nothing, really. I just feel a bit dizzy." She sat for a moment with her face in her hands. "Would you like a drink?" I suggested. "A cool cloth on your forehead?"

She shook her head. "I must—I think I'm going to be sick, Lottie." She fumbled with the doorknob and stumbled out to the privy. By the time she came back, I knew, and the knowledge that should have been joy to me tugged at the lonely strings of my heart instead.

"Why didn't you tell me?" I demanded, before she had time to settle herself. "Were you going to keep it from me, a secret?"

"Lottie." She placed her small hand on my arm. "Forgive me, please. I was afraid to tell you. It seemed like flaunting, somehow, one happiness after another, when both of us always thought"—she took a deep breath and continued—"it would be the other way round."

"I made my choices. I don't regret them." My voice had risen; there was a strident note in it. Protective. Anger is always a protective measure with me. "I'm all right, Merin, and I'll be all right. It hurts most to see you walk delicately round me, to see you withdraw from what we always had together."

Merin's face was miserable. "You are right, Lottie. I have been blundering and foolish. I should have understood, I should have trusted you more."

I sighed and attempted a smile. "We've never covered this territory before. We'll make it."

"Together," she added, "as we always have."

"So when is this little one due?"

"Sometime in July, near the end, close as we can tell."

"Are you, well, all right about it?"

"I'm a little frightened at times. But, Lottie, to have a child again, and *his* child!"

"Arthur is pleased, then?"

"Very. Overwhelmed by the prospect, but not frightened or uncertain."

"You know his background. Fatherhood is a grave matter to him. He must succeed at this or he will fancy himself a failure at everything."

She nodded, but her eyes were shining. "It will be easier than he thinks it."

She is behaving like a newlywed, I thought. "It will also be harder," I added. "May I tell the girls?"

"Of course. I think Emma suspects something anyway."

"They will be pleased. And you must allow them to help when-ever you need it. What does your Drusilla say?"

A slight frown furrowed Merin's white forehead. "I don't want to tell her, Lottie. Her own baby is due so soon. I don't wish to detract from the excitement and wonder of her own experience." She cocked her head and looked at me a bit whimsically. "It can certainly wait until after her child is born. To tell the truth, I feel a bit foolish; this child will be younger than its niece or nephew."

"Such things have happened before."

"But not to me!"

We giggled like girls about the matter. But the gaiety of our mood did not sustain me as I went my way home. Merin was still involved. She had jumped with both feet into the very thick of the vital matters of life, and that very vitality is what shed a halo around her. Some-thing inside me threatened to panic. *I am too young,* I thought, *to be relegated to this dull, background position—a person whose life has been mostly lived, all the magic burned out. Nothing left, save to wait in the background while others take the roles of doers and creators.*

I suppose in a way I was feeling sorry for myself. When Christ-mastime came I realized with a start that the new restrictions were still being imposed on me. Drusilla was ready to give birth any time, so Merin and Arthur had decided to spend the holidays in Provo; and certainly that made sense. Three days before Christmas it began to snow—soft fluffy flakes like the ones I had first seen in London. By nightfall the temperature had dropped, a wind had risen, and a bliz-zard was in full force. When I awoke the next morning and pulled back the curtain to see snow still falling, I knew our plans for travel-ing up to Abigail's would have to be abandoned.

We prepared for the dubious adventure of being snowbound. Since we were on our own, I baked fewer pies and fruitcakes. But I did make a good English pudding, and indulged myself with spiced pumpkin, made with cardamon and red onion, and pullao rice, the only Indian dishes I had ingredients for. These younger girls of mine did not particularly like Indian food; that part of my life had no real-ity, I realized, in their eyes. Even to myself it had taken on an almost otherworldly, dreamlike quality.

My thoughts this day were not in India, but in London—that Christmas in London when my life reached such a dismal, low ebb: a widow and her two small children scarcely eking by in a dreary flat in Nine Elms Lane. I shuddered and pushed the memories away from me.

We played games and sang carols, and even Emma rallied to the gentle, hallowed spirit the sacred music drew forth. When we heard an energetic pounding at the door I was startled. It was late afternoon and still snowing outside. I glanced at Grace. "I'll get it, Mother," she said, rising.

"Perhaps it is Susie come in her sleigh to sweep us off with her!" Emma cried, half in jest, half in hopeful earnest.

It was a stranger who entered the parlor, shaking a layer of snow off his shoulders, a man in his early thirties with a thin, nicely curled mustache and kindly brown eyes.

"I apologize for interrupting your Christmas, Sister Taylor," he said. "But I have something I thought might complete the day for you."

He dug into his pocket and pulled out a much-worn letter, handing it to me with a flourish. "It's from your son. He gave it into my safekeeping when I left Italy several weeks ago and made me promise to deliver it here by Christmas, no later." He shrugged his shoulders and grinned. "Barely made it, I know. But I've been home less than a fortnight, with an old mother and a new wife to look after, and truth is, for a while there I nearly forgot."

I reached for it eagerly. *Winston.* "Were you his companion, then?"

"That I was. He brought me up by my bootstraps, I'll tell you. I've never known a finer young man."

My heart was pounding. "Did you leave him well?"

"Yes, ma'am, well and happy—happy as a man can be who is separated from his loved ones."

I nodded, holding the letter against me gently. "This is most precious indeed."

"Thought it might be." His grin softened into a contented smile. "Well, I'll be on my way, then."

"No! No, you must stay and warm up before braving the snow and cold again. Have a warm drink and something to eat."

He waved away my entreaties. "That's kindly of you, Sister Taylor, but I have a horse and wagon waiting outside, borrowed from a kind neighbor whom I should not keep waiting."

"Did you have trouble getting through?"

"A bit. But I don't live far from here." He had his hand on the door, but turned again to face me. "You know, when Winston gave me the letter he said, 'I believe my mother will need this, so you must not fail me, brother.' Winston is like that, isn't he? almost seeming to know what you're thinking. It rather spooked me at times."

I thanked him again, and after Grace shut the door behind him she said, "I believe Emma and I shall wash up the dishes now, Mother, and leave you for a while to yourself."

I sent her a trembling smile and tore with eager fingers at the envelope. The letter was neatly written, with small letters crowded into close lines. He told me about the work he was doing and the families he was teaching, and how generously the Lord was blessing them.

This is as foreign a place as I have been in since leaving India. But people are the same the world over, Mother, aren't they? Especially when it comes to families, and the love they feel for each other. I have been thinking much lately of the family you created for me, of Seth's gentle love and guidance—but even further than that, back to the first night you sat by my bedside in Barrackpore after my mother had died. I remember, Lottie, dear, my initial sight of you bending over me, your face framed in the halo of your auburn hair, like an angel, solemn and gentle. Mother dear, could either of us have dreamed at that moment all that would yet come to pass! I remember Dacca and your incredible courage—powerful enough to chase away the shadows of evil that surrounded us. I remember the storm aboard ship when we all thought we were dying, and the captain said we were doomed. You alone believed that God would deliver us. You alone believed in his goodness.

Mother, there are so many memories which my experiences here have called forth! It is autumn now, and even in Italy I can feel the difference. Elder Eakins is going home soon, so I am writing this to send with him. My thoughts have been turning to the coming Christmas season—that terrible Christmas in London; terrible, yet wonderful—when

heaven was so close we could touch it—when even despair did not con-
quer you. Mother, it never has. Not then. Not when Seth drowned—not
later when his body was found and we buried him—not when Abbey
and I were lost on the mountain.

I must close. Time and paper have both run out on me. But I must
tell you, Mother—remind you, so you will not forget it, how precious
you are to me. I am grown now, and making my own way, with the
devotion of a good and noble woman to help me. But, without you,
there would be nothing. Mother, I would be nothing. All that Abbey
loves in me has been brought forth by your hand. May God bless and
keep you. Happy Christmas from one who honors and loves you, your
son, Winston.

I clasped my hands over the papers to keep them from trembling.
Joy enfolded me, whispered a melody in my heart so that nothing
unclean or halt or broken could endure its song.

CHAPTER THREE

In the first crisp days of the new year a large, purple-tinged black-
bird perched himself on my fence post and sat unfluttered,
staring back at me when I went out to empty the dish water. I saw him
there morning after morning, determining that he must have a nest
nearby. He was a handsome, bold fellow, and would greet me with a
saucy cock of his head. I took, almost unconsciously, to feeding him
savory scraps from the table, like some kind of pet. Crows have always
been birds of omen to me, both for good and for ill. Back in the misty
beginnings of my existence, before I was even born, my mother broke
away from the Crim nation of thieves and highwaymen who called
themselves *crows,* and then was spirited away by them, stolen from her
almost idyllic happiness back to their black ways and back to a bleak
existence again. My bird remained there as winter melted into rivulets
of spring rain and mud, as the weak March sun greened the grass, and
flocks of seagulls, swooping and screaming, followed the furrows the
farmers made as they plowed their brown fields.

Mid-month March turned cold and blustery, ruffling the black-
bird's feathers as he hovered above the open fence line, then retreated
to the relative warmth of the still-barren trees. I shivered with him,
wondering when spring would warm the wet soil enough for planting. The girls were bored with their studies, often begging leave to
spend time at Merin's or Susie's, where something seemed always to
be happening. Most times I would give in and let them go. Merin had
a new granddaughter now, and her own time of waiting was more
than halfway through. Arthur was happy with his work, Susie even
happier. I stayed at home with the sleek-feathered crow, wondering
now and again what he omened—what fortunes he presaged for the
coming year.

April came, and the days were still bracing, the nights sometimes bitter, with a thin dusting of frost that remained till the sun burned it off. Early in the month a letter arrived from Sita. This time I was reluctant to open it, strangely fearful of what I might find. I let it sit three days on my desk, until I began to feel that its presence was mocking me, and I at last sat down with it firmly and broke open the seal.

This letter was short with a few halfhearted descriptions, and much less by way of endearment. The emotions of her initial reactions had obviously faded by now. It stated what I had feared, what something within me had instinctively anticipated:

> We sail for England in three days. I will write you as soon as we have safely arrived. I can in truth tell you nothing beyond this point, Mother. I am anxious to see Baddenwell, but I am not anxious to return to Zion—except for missing you. Do not worry, please do not worry about me!

Love to Merin and the girls, etc., etc. Well, that was that. It was my own fault to entertain hopes that were entirely unfeasible. She had obviously met no one—heard nothing. My past had no substance. She had walked the frail, clouded borders of my existence, and was coming away untouched. All I had been—all that had once been so real—would remain forever dark and unknown. I folded the letter carefully and stuck it back behind all the others, wishing I could so easily and tidily dispose of the emotions and sensibilities it had provoked.

I had no time to indulge myself. The following morning Kenneth took a bad turn, and in three days he was dead. I did not really mourn for him; his life had been difficult—purposeless, really—once Victoria died, and he had not been himself for these nine months or more. And, I suppose somewhat selfishly, I let his death bring back to my mind in stark relief the tragic death of his son and the darkness of those days in Nauvoo when all seemed dull and lifeless—yet, at the same time, raged with pain.

Then there was Phyllis, who, in a cruel way, had outlived her usefulness and now had no purpose, no direction in life. I could not bear to think of her staying on in that sad house alone. I was not certain what her age was, probably close to thirty, and marriage had not come to release her from the lonely prison of self. I hated the hunger I saw in her eyes when she looked on her sister's child. I pitied her the threadbare justifications she gave to support circumstances she had not chosen but somehow felt she must defend.

"Come stay with us," I urged her gently, "at least for a season, while you decide what to do."

I almost swayed her. In the end, however, she could not yield to desires which to her appeared weak. *I shall try again,* I thought, *and again, until I catch her at some moment when she will acquiesce.*

With the first days of May, spring came in earnest at last. And spring is a cleansing time, when the offenses of winter are forgiven and the scars it has left behind are mercilessly smoothed out and healed. Hope is as much in the air as the fragrance of flowers or newly mown grass. It had been a harsh winter; it had been a hard five years, and most people were anxious, even looking for reasons and ways, to forget. Julian, with his usual foresight and business acumen, was there to provide. He had arranged, with Emma's help, shipments of the latest in fashion from San Francisco and from the East. I believed he would regret it, but as usual his instincts were right. People flocked to see what he had to offer: bonnets and shawls, the latest in sleeves and cuffs and crinolines, and shoes—everyone seemed to be in need of new shoes that spring. We were so busy that Julian decided to extend the shop hours, and with daylight lasting longer and longer, I did not mind. One of the first to pore over his treasures like a young gosling was my own Emma.

"I must have the new muslin, Mother," she would urge, "and that delicate silk with the pattern of pale stripes."

Every day she had a new request, until Julian found a way to satisfy her. "Work for me," he told her, "and I will pay you in kind."

I was a bit put out. "You forget how young Emma is," I reprimanded.

He was unimpressed. "So, she is only thirteen. She looks all of seventeen, Lottie."

"Indeed, Julian? *That* is the point."

In the end we compromised a little. She could assist him in unloading shipments, setting out items for sale, and arranging displays—after hours, of course.

Grace had enjoyed working with the younger children during the school term. "I believe I should like to go for my teacher's certificate," she informed me, her gray eyes soft and serious.

"I will support that," I told her. "You have the gentle qualities of your father, as well as a fair share of his intelligence."

She smiled at me. "And what did I get from you, Mother?"

"Not your beauty," I laughed, "for even your gray eyes come from Seth."

I did not use his name often, even when referring to me. The sound of it always sent a shock through me, an unpleasant jolting one could almost call pain.

There was suddenly work aplenty: planting and weeding, cleaning, painting and repairing, and working in Julian's shop. Late in May Merin joined us and we took her new buggy up to Farmington to visit Abigail and Abbey and the little ones.

It was a beautiful day, fragrant with lilac blossoms and clean mountain breezes. The mountains wore a shining layer of new green, as if there were a gossamer gown draped across them, and I drank in the sight of them, thinking of that green land of England and how soon the desert sun would dry these tall flanks to a dusty brown. We ate fresh asparagus, which Abbey had planted, and ripe strawberries with cream. Abbey's eyes were shining, but I thought she looked a bit peaked, and when I mentioned the fact to Abigail, she smiled reassuringly. "The girl is simply working too hard. Not enough fresh air and sunshine. She has to have everything, including the children's clothes and manners, perfect, Lottie, as if Winston were coming home every night to inspect."

She looked at me, and I returned her sad gaze. " 'Tis a hard lot, indeed," I sighed, "to be a missionary's widow."

"Don't let her hear you," Abigail cautioned. "She is as devoted to the calling as he."

"Of course she is!" I cried. "They are both such truly noble spirits." I sighed again. "Sometimes, truly, too good and noble for me."

Abigail smiled. I had forgotten how very kind her eyes were. "What is it, Lottie?" she asked. "Why do you look at me so strangely?"

"I was just remembering," I said, "the first time I awoke and looked into your eyes. The kindness in them nearly undid me." She put her strong arm round my shoulders. "Your eyes and your capable hands."

"Lottie," she scolded, "you see only good in others, and only ill in yourself."

I laughed ruefully. "I believe the major bred that into me from the time that I was a child."

"More's the pity, then. And time to rid yourself of it."

"Oh, Abigail," I lamented, "it is so difficult being separated from you, having you away off up here."

"Yes, and now there are the children," she agreed, "and they need to be close to you, darling, part of your life."

How can we manage it? we both wondered. And so the conversation went, and so the sweet hours passed.

When I took Charlotte Elizabeth into my arms to say good-bye, I was struck by her resemblance to Abbey, the delicately molded lines of her face. When I told Abbey so, she smiled, pleased, but had to add, "She has Winston's eyes." It was true. The blue of them was as deep and rich as the still ocean waters when a storm stirs them, blue as a new robin's egg wet by the rain.

Little Seth was nearly nine months old now. He would be walking and talking before Winston came back. I gave him an extra hug and reluctantly climbed into the buggy beside Merin.

"A satisfying day, don't you think?" she exclaimed as we drove out into the lane. "And I am glad we have come before hot weather sets in."

I agreed. There is so much in life that is merely duty and drudgery. I had forgotten how precious, how renewing our moments with loved ones can be. I had needed the renewal, like a restoring spring tonic, more than I had realized.

It happened too quickly; no, Abbey had deceived us too well, so that it seemed to happen all of a sudden. When Abigail sent a neighbor down with word for me to come at once, I knew that the need had to be most serious, or she would not have summoned me at all.

I made arrangements with neighbors and gave my daughters their instructions. It was a very bad time to be walking away from Julian, but he kindly agreed to let the girls work in my stead temporarily, taking turns; so Emma ended up, as she often seemed to, getting what she had wanted in the first place.

Arthur drove me up in the buggy on a mild June evening. The lake shone alabaster beneath the color-washed sky, with luminous streaks of shimmering verdigris wherever the sun's rays touched it and brought it to life.

"Beauty has always undone you, Lottie, hasn't it?" Arthur said, startling me out of my reverie.

I flushed, nonplussed. "I forget how perceptive you are, Arthur."

"I observed you in India, all those years," he continued, "even though I was but a boy. I knew when my mother wounded and humiliated you. Sometimes I felt your loneliness, and watched the things that you turned to: flowers and music, poetry and writing, and riding Cinnamon like the wind, with all the other ladies looking after you enviously!"

"Arthur!" He was truly astonishing me. I reached over and took his free hand, glad for the moment and the brother I held so dear.

We rode in silence the rest of the way, needing no words between us—much as it had been that night when, lost and pain-ridden, he had stumbled into the far woods behind the grim house where his father had died and his mother now held her fevered sway. Then we had drawn upon the only thing that was left to us: love. Love, with its cleansing, renewing powers and tentacles of loyalty and faith that bound our two lives together with cords that were stronger than cruelty, stronger than death.

When we reached Abbey's small, tidy house, nestled against a gentle, rocky hillside, I fancied that all about it looked tense and still. I felt a tightening of all my muscles as Arthur helped me down from my seat and I walked stiffly toward the door. He kept his arm at my waist, like a support. "I will stay with you, Lottie, as long as you want me."

It was Abigail who admitted us, and the hushed air I had sensed was, in here, very real. Abigail's eyes told all, without a word spoken between us.

She led us into the dim front parlor. "The children are at a neighbor's right now," she said. "Abbey needs quiet and rest above everything."

She appeared tired; even the skin of her face seemed to sag. "You have been nursing her?" I probed. "For how long now?"

Abigail ran one of her broad, large-knuckled hands through her hair—a distracted motion I had not seen in her before. "She didn't tell me, Lottie. I've been nursing all her young life; she knows danger signs when she sees them."

"Why?"

"Trying to be brave, I suppose. Thinking it was just the cold she had last winter hanging on a bit, because she was tired and lonely—"

"And loathe to bother anyone!"

Abigail's mouth tightened. "That, too."

"She is very ill, then?"

"Fever every night, and a cough that gets worse day by day. Indigestion and a rapid pulse rate, and aches and pains everywhere, most especially a soreness in her chest."

I am so dim where such things are concerned! I still did not see where she was leading. "What?" I pressed.

"I had a doctor in, Lottie. One of the best I know of, from the city. He confirmed what I feared."

"Consumption." Arthur pronounced the word. It was as though he had let a black demon out to scream round our heads.

"What must we do?" I struggled to control the panic that pressed against my chest cavity.

"Rest, first and foremost. She must wean the little one and have the children kept from her, especially during their loud, fretful hours."

"Should I take them to my house for a spell?" I suggested.

Abigail shook her head firmly. "Not yet. She gets distraught at the mere hint of such a suggestion. And she must have peace to get well, more within herself than without."

The one thing we both were thinking was too large, too futile to bring forth and express. But, as if in answer to it, Abigail said ruefully, "Lottie, she talks foolishly. She feels guilty for getting ill and not caring properly for her children. I believe she fancies herself as somehow disappointing Winston's expectations. She made me promise, solemnly, to breathe no word of this to him."

"Am I bound by that promise?" I asked sharply.

Abigail's mouth went slack. "She said she would not have you here unless you agreed to those terms."

I rose, too distressed to hold still any longer. "The house seems chilly," I said, for want of anything better.

"Shall I build a fire?" Arthur asked, jumping to his feet.

"No. It can wait until morning, to drive off the early chill." I turned to my friend, steeling myself. "The children are in my hands now," I said. "I will be with them at all hours, sleep in the room with them, and free you to care for Abbey."

She nodded, and I could see the weariness come over her again, like a slack, faded mask.

"The first thing is to get you to bed," I said. "Arthur and I will take care of everything tonight. I want you to go home."

Her head went up.

"I mean it. Tell your husband no one is to disturb you, not until you awaken naturally tomorrow morning, whatever time that might be."

She wanted to protest, but seeing the set of my features, she desisted, not willing to waste the needed energy. I pressed my advantage. "You will be of no good to her, dear heart, if you are dead on your feet, or drive yourself to illness."

The first few days were separate entities, with hours to get through, chores and challenges taking me from one step to another. After that, everything merged. The children, reconciling themselves to the new pattern, settled down to things as they were—no longer as they would like them to be. I became endeared to them as they, growing accustomed to my ways, opened their hearts and their small, trusting arms to me, and I would think every night, as I kissed them to sleep, *This is the blessing that rises out of suffering, and I am the recipient of it, drawn by these pure spirits who have part of my own self within them, woven inseparably through the rest.*

Mine was the easy task. Every morning Abigail bathed and dressed her daughter, coaxed her to eat, between fits of coughing, the nearly raw eggs she was convinced would help, demanding that she consume glass after glass of fresh milk and eat every ripe vegetable she could get her hands on.

"I believe, with others," she explained to me, "that we must build her strength up if she is to fight the disease. It will take time, but I think it will make a difference."

After several days we realized that Abbey's dry, hacking cough was becoming worse. She continued to lose weight until her thin body scarcely seemed to make an impression under the cool white sheets which Abigail changed so often for her comfort. The food she ate upset the delicate balance of her digestive system, and when her mother pressed her, she complained of pains and aches everywhere and, of course, the terrible tight soreness in her sunken chest. I could not bear to look on her, as the shadows grew darker beneath her soft eyes. Her wrists, already dainty, had shrunken to child-size. She no longer had strength to sit up and hold her baby in her arms. In fact, her hand, resting over the coverlet, looked like a small, drooping petal dropped and forgotten there.

We had the elders in to give her a blessing, but noted little difference at all. At length it seemed that the fluttering, waning strength of her body seemed to drag her spirit down with it; she made little resistance, and day by day she grew worse.

"I do not know what to do," Abigail confided at last. "I encourage her. I have even taken to scolding her a little. But she makes no resistance. I believe . . . " There was horror in her gaze. "I believe she has reconciled herself to death, Lottie."

Her words chilled me to the marrow, and the cold grip stayed with me. Late that night, though bone weary, I forced myself to stay on my knees and really pray to the Lord—plead with him for the help only he could give us, knowing we had to lean on him because we no longer had strength or wisdom to carry on by ourselves.

The next morning I sent Abigail off on an errand, convincing her to take the little ones with her and spend a few moments walking beneath the cool trees. "You need it," I urged. "And their company will be good for you."

After they had been gone long enough to be safe, I sat down on Abbey's bed. She raised her eyes to me, but I could see what the effort cost her. "Listen, darling," I began gently. "You must listen to me, pay close attention, with all the strength you have left."

Her eyes spoke agreement, and I continued slowly and firmly. "Winston has been gone a long time. His memory is like a talisman to you, a beautiful influence that warms your weak senses. You see him frozen, frozen in some sort of perfection you yourself have created."

Her thin fingers fluttered across the bed sheet. "Abbey, listen to me! Something within you has decided that he no longer needs you. His strength is sufficient. He will come back and mourn you, in some sweet, tragic manner, and then get on with his life, strong and faithful and self-sufficient." I drew my breath painfully. "And he will take care of your children, with my help and your mother's, and teach them to hold you in reverent remembrance, like some sad, sainted angel dying before her time."

Something in Abbey was struggling now. I could see a spark of light flicker ever so dimly within the depths of her eyes.

"You are wrong. Your death will destroy him, Abbey."

She tried to shake her head, but could move it only a fraction, a rustling upon the pillows.

"I was there when his mother died and all that was innocent within him struggled to go on, to survive. I shared with him the shame and blackness of his father's death, the careful, painstaking rebuilding, cell by cell, of the essence of his young life. I saw that essence blown into shards of pain as cruel as the ice that killed Seth. I know without doubt that he could not live through that again."

The stillness when I ceased talking was terrible. It throbbed like a sickened pulse through my head. "You, Abbey. You are part of him in a way no other person has been." I could read the anguished questions in her eyes perfectly, and I answered them. "Yes, he has always adored me. Yes, I have been more to him than a mother. I have been mother and father, child and saint, and at times the albatross round his neck."

Her hands trembled as she struggled to take in what I was saying. I bent over her and drew the fevered hands into mine. "I have been all that, Abbey, but I have not been his wife. You alone are body of his body and soul of his soul. You are essential to him, because you are literally part of him. He can no longer separate where one of you ends, Abbey, and the other begins."

I replaced her limp hands on the sheet and arose, wetting a cloth with cold water, gently sponging her neck and forehead. "You must live if Winston is to live, Abbey. And I know that you can!" I bent to kiss the almost translucent skin stretched over her cheek, not aware that my tears fell against her hot skin. "I am speaking the truth," I said, soothing now, yearning, "because I love you, because I am prepared, even if you are not, to fight for your life."

I leaned above her, my back bent painfully, willing my love into her soul just as her mother had willed vital nourishment into her flesh. Suddenly I realized she was reaching for me—her thin arms flailing, trembling terribly. I drew them gently around my neck and lifted her to me.

"Yes, my dear, my dear, it's all right now. We can make it, together."

"I need Winston." She had formed the words with her lips with barely a perceptible sound.

"You are ashamed of that desire, like a weakness?" There were tears of anguish that revealed the misery of her young soul.

"Let it go!" I begged her in a whisper. "If Winston is life to you, your Heavenly Father understands that. His tenderness, his love, Abbey, is so much greater than mine." We were both weeping now, but I managed to say, "He will bring Winston home to you, sweetheart. I know that he will."

She sank back, exhausted, but for the first time relaxed. The terrible weight of guilt and self-loathing had lifted. If her body possessed the strength still, her spirit would make her well. I sat beside her for a long time, cooling her skin with the wet cloth and gazing into her eyes.

CHAPTER FOUR

I was not there when Merin's child was born. *A son.*

"We are naming him after my father," Arthur told me later. "Merin readily agreed to it. Ralph Joseph Reid, but he shall be known as Joseph."

"I like that," I told him. "He promises to be as handsome as the rest of the Reid men."

And if any woman deserved the gift, Merin did, having her only two sons lost to her in the darkness of a past which she could not penetrate. What was the matter with me? Why in the world did I have to feel sorry for myself?

But the weakness was short-lived—occasional sharp pangs of loneliness and longing, not any true resentment of her. I was too busy with Abbey.

One morning I awoke and was almost startled to realize we were now in the full bloom of summer. I had spent nearly six weeks at Abbey's now; it was already nearing the end of July. I blinked at the high fields of wheat and alfalfa that lined the road, and the herds of sleek-coated, well-fed cattle outside my window. *For many,* I mused, *life is going on as usual: rising and working, baking and churning, planting and reaping, day following common day. For us everything in life is suspended on one thin thread, the thread of life breathing through a single frail, precious body.*

Over the next ten days we worked tirelessly together—all three of us, for Abbey, at last, was in the fight, too. Perhaps we had waited too long, begun too late. The disease had a tenacious hold and its power seemed to grow daily. The pallor of Abbey's skin took on a gray tinge. Some days she could not hold food down. The cough, the terrible cough, seemed never to cease, and when it did grant her a moment's peace she seemed almost unable to catch her breath. The hankies she held to her mouth to staunch the racking cough often came away stained a brownish red.

"This means she is hemorrhaging," Abigail said, her lips drawn thin, but her firm chin trembling. Even I knew what that meant.

Worn to a raveling, constantly fighting down the panic of despair within us, we carried on one day at a time—one hour at a time— holding the fragile, birdlike fingers, rubbing lavender-scented lotion gently to ease the fever-worn, pallid skin.

He came without warning. Not even the Spirit prompted or prepared us. I had been sitting with Abbey while Abigail played with the children. I was singing to her, my old childhood Indian songs. I sensed nothing until I heard his footfall behind me, and then I knew—knew so surely that I said without turning, "How is it you have come? There has not been time, we have only just now sent word to you."

I did not know until Winston told me later that I was crying, crying weakly, quietly. He sat down beside his wife's sickbed as I had once sat beside his. He looked into her eyes. I do not think that words passed between them before I stole away. It was Abbey who told me later of the first words he spoke to her. Bending close, but not touching her, he said: "I saved you once, Abbey. I am come to save you again." "Why?" She had formed the word back to him. "Not of my own strength," he replied. "Because she came to me again, because it is God's will that it be so."

When I stepped out of the room I realized that Abigail was in the back with the children; she had not seen Winston pass. I went to her and told her as quietly as I was able. But the sharp current of hope, almost as painful as despair, shuddered through us.

I went for a hairbrush and wet cloth so that we might spruce up the children before presenting them to their father. It did not seem possible; it did not yet seem quite real. When we were ready to re-enter the house, I went before the others. I thought Winston should not set eyes on his son for the first time without Abbey there.

He was still in the room with her, but when he heard us he called out, so I went cautiously in. The transformation in the wasted young woman was real. He had propped her into a sitting position against the pillows, and she attempted a smile when she saw me. I felt my pulse quicken. "Are you up to having the children brought in, dear?" I asked. "If not, we can wait until morning."

She shook her head at me and lifted her long arms from the bedcovers in a gesture of appeal.

I returned and beckoned the others to follow me. Little Charlotte held my hand trustingly, Abigail cradled Seth in her arms. "Let Lottie come first," Winston called out. "I cannot do justice to both at the same time."

I led her in, both of us as expectant as Christmas morning. He opened his arms to her. "Do you remember your daddy?" he asked, his voice a hoarse whisper. She went into his arms, cradling her whole body against him. "I am four years old now," she said. "You missed my birthday."

"I did indeed. Will you forgive me, darling?"

"I will if you don't go away."

Oh the precociousness of a four-year-old!

He stroked her soft cheek. "She looks like you, Abbey," he said. "There are already some freckles over the bridge of her nose, see?" He kissed the spot tenderly. "But she has my eyes."

I looked at the sick girl and we smiled at each other. After a few minutes we summoned Abigail in. When Winston caught sight of his son, nearly eleven months old, giggling delightedly in his grandmother's arms, the tears began to run down his cheeks.

"Don't cry, Daddy," Charlotte comforted. "We've told Seth all about you, haven't we, Mother?"

Abbey was crying now, too. I pressed a clean handkerchief into her fingers while Winston took the wide-eyed boy from Abigail's grasp. I watched for a moment, then slipped out of the room by myself, rendered weak by relief and joy. I leaned against the wall and began to shut my eyes, and then the sound came—low, more faint than a whisper, yet somehow distinct: an odd, familiar whistle I had not heard for years. "Do old houses have echoes?" I remembered Emma asking back in Nauvoo, after Emma Roselyn was born, and Seth's spirit had come, in this same manner, to let me know of his presence. It had not happened since then, since that one time.

I let my eyes shut. I talked to him—without a sound, without words—my soul communing with his. I felt strength and joy, like a light, flow through me. I was no longer afraid or tired or even lonely. I rested there a long time, content in his presence, assured of his love.

That same night Winston called in one of the neighboring elders to assist him and, anointing her head with consecrated oil, pronounced a priesthood blessing on Abbey's head. He spoke in the full power of his authority and of his faith. He had explained it to me. One night, in Italy, he had dreamed of that murky evening in Wyoming when the Pawnee brave stole Abbey away on his pony and Winston went after her. He dreamed of their nightmare flight back to the camp through the darkness and of that one incredible moment when a gentle light had appeared, surrounding the figure of my Grandmother Simmons who had warned them of the dangerous cliff upon which they stood—warned their spirits and saved their lives from destruction.

"I thought at first it was merely my longing for Abbey," Winston explained, "translated into the memory of that horrible and wonderful time. But then a day later I turned a corner on a narrow street in the little town of Palermo where we were teaching a family, and *she* was there—standing with a gentle composure, as though she were watching for me, as though she had been waiting in the silence, knowing that I would come.

"She did not move, but her eyes seemed to take in the whole of me, and her gaze warmed me—you understand what I mean, Mother?"

I nodded, feeling her tenderness even as he described it, while knowing, somehow, that she would never appear in like manner to me.

"Did she speak to you?" I asked.

"Not as distinctly as the first time but just as powerfully. I felt her words move through my being, and the urgency of them shook me. 'You must return home, at once,' she said, 'or you will not see your wife alive.' You can imagine my feelings." His blue eyes clouded, remembering. "I went to the president and explained what had happened and all that had preceded it. He concurred; there was a perfect harmony between us. He began arrangements for my return that very night."

"There is someone taking care of you, Winston," I told him. "It has always been so. I believe your own mother has some hand in it."

He smiled. "Abbey will get well now," he said.

Winston, I marveled, *how often have you, with uncanny strength and insight, inspired and uplifted me?*

I resisted the temptation to throw my arms round him and tell him outright how dearly I loved him, how vital he was to me. Something made me pause; he was not my little boy now, but a full-grown man. He had filled out during the year and a half of his mission. The fresh, boyish expression had deepened; there was a maturity in the lines of his face that had not been there before. Even his voice had a more full note to it, and there was a confidence in his manner borne of challenges met and conquered, hard lessons suffered and learned. This assurance added charm to his dark good looks and the untroubled clarity of his startling blue eyes. I felt a sense of humility when in his presence, an awareness that heaven had blessed me by placing this choice spirit in my care.

And, thank heaven, he was right. The healing powers of the blessing her husband gave her worked wonders with Abbey where nothing else had. "The boy's presence doesn't hurt any, either," Abigail said to me several days after Winston's return. I agreed, and felt a deep satisfaction when I left the three of them together and returned once more to my home. Winston had been like a son to Abigail for years, a relationship solidified during the months at Winter Quarters when he would accompany her on her errands of mercy and, seeing her bone-weary from nursing others, administer to her modest needs.

He was in good hands. We, as a family, were all in good hands, for that matter—the hands of him who loves and upholds all his children and abundantly blesses those who even attempt to love and serve him in return.

Life is a fluid thing, never holding still for our pleasure but, like a kaleidoscope of rich, varied colors, always shifting and changing, presenting new possibilities and clothing old pictures in diverse and altered hues.

During the weeks of Abbey's recovery, as she built up her strength, Winston became re-acquainted with his children and spent many hours repairing and fixing up things which had been neglected during his absence: a door off its hinges, a room that needed painting, a garden that needed mulching and weeding. Brother Perkins took him back on at the mill, and all seemed moving ahead.

Then one day late in August, when summer was at its most languid, I looked up to see both Abbey and Winston walking into the room. At first my heart leaped; could something be wrong? But their faces were placid, and they stood there together. I took them into the cool parlor and asked Grace to bring in glasses of lemonade and the rest of yesterday's scones.

"We have made a decision, Lottie," Abbey announced. A little color had returned to her face and her thinness was not quite so wraithlike, though she still moved with a painful slowness and spent many hours of each day in bed. "We are moving back to the city, to Salt Lake."

"Truly? How can that be?" I tried to disguise my extreme pleasure. "What of Brother Perkins?"

"It is because of Brother Perkins that we are returning," Winston explained. "He has built a huge flour mill out by the Oquirrhs, in an area they are calling West Jordan. He wants me to take over its operation."

"Why you?"

"Because he is young and enterprising and entirely trustworthy." Abbey's eyes were gentle, doe soft in her pale face. "Because Brother Perkins suffered a slight stroke last winter and feels compelled to set his affairs into some kind of order which satisfies him."

I nodded. "I shall not pretend anything but the delight I am feeling," I told them. "But what of your mother, Abbey?"

"Mother understands. She appreciated Winston's coming up there in the first place. It will be difficult for both of us . . . "

She left the little word trailing. "If only she could come back here with you," I unwisely cried.

"Harold does not see it that way. He likes his work, and he likes his home there. Mother says he is too old to respond well to change."

"Too old in spirit!" I cried, again unthinking.

But Abbey's mouth twitched with the beginning of a smile. "Those were Mother's words precisely!" she said.

"I felt it was right," Winston began, "after much prayer and thought, though I cannot exactly say why."

"That is enough for now," Abbey said, her voice as firm with resolve as I had ever heard it.

"There are many hands to help you in the moving and fixing," I reminded them. "I want you doing nothing, Abbey, nothing at all, you understand?" The obvious risks disturbed me. "Have I your word on it, Winston, that you will watch her carefully?"

"Put your mind at rest, Lottie." Abbey's low voice held a musical note, a reverberation of the joy she felt. "He will not allow me to lift anything heavier than a piece of paper. He is taking very good care of me and securing himself in the children's affections."

"Good. I am glad of it."

"We will delay the actual moving as long as we can," Winston assured me. "But I want it to be early enough to avoid any possible bad weather."

So the changes were set into place and a new course charted, a course that was welcome and good.

CHAPTER FIVE

They say autumn is a somber time when the earth is dying. But to me there is something in the colors, in the taste of autumn, in the brave showing of splendor, that breathes of life, and I thrive on the intensity of that sensation.

There was a sharpness of sensation about everything that October: the enjoyable hustle-bustle of moving Winston and Abbey into the house they had rented in the city, and the pleasant, personal little fussing that would make it into a home; the exhausting, but satisfying exertion of bottling and preserving the bounties of our garden; and the lively push of business, for Julian's affairs were moving briskly as ever. I seemed to thrive on it all, feeling better with the extra labor and challenges—less weary, really, and better able to sleep.

It seemed to me that my birthdays came more often than others'. I could not be turning thirty-eight! That sounded much closer to forty than did thirty-seven. I did not enjoy celebrating my birthday. I had not for a long time.

But as the day approached I felt none of the petty frustration I had experienced the previous year. There seemed an order in my life which had before been missing—a subtle symmetry of forces both within and without. I remember feeling grateful, not realizing how vital such harmonious conditions would prove, nor how much I would soon need to rely on their strengths.

We had arranged a birthday luncheon: Susie, Merin, and myself, with Abigail coming down to join in if she could. The weather was mild. By mid-morning the sun was hot, though the air, when a breeze blew, still tasted deliciously cool.

I had gone into the garden to check on the last of our squash and tomatoes, taking my time there, drinking in the solitary beauty, pressing my favorite white roses against my lips and breathing in their fragrance, still as gentle as the first sweet days of June. I had dressed in a frock of soft gray wool trimmed in green, which enhanced the emerald lights in my eyes. As I pinned my hair up into soft waves on my head I examined the auburn tresses with a keen eye but could discover no gray threads there. I splashed on the lavender scent Emma had brought me from San Francisco on her last visit. The autumn feeling was strong in me, of life and vitality, of beauty as weighty as a fruit-laden bough, of loveliness too gentle and elusive to grasp.

What happened as I stood dreaming in the garden is not easy to tell; I should not be able to capture the anguished sensation if I described it, spoke of it, wrote of it dozens of times. Such experiences go beyond man's meager means of expression.

I heard no sound behind me but, at length, a sense of a presence nearby. I paused, taking in the subtle change in the stillness, yet never imagining—never! Then he spoke my name—one word, two anguished syllables that shivered through me, somehow containing the pain and passion of every time he had ever uttered that name before.

I could not turn—I could not move. I felt him closer. *"Charlotte,"* he repeated. "I am real, I have come to you. This is not a cruel dream. *Namaste,* my dear one."

I felt his touch, the pressure of his hands on my arms as he turned me to face him. I know I was trembling all over; I knew I could not speak yet. And, for some reason, I dreaded raising my eyes to meet him—as though the gods would surely destroy human beings before they would allow such dreams as these to come true.

How can one tell of such unbearable moments when the earth touches heaven for one brief heartbeat, and all is goodness and light—the dross of mortality falling away before the magnificence of spirit, of love in its purest form?

"Listen, if you can," Karan said, his words measured, unhurried. "I am here because God wills it so. I can see in your eyes that you understand this. I am here because, against all odds which mortals would hazard, the Eternal Spirit led your daughter to the places where he alone could take her—because she was drawn to me, Charlotte, even as you were in that time long ago."

He paused, his dark eyes watching me closely. *How little he has changed,* I thought. *There is nothing worn or world-weary about him.* I could not see if there was gray in the thick black hair that his turban covered, but there were very few lines in his chiseled face, and those eyes—those eyes which could reflect the soul of all living—still pulsed with youth and tenderness and life.

"Oh, Lottie, forgive me!" His words were a murmur. "All my life I have dreamed of this moment, never once having faith that it might come to pass. I am undeserving, to be standing thus before you, drinking in your beauty, with no barrier between us."

His voice, sweet as honey, musical as the subtle harmonies of wind and water—how could I have forgotten the sound of that voice? I reached out and touched his hand; only my fingertips caressing the smooth tawny skin, that tentative, delicate contact uniting his soul with mine.

What was not possible has become possible, I thought. *Dream has found root in reality, and the past and future are restored to one another. Harmony.* The sense of harmony I had been feeling, had it been a presage of this?

Slowly, piece by piece, Karan revealed what had happened, at least the bare bones of the events that had brought him here. Marion had taken Sarah Elizabeth from Bombay across the narrow part of the country and northward toward Calcutta, stopping to see all the obvious tourist wonders along their route. As they approached the port city they diverged sixteen miles in order to see Barrackpore, the British station along the banks of the Hooghly, where I lived many years of my life. The last stop was Calcutta, where they would take ship for England.

Karan spoke slowly, as though weighing each word, and I knew he was taking care not to say too much too soon. "It was a strange way in which Sita and I were brought together, " he said.

"It would have to be," I replied. "And you feel the gods ordained it?"

"I believe *your god* ordained it, this new god about which Sita would tell me very little, this god you discovered, who led you here."

"Here where you once saw me, remember?"

"I remember." He was very solemn; no smile played along his sensitive mouth nor softened the keen penetration of his eyes. It struck me, suddenly and quite for the first time, how difficult this must be for him.

"Why did you come? Were you—are you sure about being here?" It was a blunt, awkward question—stupid, really. But he sensed what stood behind it.

"Did I come from the bowels of hell, clear across the world merely to set eyes upon you once more, Charlotte, is this what you ask?" His voice was controlled still, as enigmatic as his expression. "I came to refashion my fate, if the gods and yourself so will it."

I came to refashion my fate. The words had the music of poetry in them: the poetry of his soul, the poetry of his integrity, the poetry of his love for me.

"What of your wife . . . and children?" I stammered.

His eyes narrowed and darkened. "I do not know what you are talking about. Did I not tell you, when we parted, that I would treasure your love like a jewel, that I would be constant?"

A sense of misery was sweeping over me in sick waves, as though my question had become in some way an accusation, as though I should feel ashamed of it.

"Constance told me that she had word of you, that you had remarried, that your wife had borne you fine sons, sons who would never be . . . mine." I was aware, as if from a great distance, that I was weeping softly, but I could not control myself.

Karan said something curt and angry in Hindustani which I did not understand. "The wicked woman! To impose her poison upon you all these long years, to leave it festering in your system long after she is dead!"

There was venom in his voice, but a golden glow in his eyes that had not been there before.

"I have liked to believe, at least I always told myself, that it was this knowledge, this knowledge alone that made me accept Seth's proposal."

"Charlotte, we were lost to one another!" The passion in his voice was arresting, drawing me like one of the powerful chants of the snake charmers, while yet maintaining that deliberate, almost soothing cadence. "I had reconciled myself to a half-life, you knew that when I first left you." For a moment bitterness involuntarily tightened the edges of his mouth into an expression that brought back vividly those nightmarish days in the hospital. "Had I ever known anything better than a half-life, Lottie, even after you came to me?"

He paused to control his pain before continuing. "With a woman it is different. A woman has a right to bear children; she is never her whole self without them. You had a right to seek happiness to—"

"To love someone else, Karan? Did I have a right to do that?"

I could feel his compassion reach out to me like a caress. "Yes, you had a right, Charlotte."

"Why? Because I am weaker than you are, because allowances must be made for me?"

He was troubled. I could see that I was wounding him, tearing the meat of his spirit as the tiger had torn the flesh of his body those long years ago. "Charlotte, please. Can we not—"

"No! This must be faced first, before, before, . . . "

"Yes." *That cursed calm of his that had always tormented me.* "Yes, I understand, Charlotte. All right." But he could go no further, he took a moment to gather his strength again. "You know that I expected you, that I desired you to live a full life. You can remember, you can now contemplate safely how much your unhappiness with Major Hillard tortured me, drove me nearly to the brink of madness! Do you really believe that I would have begrudged your happiness? Do you believe me capable of such pettiness, Charlotte?"

"No! No, Karan!" I cried. I had not spoken his name yet, and the sound of it trembled between us, as though transmitting the waves of our pain.

"What is it then, Charlotte? What is it, exactly, that torments you, that stands, even now, between us?"

I caught my breath painfully. With all of my strength I forced myself to continue meeting his eyes. "My love for another man, my love for Seth, stands between us."

I could not see beyond the warm brown pools of his eyes. "You see this as betrayal, you see this as weakness on your part?"

"Yes."

"I see if differently. I see it as affirmation."

"That is not possible."

"Of course it is. It is not possible only if you insist upon the continuance of this punishment you are inflicting upon yourself."

A fierce desire to run away from his words trembled through me; I longed to deny their harsh veracity.

"Love does not walk away, " he said. "You once taught me that principle in a miserable hospital room in Barrackpore—"

"No! It was *your* truth, it was part of *your* strength. I was only attempting to practice it!"

"I am only attempting to practice it now."

Again, a silence, heavy and painful.

"Do you regret what you see before you? What you feel? Do you wish that I had not come?"

I shook my head.

"Do you believe that your love for Seth, that what existed between you two, would stand in the way of any love, any harmony we could achieve?"

I heard the question as if from a distance. I did not want to embrace it, face the full impact of it; yet I knew that I must. Long moments passed. I remember closing my eyes. I remember trying to pray. I remember seeing the image of Seth's features rise up before me, as real as in life. Then his voice came, more than memory only, repeating the words he had spoken when he had asked me to be his wife: "I know you have loved before, Charlotte; I am not a fool."

"Seth was a good man," I said, looking up.

"Of course he was a good man, an extraordinary man to have won such love from you."

Am I so transparent to him? I anguished, forgetting that I always had been. *"He is not here, Lottie . . . "* Seth had said to me, *"and I am. I love you, and despite your fears, you love me. It is enough to build upon, as long as you know that I want to take care of you, that I will never betray you or hurt you for as long as I live."*

"What are you remembering, Charlotte?"

I repeated Seth's words for him. He took them in thoughtfully, carefully, as open to any pain I would inflict upon him as he always had been—loving me beyond that—bound to his own integrity beyond that. "Do you feel you would be betraying his love then, in returning your love once more to me?"

I could not answer.

"Do you think love between us would hurt him, as he promised not to hurt you?" He gave me a space in which to reply and then added, "He wanted your happiness; he would want it now, Charlotte. He would not wish you to run away today, any more than he did then."

He was right. It had all been too much, too soon for me to grasp. *I have no concerns on my account,* Seth had said. From the beginning Seth trusted me. He had trusted me in London when May had attempted to deceive me and tempt me away from him and the Church. He had trusted me in Nauvoo when I was devastated by his death, and Emma tempted me to give in, to take a selfish, worldly, and easy way out. He had always trusted my strengths and insights; he had been proud of every goodness he saw in me; he had trusted that goodness. The tightness in my chest that had been threatening to cut my breath off began to relax. He had always trusted me; I knew he would continue to trust me now.

I do not know how long we two sat there. I do recall vaguely that Karan arose at one point and went into the house and brought back glasses of cool buttermilk for us. We moved into the shade, we forgot all time, all commitment beyond the needs of the moment.

At length I must have been roused and remembered what day it was and the plans I had made. When I showed a sudden alarm, Karan smiled all the more tenderly. "I fear there are many things I have not told you. I came, you see, from Merin's house. She knows I am here. She knows"—the golden lights leapt in his eyes—"she knows, at this moment, far more than you do."

"How long?"

"Two days ago; I arrived two days ago in the city. We have rested and made plans. I thought it a fortuitous omen that we meet again on your birthday, as we did that time in Barrackpore when you turned eighteen, and we plighted our troth with the ring of my mother." His warm, slender fingers brushed the skin of my throat briefly as they felt for the chain and drew out the ring that still hung from it, concealed by the gray folds of my dress. The ancient gems, costly and well cut, sparkled as the midday sun struck them—emeralds and rubies and diamonds set in a thin and worn band of gold. Their beauty never failed to take my breath away. "All these years," he murmured, cupping the ring in his hand.

"You said, *'I do not believe that the fates will favor us.'*"

"You remember well, Lottie." His deep voice was grave. "Well, I was wrong. But they have surely taken their time." His sensitive mouth trembled and then tightened.

"I am afraid," I whispered.

"You always were," he replied.

I shuddered, thinking of that day in Nauvoo when I had been fearful of too much happiness, that moment of premonition when Seth was torn suddenly, cruelly from me.

Karan was leaning toward me, his eyes clouded with concern. "You have suffered much more than either Seth or I would have wanted." A sigh trembled through him. "I am with you now. If you will let me, I shall do all in my power to soften your suffering."

I touched the knuckles of his lean hand where it rested against his knee. "I have known sweet with the bitter. You have known only emptiness and denial. It is time for something different, Karan. It is time for more than a half-life for you."

I do not know how it came to pass that his arms were around me, that I was crying against his shoulder, that he was repeating my name, over and over again, as he kissed the folds of my hair, the arch of my eyebrows, the hungry curve of my lips.

"We must go to Merin," I said at length. I was beginning to accept the reality of his presence; a certain excitement was building within me.

"There is more yet, Charlotte, more for you to know." I could feel my whole body go tense. "No, it is not bad news, nothing to worry you, Lottie. But it will be a shock, a very great shock to take in."

He made me sit. I could tell he was nervous and uncertain of how to proceed. "I will tell you, because I believe the choice should be yours. Remember I said *we* a few moments ago? I did not come alone."

My first thoughts were of Dr. Fielding. But, watching me, Karan shook his head. "It is no one you know, no one you remember, except in your heart."

Incredulity was in his eyes. "Tell me quickly, Karan. Say it quickly. Say it!"

"All right. *Your mother is here.* She lives. She has been found. She is waiting at Arthur's house for you."

He put out a hand to steady me. I felt light-headed, and for a moment my vision blurred. "Can it be? You are not mistaken?"

"Your god has seen fit to bless you and to bless her who has waited so long."

I sat silent, and he withdrew a short distance. I closed my eyes. I tried to remember—I tried to imagine. "Is she—tell me something of her, Karan! Please!"

He came close and sat on the stone bench beside me. "She is small of build, Charlotte, with delicate features, not robust like yourself. Her eyes are the eyes of an Indian woman, dark and unfathomable. But there is a kindness in them and a patience that will speak to you of the many things which she cannot say."

I listened; I drank in his words. I tried to clear my mind so that I might see her as he drew her.

"She has your grace of movement; or rather, you have hers," he said, a smile teasing his lips. "Her voice has music in it, but no laughter. Life has drained laughter from her, but it has not drained love." I lowered my head. "Do not be afraid; that would be a mistake, Lottie."

"Is she fearful of meeting me?"

"Indeed."

"Why did she come? Who talked her into it?"

"Charlotte!" His tone was gently chiding. "She would have traveled distances hundreds of times as great, thousands of times as great. She would have suffered nameless horrors just to once more have sight of you. Surely—"

"Yes!" I put my hands up in protest. "I know I sound ridiculous, petty, inane!" A childish, unreasoned fear came over me. *What if I do not please her? What if she is disappointed in the daughter she has longed for and kept sacred in her heart all these years?*

"You have nothing to fear, Lottie. It grieves me deeply to see you so."

I raised my head. I looked into those eyes that could burn into the depths of my soul. "You will stay with me?"

"I will not leave your side for a moment, unless you send me away."

"Bring her to me. I should like to meet her here, in my own home. Only the three of us."

He bowed, as is the Sikh custom. "It will be as you say."

CHAPTER SIX

I tried to reflect, to use the precious moments of waiting to gather my thoughts, to prepare in some way. But I was incapable of thinking or planning or sorting anything out.

I waited until I saw Karan approaching, the sight of him nearly as startling as the first time. My mother walked behind him; I saw only the folds of her soft cotton sari. Not until Karan came close and stopped did she step into view—a gentle diminutive vision of loveliness: her black hair pulled back tight and glistening with coconut oil, and a perfect kumkum of red powder gracing the gentle slope of her forehead. She had a proud, delicate face, one seasoned by thousands of years of breeding. Something ancient in both the lines and the feel of it gave me a sensation of awe. The mysterious Indian countenance, closed and inscrutable to the white man. We gazed upon one another, and she was the first to break the silence. Bowing her head in a slight, graceful gesture of respect and greeting, she said, "*Namaste, Namaste,* my daughter."

Against all my will my eyes swam with tears. I could not help myself. I held my arms out and cried in a hoarse whisper the one word it had never been mine to speak: "*Mata! Mata!*"

I felt the warmth of her frail body against mine, thin and birdlike, tinged with the faint scent of curry and cloves. The touch of her, the reality of her was a restorative, as though I were touching some missing part of myself that would now make me whole. For the first time in my life my childhood and my womanhood merged. When I drew back to seek her eyes again, I found I could meet them without faltering. "I marvel that your god can be so good," she murmured.

So do I, I thought, my soul swelling with gratitude for the knowledge I possessed of that god who had reached down so benevolently to bless our lives.

They say all good things in life come in threes, and there was one surprise yet awaiting me. When at length Merin and Susie felt it appropriate to join us, they brought a stranger along—an obvious stranger, with cinnamon-warm skin and eyes like wet chestnuts, eyes like Sita Beg's eyes.

"This is your brother," Karan told me gently. "He desired to accompany his mother, to come here with her to this country, even to this place in the great American wilderness. I did not think you would mind."

I looked at the young man. He was slighter of build even than Karan and not nearly so tall. Nor did he possess the impeccable, lithe bearing that is the Sikhs' trademark. He had a strong jutting chin, and his dark eyes sat beneath a prominent forehead that seemed to me a mark of intelligence and a calm, thoughtful nature. *My brother, bearing the same blood as mine in his veins!* He bore my scrutiny patiently. Presently he inclined his head in a respectful gesture. "I am Kishan. And you, my sister, are as lovely as the Sikh here has said you would be."

I smiled at him. It seemed a natural and easy thing to move spontaneously forward and draw up his thin hands in mine. "Welcome to my house," I said. "Welcome to this new homeland which my people have established. I hope you will find happiness here."

He was touched by my kindness; I do not know what he had been expecting. He lifted one of my hands to his lips so tenderly that I felt tears gather in my eyes and found my gaze searching for Karan, needing from him, as I always had, some sense of affirmation and strength.

I cannot tell of those first days step by step; they have merged too much in my mind. There was some awkwardness in the beginning, as we grew accustomed to one another, as we took care of the ever-present essentials of life and daily existence. My mother spoke English well, with an accent all her own that had the lilt of a girl and made me wonder at the words she must have spoken to me when we were together and I was a child. I wished I could have remembered that voice.

From the very start we made over Merin's room for my mother; it was an arrangement which delighted me. She had brought some of her own things with her, and their presence breathed of that world I had never thought to touch again in this life. Her soft sandals, her colored saris, or skirts, and kurtas, or blouses, were all neatly lined up. She had a small, but exquisite, assortment of rings, bangles for the arm, and necklaces hung with charms. She placed a small statue of the Hindu god, Shiva, in a little shrine, called a puja, thus making of her small home away from home a temple where she might worship. She had brought Indian food with her! Boxes crammed with spices and karhi, or curry, Indian rices and nuts, even dates and a few pomegranates and dried fruits. To think of eating Indian food again filled me with an intense sense of pleasure.

It had been decided before I came on the scene that Karan and Kishan would make their home with Merin and Arthur for as long as they wanted.

"We rattle around in that big house," Merin assured me, "and Arthur is delighted to have men around, men who share a portion of his old world with him."

I hesitated, firmly leading her aside under the pretense of showing her some hand work I had been doing. "Does Karan realize whose son Arthur is?" I asked.

She blinked for a moment, as though not comprehending the question and the significance I obviously attached to it. Then I saw remembrance, like a light, come into her eyes. "Lottie, of course he knows that! The son of his old enemy. Do you think he blames Arthur for the sins of his father? He is far too noble for that."

"I know Karan is noble," I responded, "too noble for his own good sometimes. But, you do not understand. Enemy, indeed. He took Karan's whole life in his hands and twisted it into a tortured shape, literally re-forming it as he desired, taking away one vital element after another until—"

Merin placed her hand on my arm. I was surprised to see concern darken her features. "Lottie, dearest," she soothed. "I cannot bear to see you torture yourself by recalling it so vividly." She paused a moment, then added in a more gentle tone, "You take it hard. I believe you are less reconciled to Karan's life than he has been."

"Perhaps so," I conceded. "I watched the torture being applied. I incurred some of the punishment and horror in my own life, being forced into a loveless marriage with a man I later grew to fear and despise. Yet, I have had an abundance of love and joy in my life, Merin! He has dwelt year after year in that narrow corridor where Major Reid put him."

"He will have happiness now," Merin responded. "It will all be made up to him."

"Will it?" I asked, realizing with that question how frightened, how uncertain I was of what the future might bring.

The appearance of either Karan or my mother would have been a shock, a miracle nearly past believing. But to have them both here together—both come back from the dead, from the realms of pain and dream and desire—seemed continually inconceivable. I would find myself stealing glances at them frequently, as though to assure myself that they truly were real.

Sita Beg was shy in her ways. Even with my daughters she did not seem able to drop her reserve. But then, that is the Indian way. And time would heal, would open up the closed petals of her heart which had lived without the life-giving warmth of the sun to reflect their beauty for so long. I wanted to ask her if she saw anything of my father in me and if the memories I drew forth were painful, but I did not dare to broach such intimate matters with her yet.

She fascinated Grace and Emma. They made allowances for her differences, pampered her as though she were a favored child whom they found irresistible. Each, in her own way, set about making Sita Beg welcome, helping her to feel part of a family as diverse and challenging as ours must have appeared to her.

I could relax where my mother was concerned. I could put her out of my mind, if need be, for several hours at a time and see to matters that needed my attention and concentration. But not Karan. Mere awareness of him, even when he was not with me, drove all desire for other thought and action away. I saw little of him the first two days following his appearance in my garden. Arthur and Susie whisked him off, introducing him to notable and influential figures in the business world and at the newly established Deseret University.

"A man needs to have work at hand first off," Susie told me. "His inner confidence, his very equilibrium falters, my dear, without that. I've a few possibilities we must grasp hold of before they get cold. Once Karan knows where he's going and who he is going to be here, once the balance is restored, then he can turn his attention to other things."

She smiled at me knowingly, that expansive, effusive countenance beaming upon me with compassionate affection. Yet I felt a contrary, inexplicable desire to run away from the society and the people who had already taken both his life and mine in hand. I tried not to worry. I saw patience all around me, but I could not produce it within me or find any way of stilling the anxiety that ate at me day and night.

Susie had used the phrase "who he is going to be here." I knew those words touched the tender core of one of my worst fears: *Who is Karan going to be? What does he want? Will he find a way to "fit in," to make a place for himself here? or will I look into his eyes and see discontent and disappointment? Will he in time regret the fact that he came here?* Such questions were always with me—when I awoke, when I lay in my bed, weary and tired, and sleep would not come.

On the third day following my birthday Karan arrived early in the evening, unannounced, but not entirely unexpected. I had been in the parlor with my mother, showing her some of the quilts Merin and I had created together, and I watched him walk up the path. *He appears always the same,* I thought, *because his exterior never changes. What would he look like in trousers and top hat like other men? Would his dignity, his grace of movement be so apparent?*

Emma flew to the door; I believe she was a little taken with this exotic stranger. Karan greeted her warmly, then spoke to my mother with some deference before turning to me.

"Merin has graciously loaned me the use of her closed carriage, Charlotte. Would it be convenient for you to come riding with me?"

Convenient! "It would please me very much to ride out with you, Karan. Give me just a moment to give the girls some instructions and get my warm shawl."

I went with him, eagerly—as eager as a girl, if the truth be known. Yet, once alone together, there was a shyness between us. I attempted to push it aside by asking him questions about the people he had met that day and the things he had done. He answered willingly, warmly, and I felt myself begin to relax, begin to forget all the differences, and feel only those wonderful ways in which our spirits moved in harmony.

We drove up above the city as far as the road would allow us. The day was mild for the end of October. The air was bracing and clean. We stopped the horses and walked beneath the burnished gold of a harvest moon.

"Charlotte," he said, "I have a little treasure for you, an unlikely gift from your daughter."

"My daughter?"

"Sarah Elizabeth."

I could not begin to think what he was talking about. "This is something she gave to you?"

"Into my safekeeping. It was very important to her that it reach you, that you read it. It is her way of sharing this part of her life with you, of coming back to you, in a way."

Unknowingly, I frowned. Karan noticed and shook his head, albeit kindly. "Believe it or not, I am glad to see you have not changed in this, Charlotte. You still wish to take the reins of life and drive all the horses, to take every person you love where you believe they ought to be going."

"I know that is a fault of mine," I defended. "But sometimes it is more than mere belief. I *know* where Sita ought to be going, as you put it."

"But if she is not ready, if she is not interested, right or wrong, your desire will not get her there."

"I know that."

"Of course you know that; you have known that for years. But your heart will not accept what your mind understands. Despite all you have suffered, your heart is still the stronger of the two. Your heart still keeps trying and struggling, despite the anguish it causes you."

"And you do not wholly disapprove of this?"

"I love you all the more for it."

His words had the taste of sweet nectar on the chill autumn air.

"It is a journal I have brought with me, a journal of her travels. It will explain many things we have not yet discussed. I would like you to read it first."

I felt an eagerness well up in me. "Do you have it with you?"

"I have."

We walked awhile longer, then stood to look down on the city, his arms wrapped about me, his lean strength supporting me. "From one desert to another, from one end of the world to another," I said. "Who would have dreamed?"

"Not I," he replied, very quietly. "I did not have such faith. I did not know any god could be this powerful."

I rested in the warmth of his arms, knowing that the perfect contentment I was feeling went deeper than this moment, possessing a strength which had the power to sustain me, to alter my life in ways I had never experienced before.

CHAPTER SEVEN

My mother was awake when I got back to the house. I showed her the journal, held it out to her, and she nodded. But she could see something unaccountable in my face. I heard myself saying, "This brings back a flood of aberrant feelings. During a difficult time of my life I was given another journal, one that had been unfairly withheld from me for years. Reading it was the sweetest torment I have ever experienced."

Her eyes grew wide. She wanted to ask, but I would not make her. "It was my father's journal," I continued, realizing that I was choking on the words. "The journal he kept of his life with you, Mother."

This was the first time I had used that word with her. I had called her *Mata* a few times, but with a terrible hesitancy that both of us felt. Somehow tonight I found myself going beyond that. I could continue to read what her eyes spoke, and shook my head.

"I no longer have it in my possession. When I left England my circumstances were so uncertain that I gave it into his sister's safekeeping, the sister you met in India."

Sita Beg's mouth trembled at the corners. "I did not meet her, Charlotte," she said. "I spoke only with Sarah Elizabeth."

"What do you mean?"

She sighed, not wishing to speak the words outright. "Your aunt refused to see me."

"No!" The pain of her words sent my feelings into turmoil. "So she was with me the first time." I remembered. "She is a narrow woman, I fear, with a stingy outlook on life. She has lived too long with loneliness and difficulty."

"Then you and I must be mahatma—great-hearted toward her."

I nodded, subdued by her guilelessness.

"I will bring you a drink to warm you while your read," she said, moving off toward the kitchen. I found my favorite chair, placed a bright lamp filled with oil beside it, and settled down. Sita Beg returned shortly with a cup of steaming cardamon tea. She set it down on the table, then leaned over to kiss my forehead. "I sleep lightly," she murmured, "in case you have need of me."

She turned and was gone before she could see the tears I was unable to hide. I opened the cover. Sita's familiar writing brought a wave of longing for her, but I firmly refused to admit it, and started to read.

Tuesday, 24 July, 1855—Dear Mother,

Pioneer Day today. We begin our own pilgrimage, leaving Bombay along the Great Trunk Road, in search of the past. I do not know what is in Aunt Marion's mind; she seeks visual evidence of the brother who lived so much of his life here. I seek him as well. But I seek you first, Mother, then what might come to light of Frances Simmons, your father, and of Sita Beg. I know she is nothing but a memory shrouded in mystery. But that mystery is all about me here: in the fragrance of the air I breathe, in the natives' eyes and the strange, melodic words they speak. Marion notices none of this; she is eager to "be on our way." We are on our way, as I look at it. Every inch of this country has something to show us, something to teach us.

Friday, 10 August 1855—Oh, Mother, the mosquitoes! There is nothing like them at home, nothing that can drive soul and body to madness! We travel as quickly as possible and sometimes, for hours together, we see nothing at all. There are several officers' wives and their families traveling with us, going all the way to Simla, though we will stop at Delhi. Thus we have escorts and servants, and people knowing what they are doing, and meals served, and some sort of comfort dispensed. I think of your traveling thus when you were pregnant with the child you lost. I think of you young and in love and believing that you would live here, in India, for the rest of your life.

I looked away, into the shadows of the silent room where I sat alone. *Alone.* So many memories crowded round me that I feared they might choke the very breath from my soul. Sita's words were bringing up apparitions I had not been disturbed by for years. I was not certain that I even wanted to read further, though I knew that I would. Despite the torture, I was bound to go where her words would take me.

Monday, 27 August, 1855—We reached Agra today. They tell us we have traveled nearly six hundred miles from Bombay! There was a grand dance to celebrate our arrival—dozens of handsome young officers, Mother, looking for wives. I thought of you, Mother, watching them flirt shamelessly with the newly-widowed Major Hillard, my father, who claimed that he wanted something more. I flirt with all of them rather shamelessly, for they know we are only visitors and will be going on in a few days' time.

I felt a shudder wrench through me. The thought of Sarah's parentage had not surfaced since the days in London when I married Seth. She was his as surely as Winston, as those babies who were to come after. It was strange to think of Geoffrey as her father. The few times she had asked about him as she was growing up I had answered vaguely, not wanting to tell her unnecessary truths which might make her ashamed of her parentage. Winston, on the other hand, remembered his father too well. The nightmares of life in Dacca and London had been forever burned into his mind. Since he was a little boy one of his purposes in life was to expiate his father's black sins. Sita knew little of this—a few impressions and rumors and half-truths. If she knew, she would not be so blithe about her father's dealings with other women, or with me.

Sita went on and on. I read of the ardors of her long journey from Agra to Delhi, the capital of the country, where the Himalayas were close enough to see in the distance. She became nearly eloquent sometimes, as when she described the hills rising out of rain, fog, and mist, *"their purple heads rising like turbaned ladies wreathed with the flimsy white veils of the thinning clouds, and green valleys—green, Mother, nothing like Utah. But then, I am sure you remember well."* I could see so clearly her mind and spirit expanding, as well as her knowledge of life. That pleased me, if little else did.

Sarah's uncanny journal, coupled with the appearance of my

mother and Karan, was recreating my life for me—forcing me, as it were, to live all of it over again. It was not an enjoyable process. I shrank when I saw the word *Barrackpore* written in Sita's clear, legible hand.

Friday, 23 November, 1855—Barrackpore at last! I made our driver take us for a quick tour round before depositing us in our quarters. I was longing to feel a sense of you in the grand English houses and gardens, in the row of officers' bungalows, in the parade grounds shaded by huge banyans and lines of almost gaudy poinsettias that, after the rains, stand over ten feet tall! I could not find you until I rode with one of the wives to the cemetery. She had known Major Reid's family, Mother, and remembered you. She said: "There was a to-do while she was here with one of the native officers. But your mother was quite young then, you must remember, and very beautiful with her mane of auburn hair. Constance was furious, but I remember feeling a bit sorry for the both of them. He was handsome enough to turn any girl's head, I can assure you."

You can picture us, Mother. Gossip of you—in this place that seems out of a storybook, never quite real! After she found young Roselyn's grave I got her to leave me alone there. There were little roses growing and jasmine. I sat down beside the pink-lined marble and read the inscription, "She rests now with the fair ones of heaven." That is out of a storybook, too. I sat in the silence and tried to empty my own mind and just feel. Something happened to you in this place. I know it did, Mother. You may as well have been sitting beside me, telling me just what it was. I wept for all I felt there, so vivid still, so beyond my help.

I rose and placed the thin volume facedown. I wondered if I was up to finishing it through this night to the bitter end. But then I remembered that her words held the key to the two people who had come out the mists of the lost and damned to be here at my side. I stood and stretched and walked the perimeters of the room to get my blood moving. Then I sat and took up my strange burden again.

When I returned to the woman's house again (her name was Anne Thomas, and she does not appear to be much older than you), I remembered to ask her about my father. "Major Hillard?" she repeated, as though not pleased with the question. I could see her mind at work as she regarded me. "I must tell you truly, young lady," she said, "since we are not likely to meet in this life again, and I have seen too much of life to dissemble. Your father was a charming one, charming with the ladies, that is for certain. But he was hard on his wives, a very hard man to be married to."

I am certain I blinked at her, stunned as I was. Then I heard myself saying something I had not at all intended. "Especially if his young wife was in love with another man?" It was certainly her turn to stare then! But she answered me evenly, without dropping her gaze. "Yes, my dear, especially so."

I was sorry for you, Mother. I thought of you at that moment as I thought of myself: young and betrayed by the cruel disregard of life's patterns—bereft of something so dear that it was a part of you, yet you could never, never reclaim it again. I wanted to hate you all the more for your role in my own pain and denial, but I could not. And then the thought came: Perhaps you were only trying to spare me what you had suffered. I was, it is true, so young. You wanted me to take time, to be sure, to perhaps avoid some of the things you had endured.

I walked out into the dark, moist night, and Mrs. Thomas followed me. We gazed out on the checkered mall where the shadows of moonlight played. "I can see your mother now," she said, "on the top of that feisty stallion she called Cinnamon. There was not another woman among us who could ride like she did."

"She was not really one of you, though, was she?" I answered.

"There may have been those who spoke of her mixed parentage behind her back," Anne Thomas replied. "But for the most part we women stuck together. Some envied her; perhaps all of us did in some ways. But most of us admired her, too. She had Constance to put up with, and you cannot know what that was like." She laughed then, a light, girlish sound in the stillness. And I was surprised when I felt her reach out for my hand. "Your mother possessed a rare combination of qualities, especially for one so young. Spirit and independence, yet the patience requisite for survival in India. Tenacity and tenderness, and the ability to suffer without growing bitter or narrow inside."

"Yes," I responded, unable to help myself. "She still has those qualities, and they have been further tried. When my father died in London he left her penniless and heartbroken,"—now, Mother, why did I say it that way?—"and then she lost a good husband to a tragic accident while she was carrying his child." On and on I went, Mother, telling her more of our lives than I had ever told anyone. She was a good, gentle listener. When at last I wound down, she squeezed my cold hand and told me how proud I should be of having a mother like you. "I shall never forget her," she said. "Give her my fondest greetings when you return to her, will you dear?"

I brushed the tears from my eyes with a clumsy hand. *Will you ever return to me, Sarah?* my sore heart cried. I skipped ahead, turning the pages until the word Calcutta leapt out at me. I scanned the thickly written lines of description, Sita's impressions of the Tower-of-Babel confusion of that great city; the balconies, belvederes, columns, and monuments jostling with leaning rooftops and laundry lines of the nearby bustees, or slums. I kept looking until I saw the dread words: government house.

We were two whole days in the city before we were taken to see the Maidan in the center of the city, which in some ways outshines the parks of London, at least as I remember them. The government buildings are lined along Esplanade street, just north of the Maidan. Aunt Marion needed to check on details concerning our departure, and I went along, anxious to examine the architecture, as well as the people. That was all. An innocent enough motive, a common enough errand, Mother. And yet—fate or karma, or Heavenly Father, as you would have it, had other plans.

It was a small thing. There should have been trumpets and music, people standing by in amazed rejoicing. Karan heard my voice. We were walking one of the main halls, near the end of the regular business hours, Aunt Marion and myself conversing, and he heard my voice—enough like yours that he paused to listen more carefully, to watch us approach him. I, too, observed him as we came close to each other; what female could not? Those luminous eyes, tender as a woman's, searching my countenance, the fine etched lines of his forehead and cheekbones, and his slender, patrician nose. His eyes compelled us to pause. He inclined his head slightly and said, "Nomaste. I am Karan Ranjit at your service. Are you ladies strangers here?"

"We are visitors from England," I informed him.

"You do not speak with the accent of the British," he replied. "But you speak with a voice that I know." He was distressed—I could tell, though he did well to conceal it. "May I ask you, what are your names?"

Aunt Marion tugged at my sleeve; she thought this most forward of the stranger. But I was compelled to go on. "This is my great aunt, Marion Simmons of Baddenwell in South Yorkshire. I am Sarah Elizabeth Taylor—"

"And you come from the colonies?"

His eyes were burning into me, Mother! I nodded. "The farthest reaches of colonial America," I told him, "a part of the American desert—" I paused, not knowing how to explain it.

"And your mother?" he pressed.

"Really!" Aunt Marion blustered. But I placed my hand on her arm to detain her. "My mother's name is Charlotte. Charlotte Hillard when I was born, but my father died many years ago, and I have taken on the name of my stepfather who—" I paused, because the tall stranger was leaning against the wall, looking shaken and ill. "Are you quite all right, sir?" I inquired. "Shall I send someone for a doctor?"

He opened his eyes and looked at me, and there was so much pain in that gaze that I gasped. He reached for my hand, very gently. "What are you doing in India?" There was no further attempt at the expected proprieties; he knew he had to ask me—and I knew I had to answer.

I gave my reply in some detail. He drank in every word, every syllable. I was not aware that Aunt Marion had imposed upon a passing officer to do something about the "situation." When he coughed at my elbow and presented his services, I merely looked up at him blankly. "Is this native imposing on you, miss?" he asked politely. Oh, Mother, I am your daughter, even though at times you resent my high spirits and excitable nature. "Imposing upon me?" I replied, as icily as I could. "We are engaged in a personal conversation of a highly important nature." Then, having a new thought, I attempted a charming smile. "On the contrary, sir, might you provide us with a private room and chairs to sit upon? And, perhaps I could prevail upon you to take my aunt to the address of our hosts here in Calcutta—I fear the pace of the past two days has exhausted her."

Aunt Marion (as she told me later, and I knew for myself by merely looking) was too stunned to protest. The officer, a little confused, but gallant by force of habit, kindly complied. The room he led us to was small but adequate to our needs. As soon as we sat, Karan asked, "Is your mother alive yet? Is she well?"

I answered, "She is alive and well, sir. Shall I go on?" I then outlined the entire history of your life, Mother, and my listener drank in each word with a thirst that was pitiable to see. The responses which played across his susceptive features made my own heart tremble. When I got to the point of Seth's death, his anguish reached out to sear me. There was a wildness in his eyes as he buried his face in his hands and muttered something I could not understand. I went on and on, heedless of time, not the least disturbed by the fact that I was unfolding to a stranger in a strange land every intimate detail of my life. I even told him of Maurice, Mother, and your refusal to marry him; it seemed expedient to do so. When I reached the present I even told him somewhat of my own sufferings which, indirectly, had led me here. He listened with every fiber of soul and body.

We continued to talk. We talked until footsteps down the empty corridor alerted us and we walked out to see the building deserted, no one but the night watchman near. He smiled at our passing; Karan is an imposing figure, and I was quite obviously an English lady and, therefore, due respect. I had learned much of him, of his life since you left, of the extent of his feelings for you. "We must meet again," I urged, for I felt the need nearly as strongly as he did.

"Can this be?" he replied. "You will not disappear when you leave me? This will not become only another cruel dream?"

I assured him it would not. I tried to think quickly. "We would be hampered if we attempted a private meeting amongst the people I travel with." His expression conveyed understanding but also distress.

"I live alone," he thought aloud. "It would be most improper for you to come to my rooms, and I do not wish to meet in a public place." He thought a moment, and at length his features relaxed a little. "I have a friend," he suggested, "who works also at Government House. He lives with his mother. I have never met her, but I believe she might agree to allow us to go to her home, with herself and my friend as chaperone."

"I find that agreeable," I told him, and we made plans to meet at the government offices the following morning, and he would then escort me to his friend's mother's house.

As I read, the words were so vivid that I felt I had been there. I could easily feel Karan's amazement, his anguish. I do not know how he contained them, as I could scarcely contain my own. With a dread eagerness I continued to devour the pages:

We arrived at the house to find it a very modest one. The young man who opened the door was a native such as Karan, and he appeared scarcely more than a boy, thin almost to the point of looking wasted, with large, soulful eyes. But when he smiled, the smile was boyish and playful and helped to break the terrible tension. We sat in the modest room and talked for half an hour, and he began to question me concerning religion. I parried most of his questions, reluctant to be drawn in that direction. At this point a woman approached us, bearing a heavy tea tray. Karan rose to his feet to assist her, thanking her in that gracious manner which in him is so alluring, then introducing himself and his foreign visitor. I only half-listened to his words, busying myself with the very tasty-appearing delicacies the tray held; I only half-heard him murmur my name. But I glanced up in time to see the woman's face convulse, to see her slump to the floor in a faint, before Karan bent over her and called out urgently for her son.

CHAPTER EIGHT

Karan had said, *"This is Sarah Elizabeth Taylor, born Sarah Hillard here in India, of a mother who is half-native as we are: Charlotte Simmons." You can imagine the effect those words had upon her.*

Once we had revived her, it was only with great difficulty that Karan got her to talk. But then, she spoke only Hindi, so I did not understand. "We must go elsewhere," he pronounced at length. "I have money. We will rent a carriage where we can converse without interruption."

I followed his instructions as though his will were my will. He was behaving a bit strangely, the fevered excitement still upon him. I noted that he kissed the woman's thin hand when he left her and drew the slender young man tenderly into his arms.

In the solitude of the closed carriage he revealed the amazing facts to me: that his friend was your own half-brother, that his quiet mother, with the delicate, patient features of a statue, was the mother you had longed for and never known—Sita Beg, whose disappearance had driven Frances Simmons to the madness of self-destruction.

So, Mother dear, you can imagine the exhaustion of those amazing hours. And I know you can also appreciate how difficult my task was as I attempted to unveil all of this to Aunt Marion. She would have none of it, of course not, she dismissed it all out of hand. "Preposterous," she said, over and over again. "You are being manipulated, Sarah, because of your youth and ignorance. Why, I am sure the natives use this ploy constantly, to inveigle themselves into some favorable conditions, to claim heirship and privilege where there is none!" And so it went, until at length I determined to strive no longer.

We were scheduled to sail for Great Britain in three days' time. I explained this to Karan. I explained it to the wide-eyed woman who was my maternal grandmother. I was not prepared for the response I received. "You wish to sail with me?" I had questioned foolishly.

"No, we wish to sail to America. Can you help us secure the arrangements before you leave?"

I yet stared at Karan stupidly. "America? All three of you?"

He nodded, patient and serene as always. "I have studied the maps. If we sail to the west coast, to California, we will not be far from the place you call Deseret."

"Can we travel inland?" asked your mother's son Kishan. "Can passage be made through the desert?"

"Yes," I answered woodenly, "passage there can be made." They were exuberant, each in his own way; I could even see it in Sita Beg's eyes. "You are certain?" I kept asking. "It is a very long way. You will find it very different from this." I could in no way influence or dissuade them, and so arrangements were made. I prevailed upon the highest-ranking officer I could find at Government House; I used all my charms, I used every influential name I could remember; I secured three tickets from India through Singapore clear across the North Pacific Sea to the Hawaiian Islands and then to the port of San Francisco, and Aunt Emma—I felt good knowing she would be there to greet the travel-worn pilgrims. She would make arrangements for them to travel safely to the Valley, Mother dearest—and you.

As for myself, well, you shall have already received word of my returning to England with Aunt Marion. I cannot explain the decision, except to tell you I feel for right now it is right. I should like to see your face on the day Karan greets you. I should like to see you draw the solemn little Sita Beg into your ever-capable arms. God bless you, Mother. I love you, far more than I did when I came here—yet less still, I have a feeling, than I ought to. God bless and keep you and the others at home. And God speed your most unusual and most unanticipated visitors. Your loving daughter, Sarah Elizabeth (or Sita 2).

I put down the book. I was tired past sleepiness, yet a deep sense of well-being engulfed me. *This is not like the last time*, I thought, *reading my father's journal. This is not despair and betrayal. This is not horror and loss. This is remembrance and renewal, and heaven blessing the patient and faithful, as it always does when it can. This is the future linking hands with the past forever.* With that thought, with a comfort I could not explain upholding me, I went to my waiting bed and slept.

I awoke late. Sita Beg was very efficient. By the time I arose she had started the bread and nearly churned the new butter from cream Grace brought in from the barn. She had scoured the table and washed up the morning dishes and was waiting for me, with a cup of new milk and freshly-boiled eggs to tempt me, and some sort of prune pudding she had concocted herself.

"Mornings in India are filled with the babble of insects and birds and the chattering of bothersome monkeys. Here it is very quiet."

Her words were an observation only. "Does the quiet disturb you?" I asked.

"It is a boon. In it there is nothing to fear, nothing to turn away from."

I wanted to say, *I have read the journal, Mata. Tell me what you were thinking when Karan revived you and you knew the daughter you thought forever dead to you had been found.* Instead I asked, "When the Crims took you back, when your husband and child were denied you, did you, too, wish to die?"

Her expression did not alter. Her words came slowly, but they were not hesitant. "Truly I did. I tried to lose my life without actually taking it. I would not eat. I would not take interest in anything about me."

"Were they cruel to you, Mata?"

"They were very kind. Mohan, who loved me, was in terrible agony. Every day he would kneel beside my bed, tears streaming down his cheeks, and beg me to try, to live. They did not understand; it is not their fault entirely. They had no idea what they had taken away."

I was stunned by her answer, yet hungry for more. "When did you resign yourself, give up hope?"

"I never hoped, not for a moment. I knew if the Crims did not wish it, they simply would not be found."

"Did you worry about your husband and baby?" The words sounded strange as I spoke them.

"I knew Frances loved me, but I did not know how much. I

66

willed myself to believe that he would be better without me, that some good British woman would raise my child better than me."

"Did you know that he deserted me? That he allowed death to relieve him of his grief for you?"

"Thank all the gods that I did not know."

"If you believed him alive, did you not search for him everywhere—wherever the Crows' path took you?"

Sita Beg sighed; only a little sound, but it nearly moved me to tears. "Even though I married Mohan, I was very closely guarded. Never again was I to be allowed the freedom of the roadside, much less the freedom of the marketplace and the towns we passed through."

She was a virtual prisoner, I thought with horror.

"It was not as terrible as you think," she responded, seeing my eyes. "I am of a different people, a different way from anything you have ever known, daughter. The brief time I had with your father was like something out of a dream. I could reconcile myself, as you put it, and expect no more out of life than those around me did, than my people had been doing for thousands of years."

"No!" I protested. "From the beginning you were different. You had royal blood in your veins, the blood of a brave and incredible woman. And you knew how to read."

Her eyes darkened. Was I making her angry? "You do not understand," she persisted. "But yes, there were compensations . . . after a time."

"After a time?" I sat down with the last of my prunes, my eyes entreating her not to stop. "Tell me of those days, Mata, please. You had children? Tell me of your life and your children."

She moved with the slow grace of the Indian woman. Her great brown eyes in her unlined face were as young and tortured as Sita's had been when she learned that the boy she was in love with had died. But there was a difference, and that difference was acceptance. The same maddening acceptance I had always challenged in Karan. Now I found myself wondering if there was not wisdom in it—perhaps even faith? Surely a peace, an inner peace worth something.

"I had three sons, strong Crim stock like their father. No daughters, no more daughters. Mohan trained my sons to follow the trade and profession of their father." I tried not to cringe at her words, remembering so well that fierce distinctive clan, fourteen million of them, who believe in the honor of the criminal, who hold the belief that those who die in the midst of performing their sacred calling of living by their wits, of committing crime, will be assured of a place in paradise. "I lost one of my sons," she said, her voice almost toneless, and I did not ask for details, being able to imagine them well enough.

"But then heaven granted me another, though he was so weak and frail when he arrived I wondered if I would be able to hold on to him. Every day I prayed. Every morning I went to his bed expecting to find he had died in the night. But he lived—not to thrive, not to grow strong and swift like his father and brothers. My husband, in disgust, washed his hands of the small boy and left him to me. I had found a friend, an old British healer, much like Dr. Fielding. He smuggled English books to me and even writing materials. The child and I spent much time to ourselves. Mohan's anger and disappointment increased. At length he took a new wife, needing sons, he argued, to work his trade with him."

My eyes must have reflected my horror, but Sita Beg shook her head. "At an earlier age this thing might have wounded me deeply, but I no longer minded. I looked upon the additional freedom it gave as a blessing. I taught my young son to read. I taught him to think. I taught him to want something different than a place in the Crim caste for the rest of his life."

"That was bold," I breathed. "Most would term it foolhardy." My voice, and the response in her eyes said clearly, *Ah, you know less about me, Charlotte dear, than you think.*

"I believed very strongly that it was part of his kismet, the ordained pattern of his life. I did all I could and waited upon the gods' pleasure."

Her words both sobered and lifted me. I had, at times, gathered strength to do that. But I had so much light and knowledge to help me, and she had moved in the darkness and narrowness of superstition and age-old restrictions and patterns that even the heavens were seldom able to move.

"Shortly after Kishan became a man, my doctor friend paid me a visit and spoke of a position which was available in Calcutta at Government House. 'They are in need of a native who can both speak and write English,' he told me, 'to work with the British and the Moslems, to walk that tricky line between two races and cultures. No one I know is better prepared than your son.'

"It was to me an omen. When I told his father about it, he let me go. He had his new woman, who was young and lively and had already given him sons—stout, healthy little sons running around his tent.

"That was nearly four years ago. We made a home together. Kishan has done well, risen in status and responsibility. He has been well-treated. We were happy there."

I nodded. "When you decided to leave did you not fear—" I was not certain how to continue.

"Fear change? Fear disappointment and loss? In my land there is much to fear, especially if one is of a lower caste. Here, I was told," she smiled dimly, "even by Sita, that there is nothing to fear. All men are regarded by the things which they carry inside, by the things they are able to do."

I thought of Nauvoo and the mobbers who had beaten Winston, a mere child, half to death, and done much, much worse to others. Sita had been young then. In the very young, memory is blessedly short.

"I knew we would be different and in some ways despised. But I also knew you would be here."

I did not realize that tears were in my eyes until she reached out a thin brown finger to brush them away. This was love in a form that was new and delicious. I savored it, wishing I could tell her the feelings for which no words would come.

I sought him out. I could not wait for circumstance or decorum; I could not wait for Karan to come to me. One of the young neighbor boys delivered my note on his pony, with a plate of cookies for payment. Within the space of two hours Karan stood at my door.

"I wish to talk. I need you," I said bluntly. "Am I being selfish? Are your attentions required elsewhere?"

"Nowhere more than right here," he replied, his dark eyes liquid and soft.

"May we talk? The day is mild and we are not far from the foothills."

He nodded assent. As we went out into the bright day, he took my hand. "You have read Sita's journal."

"I have read Sita's journal."

We walked up the slope to where the street houses ended, to where the tenacious sagebrush spread a carpet of withering gray. Above us, wherever the clouds thinned and parted, the brilliant colors of autumn spread like the palette of the Almighty, with more shapes and shades and hues than I could put a name to, with almost more beauty than my weakened heart could endure.

We found a long black rock upon which we could sit. The morning was silent, save for a few rooks' cries. "This is very different from India," I said. "You are a long way from home."

"Home? For many years India has been far less than a home to me. Home is where there is something to love, Charlotte. Therefore, for me, home is wherever you are."

"That is why you came?"

"That is why I came."

"Is it different than you imagined? Will it be more difficult?"

"Not really; I had not expected much. I know that white men, even the most enlightened, are not at ease with our kind. I knew you had embraced a new way of life, of which I understood little. I knew you had loved again and lost again. I knew you had children who were grown now and married." There was frustration in his voice, as though he were speaking to a child, attempting to explain things that were obvious. "I knew that all things had changed." He paused, then added, as though he could not help himself, "All things save one. All things save the love I hold for you."

I knew these were not just pretty words Karan was speaking.

"Sita wrote that she told you something of Maurice."

"The man who wished to marry you?"

"Yes."

"The man you refused."

"I could not love again, Karan," I began slowly. "Though I longed for love in my life, longed for someone to be kind and care for me. But there was no room in my heart. Seth was there, and you were there. And, though the prospect of years alone, with no one, looked dreary—although I believed I would never see you, never again know happiness—I could not consent. I could not give to another man what I had given to Seth, what I had once given to you."

He was listening carefully. He made no response, gave no reply, so I began again. "I suppose I am trying to say that I love you still, as passionately as I did that day in Calcutta when I begged you to let me stay, to not send me from you, lest I perish with pain."

He nodded. "You were meant to go, Charlotte."

"Yes, I see all that now. I accept it; indeed, I am glad of it. I was given Seth and my children and this gospel, which to me is dearer than life."

"And you were given me. I am here, Charlotte. What will you of me?"

I gazed into his deep eyes, which showed me the depths of his soul. "All need not be drug out and deciphered this very moment," he soothed. "You were ever this way, Charlotte, wanting all of the answers, all at once. Surely you know that life does not work in this way. If you love me as you say, what do you fear still?" Where I would have protested, his gaze stopped me. "I see fear in your eyes."

"You have waited so long, yearned with all of your being for the happiness that life had denied you. Now, as you say, all things have altered and changed. You have longed for and dreamed . . . " I paused, my heart pounding. "What if reality, after the anguished years of waiting, does not measure up?"

He said nothing. I realized that fear, like everything negative, has the power to wound, to inflict terrible pain. But I could not stop now. "I would not be able to bear it," I said bluntly, "if I could not make you happy, if I read that disappointment in the depths of your eyes."

"You have no choice," he replied. "I can pledge all, assert all. My avowals mean only that this is the way I now feel. Life, it is true, could yet deal roughly with both of us. It is conceivable"—I knew it hurt him to speak thus—"it is conceivable that disappointment, even failure could come between us. I can make no guarantees, no mortal can, Charlotte!" The pitch of his voice had risen, his eyes were darkened with pain.

I stood. I would not weep before him. "Let us go back now," I said. We walked down the gentle hillside in silence, until there were houses, and people moving, and the sounds of men working, and we were no longer alone together, but two separate people walking into the city side by side.

CHAPTER NINE

Several days passed. I saw little of Karan. Susie and Arthur would keep him busy round the clock, I knew, if no one moved to prevent them. We were well into November, and the colors on the high mountains had faded to dull russets and browns. Darkness came earlier, nibbling the edges of daylight as my fears were nibbling my peace. Grace was busy with her teaching, Emma with piano and looking after the baby when Merin had need of her and constantly pestering Julian to allow her to work again at the store. Julian's Christmas stock had arrived, and he pressed me to spend longer hours at the shop. My mother, taking all of this in, urged me as well.

"I have many hours on my hands," she explained. "I wish to spend them usefully. I am a good cook, and this is a work I enjoy. Allow me to do this, allow me to contribute."

I could not argue. In her wisdom she knew that usefulness brings happiness. So we settled into a new routine, and in truth, the workings of it pleased me well. I had space to breathe now, with my household chores lightened. In the hours that were freed I could read and sew, visit with this new quiet friend who had come into my life, and drive to Abbey's to play with the children.

My mother loved to go there. Once a week we borrowed Merin's carriage and drove out to spend the day. My grandchildren were for her one more generation, and I believe she held them a little in awe. Yet, only when playing with the little ones did Sita Beg seem to truly relax. Watching her I felt my heart ache for the child I had once been, for the child this woman had loved. What if she had been allowed to raise me, how different might I have been? The thought teased at the edges of my composure as I moved through my days.

Abbey was not strong yet; I wondered if she ever would be. My mata loved to serve her and seemed to possess that rare quality of being able to see what needed to be done and do it, with very little fuss or attention drawn to her. I was not so capable in that way.

Three weeks had passed since the arrival of my visitors, nearly a week since my conversation on the hillside with Karan. When Sunday came he appeared at my door. "I should like to accompany you to your meeting," he said.

I wondered why. I wondered if Merin had encouraged him, and how much she might have been telling him of our ways. He spent at least part of his evenings with me, even if for a few moments at the very close of the day. We talked of the mundane events in the lives of those around us. At times our talk strayed to music or poetry, and he would share some piece he was reading. I had not realized the extent of his knowledge of English literature, which was impressive indeed. We did not approach matters of the Spirit or religion. I knew, in this matter, Karan was waiting for me. I did not know how to proceed; I could not decide what would be best. So now, as we walked to the tabernacle together, I had no idea what thoughts were in his mind; in this he had become a stranger to me.

The theme of the meeting that day was the godhead, and President Young spoke powerfully, as is his way, regarding the relationship between God the Father, Jesus Christ, the Son, and the Holy Ghost. He spoke in those wonderful plain terms of his regarding our place in the plan, how in a very literal sense we are sons and daughters of Deity.

When the meeting ended Karan asked if we might walk awhile. I sent the girls home to their grandmother—how sweetly strange that seemed!—and he and I walked in the brisk air, my hand through his arm.

"It is a strange and powerful doctrine, that," he began. "Do you believe it is true?"

"Yes," I said. "There have been prophets and teachers in all times and cultures, and some of them have had some of the truth. A few are enlightened, but none have authority unless it is given of God. Once he confers his power, he also confers the gift of revelation, where he can enlighten man's knowledge with those things which are true—not a combination of man's seeking and his errors."

Karan understood that. "I wish to learn more," he said. "I cannot judge what I hear, what I see about me, until I know more."

"There is the Book of Mormon," I suggested, "and the scriptures given to Joseph Smith."

"How did you learn?"

It was a question I had not anticipated. "By bits and snatches at first," I admitted. "By being drawn to the people who called themselves Latter-day Saints. And at last, in a state of near desperation, reading their book for myself."

We walked on. We talked of the things he had heard, of the questions he had formed, until my teeth began to chatter with the cold, and my fingers go stiff. When we arrived home it was the heavenly smell of chicken tamarind simmering and fresh chapits, large, flat wheat cakes, cooked on top of a hot grill.

"Mata spoils me," I said.

"That is good for both of you," Karan smiled.

We ate, we talked, we parted. And thus my days went. It was not enough. I was in torment, and I dare not think of what Karan was suffering. I knew in my heart that somehow, and sometime soon, this must come to an end.

The following afternoon Mata and I went to visit Abbey and the children, but we arrived later than usual, and it was decided, as such things are, that we would stay on and eat our evening meal with them.

"Where is your husband?" Mata asked, as she spooned out the last of our supper.

"Oh, this is his night with—" Abbey stopped herself. "He has a meeting he will go to right from the mill. But perhaps he will be back here before you leave."

He was not. And Abbey's somewhat strange words stuck with me as I was preparing for bed. I realized that I had seen little of Winston since Karan's arrival, nor had we discussed, even briefly, those things which had come to pass. This was unusual for us; but then, there had been much confusion, many extra things to do.

Throughout the following day Winston came into my thoughts quite often, and I began to desire to talk with him, perhaps find out what he was thinking. As usual, the hours working with Julian passed quickly, and before I knew it the time had come to close up the shop.

Julian came out from the back room as I was straightening the shelves. "You go on now," he said cheerfully. "I believe this young man here has need of you."

I looked up to see Winston waiting by the front door. He grinned at me. "Julian is right, Mother," he said. "Come." He took hold of my arm and led me to where his carriage waited.

"Is something the matter at home?" I asked, worry beginning to knot inside me, as he handed me in.

"No, there is nothing wrong, Mother. Relax." We drove for a few minutes, and I saw that he headed the horses north to the empty flat which would eventually lead out to the lake. "We need to talk, Mother."

"I believe we do," I responded, feeling unaccountably relieved.

At length he drew the team off the narrow roadway and brought them to rest. The desert sun was beginning to sink below the west mountains, seeming to light them from the inside with a magical, almost unearthly glow. "Twilight in London," I mused. "Do you remember how lonely it was, Winston?"

He answered softly. "I do."

I glanced up to watch him regarding me with a very intent expression, his blue eyes troubled and dark. "Karan and I have completed the entire Book of Mormon," he began, "weeks ahead of schedule." His mouth curled in a lopsided grin at my apparent confusion. "You would not take him in hand, Mother, and so I did instead."

"Meaning?"

"Meaning first of all that I do not understand you. Meaning that the man is brilliant, that the quality of his spirit matches the quality of—"

"Is he converted?"

Winston blinked at me. "Is this what worries you, Mother?" I could see disappointment in the blue eyes, but I forced it aside. "He is not 'converted' in the regular meaning of that word; no, not yet. He has a long way to come; he is firmly bound to his own ways. But he is powerfully drawn by the things he is learning."

I leaned back against the cushioned leather seat with a sigh.

"What is it, Mother?" Winston insisted. "Karan will not fit some tidy formula you have contrived in your mind. Do you love him? Do you trust him? Do you wish to be with him? Those are the only questions that need concern you right now."

"I am afraid," I whispered. "Afraid of failure—afraid of happiness. I can't let go, Winston, and I do not know why!"

He reached out his arm and pulled me close to him. "Mother," he murmured, almost happily. "It has been so long since I have comforted you."

" 'Tis not your place," I protested.

" 'Tis the role heaven gave me, as well you know. I am content in it; I have been from the beginning. When I feared you would die in Dacca, I could not eat, could not sleep for the terror that gripped my soul."

"You were only a child, five or six years old."

"Yes, but what has age ever been between the two of us?" he answered. "What is important is that you lived and that something in me relaxed. In London, in those days when I could not rouse you, there was a difference I felt. Something beyond myself—something upholding me—and when Seth brought the gospel, well, I knew then, I understood what it was. I learned about my Father in Heaven, who loves me, and knew what it was I had felt."

I snuggled close to him. "And from that time, like Brigham, you have gone forward without any questions or doubts."

"Lean on me then, Mother. Just for a while. Let my strength help you again." I gazed up at him, sobered by the resolution of his tone. "Karan needs you, Mother. You are denying him by denying yourself; you are denying yourself by denying this man who is worthy of all you could give him, but would wait for your love ten lifetimes over before he would ask it of you."

"Why?" I cried.

"Because he was raised his whole life to deny himself! Because he never truly believed for a moment—surely you must remember it!—that you could ever be his."

Understanding came slowly, tremulously. "Winston, what of your father?" And, by that question, he knew I meant Seth.

"What of Father? Shall I tell you what I think?" I steeled myself and said yes. "He is displeased with you; it grieves him to see you cause yourself such suffering. From the first he was willing to love you, you remember, with no conditions, no expectations. All he thought of was what he could do for you."

I put my hand out to stop him, because the light had come blindingly, more than I could bear. "Yes," he pressed gently. "Forget yourself for this good man's sake, and all things will work for your good."

I hid my head against the rough weave of his jacket, my whole soul shriveled, ashamed—yet released, freed once again, as so often, through Winston's wisdom and love.

We did not hurry. We talked for what seemed like hours. We communed on a plane of pure spirit where time and its thousand limitations did not exist.

It was late when I took Winston's carriage to Merin's and knocked on the door. Arthur opened it to me, and my heart was glad at the sight of him. "I am here for Karan," I smiled. "Will you kindly announce me?" He accompanied me inside and settled me in the sitting room before going to do as I asked. I waited with a tingling of expectation playing along my spine—with a sense of life, like a song spinning round my head.

When Karan appeared he could not entirely conceal his pleasure. "I have a warm, dry carriage," I began. "Would you like to ride out with me?"

He regarded me with pleasure. I rose and put my hand out for him to take. "Do not wait up for us, Arthur," I said.

There are few places one can go in the city when it is night and the weather is cold. We drove way out, to the low marshy bottomlands that border the lake. We talked as we drove. "Karan, tell me of the things you have been learning," I urged. I listened with my heart and found myself growing excited about his ideas and perceptions of things I had known now for years. "What would you like to do," I asked, "if you stay here?"

"I should like to teach, to influence young minds and spirits. The university is in its infancy now, but it will grow. They are interested in me because I represent a perspective and a font of experience different from that found among them.

"In the meantime, in order to make a good living I shall take advantage of your friend's generosity. I have brought a store of precious and semi-precious gems with me, which are easy to come by, as you know, in India. They will serve as my start."

"Will you dislike being a merchant?"

He laughed softly. "Not here. Not under Susie's tutelage and your brother's encouragement."

"You like Arthur."

"I like him very much."

"It does not bother you too greatly to know that he is the major's son?"

"Arthur is no more Major Reid's son than Winston is Major Hillard's."

His words were a rebuke, but he did not try to soften them. I placed my hand beseechingly on his arm. "You are right," I replied. "I yet have much to learn. Will you help me, Karan?" I moved closer. I could feel the pulse of his heart through my body, though we were not touching save for the pressure of my hand on his arm.

"Is that what you truly desire, Charlotte?"

"With all of my heart. More than ever before."

He could feel my yearning. He touched my face with his fingertips, and the warmth of that touch made me go weak inside. He lowered his face against mine so that our foreheads touched. He murmured words that were indiscernible. Even in the sightlessness of the close, silent night, my eyes sought his, striving to draw his soul out—to possess the guileless, unfeigned goodness, the intangible essence that I had before been denied.

His lips closed over mine with a rough urgency, and desire as searing as fire, as gentle as soft music possessed me. I drew back from him, breathless. "I love you, Karan." The words were a cry of delight and realization, of possession and joy. He drew me into his arms again. The abundance of our joy was overwhelming—a benediction to the years of suffering and acceptance. I realized that I loved this man with all that was pure within me, with all that was frightened and weak, with all that was true, all that was petty, all that was noble—*all that was me.*

CHAPTER TEN

The wedding was set for the day before Christmas. "It is only right," Winston urged, "that evil should be cheated this way by that God who made all things good." He knew what I was thinking of—that dreadful Christmas in London when I was bereft and lonely, spurned by my only living relatives, in the clutches of poverty, my baby ill, Emma gone, and no earthly friends save the Mormon missionaries I had been forbidden to see. I could now look back and smile, now that all that was past; those days still lived in my heart, sanctified by the gospel truths which had saved me and the man who had been the means of bringing that salvation to me.

"I understand we are to have an arranged marriage," Karan said a few days later. When I looked up, startled, he smiled and explained. "Winston's advice to me, most solemnly given."

"Everything Winston does is done solemnly," I added.

"Well, in the very beginning he was not of that mind."

I laid down my mending, all attention now. "He questioned me severely and gave me to understand in very clear terms that I was not to compromise or confuse or distress you in any way."

"Winston did this?"

"Oh yes, he took me very carefully through all the things you have suffered. 'She can bear no more,' he told me, 'nor should she have to.' He wished to know in every particular what my own intentions were."

Karan's brown eyes glistened; I believe tears were moistening them. "Would you like to hear those intentions?" I did not move; I did not need to. He continued, in a voice low and melodic. "My intentions are to spend the remainder of my days in serving you and loving you, in doing all I can to live a noble, useful life, in gratitude to that Power which restored you to me."

I could feel myself flush. "You have done that already," I murmured.

And now that I had let go, now that I had released all my barriers, love flooded through me like light. Not only love for Karan, but love for all; and the more I gave, the more strong and clean was the feeling that coursed through my veins.

Both of my daughters were fond of Karan, though Emma remarked snidely, "He is not a Mormon, Mother." I opened my mouth to try to explain to her, then shut it again. She understood as much as she wanted to, and I could not force her further than that. At first I had feared, fretting about what others would think of me if I married outside the Church. I did not look at it in that manner, though many would. But I had let go of that too. I knew what I was doing had found approval in the sight of the Lord. I knew of the integrity of this man, of his worthiness. I had prayed to receive my own witness, and now my heart was at peace.

Those who were intimate, friends and family, for the most part understood. The quiet joy I saw in Merin's eyes gave me insight into what she had been suffering. "I could not bear my own happiness," she confessed. "It mocked me, knowing, as I did, of your sorrow and loneliness. Your joy has released my own, Lottie!"

"You were as foolish as I was," I chided her gently, knowing that our hearts had never been closer and would never suffer estrangement again.

Arthur was jubilant. "Ever since my father died," he confided, "my heart has ached for you, and I have felt the curse of my parents' wickedness on my head."

"I had no idea," I breathed. "It was foolish to so torment yourself, Arthur."

"So I have learned," he conceded with a grim smile. "But, nevertheless, it means a lot to me to see this burden lifted from you."

We were to spend two days and nights, upon Susie's insistence, in the small cabin she had built on her ranch at the foot of the Oquirrhs, secluded behind a stand of young cottonwoods, fed by a clear water spring. It would by idyllic.

As the day approached, I found myself eager for it, unable to settle to any mundane tasks. One afternoon, early, Julian shook his head resignedly, "You're useless to me here," he scolded, "go on home with you, Lottie. There must be more for you to do there than here."

His kindness was fortuitous. My mata had not been expecting me; when I walked into the house I found her in the privacy of her room going through some of the things she had brought with her from India. Among the colorful scarves and saris spread over the bed was one that appeared unmistakable. I lifted the red folds gingerly and let the rich satin fabric fall through my fingers.

"It is a wedding dress. I wore this when I married your father."

I sank down onto the bed. "All these years." I lifted the long gown up and held it away from me. "It is so small," I lamented. "Look at the size of that waist. I could never fit into it."

Had she been wondering, wanting—yet unable to express her desire in words to me?

"You are a mature woman," she replied in a reasonable tone, "with many years and many babies behind you. The stitchery can be adjusted, let out—"

"I would not dare!" I cried. "Mar the perfection of it."

"Do you wish to wear it?" she inquired in her softly accented voice. "Or do you appear so to please me?"

"I long to wear it!" I replied breathlessly. "Karan will be dressed in all his Sikh glory. I have been wondering what I could do to keep from appearing drab beside him." We smiled together. "This is the perfect answer." I ran my hand along the rich folds. "Do you really think it can be done, Mata?"

"Without any trouble."

"I have never worn the dress of my people." I raised my eyes to meet hers. "Karan once told me that I would look beautiful dressed in this manner, that I would always be an Indian woman to him."

"I have bangles and bracelets and armlets." There was a strain of quiet excitement in Sita Beg's voice. "I have coconut oil for your hair, sindoor and kumkum powders."

I was overcome by the idea, by the image of myself adorned like one of the fair ones of my people, prepared for the wedding feast.

"You must be certain; you must truly want this." My mother was watching me closely.

"I truly want this," I said.

Thus the decision was made, between the two of us only, and our plans went forward. But not till the wedding day would we reveal to the eyes of others our glorious surprise.

The days went forward; there were so few of them. It was the Christmas season, with more than enough things to do. But Abigail, Susie, Merin, and the girls threw themselves into the wedding plans with a fervor that touched me deeply. Poor Abbey was somewhat left out. She had little ones to care for and only possessed so much endurance, and when her strength did give out she had no choice but to stretch out on a bed or sofa and rest until her frail limbs and muscles were strengthened again.

"You have a patient heart," I told her one afternoon. Then, with a twinge of insight, "Do you grow tired of hearing that?"

She sighed. "I do, indeed, Lottie. At times I feel so useless. This frailty is a terrible curse to me. Winston is so robust, so full of life and endless enthusiasm. I feel like a withering flower that must be watered and coaxed and pampered to stand upright on its stem."

"It must be terrible for you." I knelt down beside her.

"I know we all have our crosses to bear." There were tears in her eyes.

"There is very little comfort I can offer," I soothed. "But you are so lovely, so truly beautiful despite this, and you possess the most tender devotion of your husband's heart." I glanced into the next room where Mata sat reading a book to the children. "You are responsible for those wonderful little people," I reminded her. "You brought them forth. They are part of you, and will be forever. And you have such joy in them here."

"Yes," she whispered thickly. "I often think how terrible it would be to have died and left them." Her voice had a tremor in it. "Then I count my blessings indeed."

"I count mine, too," I said, a little fiercely. "And when I do, you are high on the list."

I held her in my arms for a few moments—so little flesh on her, and bones as frail as a bird's. But her magnificent spirit throbbed through her flesh and transformed it into something beautiful, sanctified. I felt privileged to love her and to recognize the hand of Deity on her life.

The day arrived! A morning of frost and sharp shadows, and a white-dusted crow on my windowsill, seeking his morning's offering against the cold of the day. I smoothed his purple-hued plumage. "Handsome fellow," I purred. He cocked his head at a jaunty angle and regarded me with one bright eye. "Yes," I laughed, "when Sita Beg gets done with me, I shall be nearly as grand as you."

And I was. Transformed is the only word for it. When I stood before Susie's long looking glass I did not recognize the elegant, exotic lady who gazed back at me. My eyes, enlarged by black lining, appeared as shiny as the crow's feathers, and their green lights were dancing. With my hair slicked back, the bones of my face stood out in sculptured relief. "You look ten years younger!" Grace murmured.

When we walked out amongst the company Winston leaned close to brush my cheek with his lips. "You have come into your own, Charlotte," he said. *Charlotte.* There was added respect in the name he had not called me since he was a small child.

Arthur was my older brother; it was his right to escort me to meet my bridegroom. A sealing in the Endowment House would have embodied elements I longed for in being united with Karan, but that could not be. I slipped my arm through Arthur's. He looked very slender, very handsome gazing down upon me. I thought fleetingly of the dance in England when he had been proud to escort me, and I had been proud to be with him, to watch the heads of the ladies turn to see who my young companion might be. I noticed the gasps as I walked out in my eastern splendor, but it did not affect me. I seemed to move regally, with a grace I had never before experienced; I felt at home, especially beneath Karan's gaze as it rested on me.

It came to the moment of standing beside Karan, of turning to face him—of watching his expression as he slipped his mother's ring on my finger, after twenty interminable years of longing. This ring had rested against my throat; it had been with me, part of me through everything I had achieved and suffered, through every change and challenge of my life—a bit of his spirit clinging to mine.

The moment was too short. It could never have been solemn enough—or joyful enough—to suffice. We were pronounced man and wife, no longer separate, no longer denying the unity of our souls! *Major Reid,* I thought triumphantly. *In the end we have beaten you, both Karan and I. And Sita Beg. In the end Karan triumphs, and man's deeds return full circle to haunt him, as yours did to you. Karan and I are together—our love and the power of it sanctified by one far greater than you.*

There was a celebration. In a sort of daze I enjoyed it: the food, the laughter, the kind well-wishing, and the reminiscing. It was not easy to realize that all this was for me—me and the tall, gracious man standing beside me, his hand cupping my elbow or protectively holding my arm.

I thought how familiar and dear all the faces around me were; the many scenes we had endured together seemed to flash through my mind. It was singular to contemplate that, in one very large sense, my life was just beginning again. I let awareness of that sink into me. I was ready. I felt young; I even felt beautiful. When I looked up to see people's eyes resting upon me with admiration, I wanted to throw my head back and laugh. *I have never been a girl,* I thought. *Not in the way my daughters are. Life has always been a weight to me, a duty, ever since I can remember.* Even when I married Seth it was in the midst of grave responsibilities—a woman, with two children to look after. And oh, how short the season of our joy was before death cut it short!

This is for me! The thought was passionately exultant, with no guilt in it at all.

It came to pass—like a dream—our days together. Our solitude was unbroken, unhampered, our intimacy unmarred. If life can hold perfection, even briefly, it was embodied in those three days.

"You are beautiful," Karan said to me often. "Remember how once I told you that adversity had only deepened the impress of God's mark on your features?" I remembered, and shuddered. "Now you stand in the full glory of your womanhood, and I have a spiritual helpmeet, a saha-dharmini to walk through life with me."

I knew the Hindu ideal: that the Supreme Being is to them the Divine Mother, source of all virtue and wisdom, her spirit enhancing every feminine spirit born into the world. I knew that a man's spiritual life was considered incomplete unless in all things he moved in harmony with his wife.

As a Latter-day Saint I understood my own form of that ideal, which at the moment Karan could not completely fulfill. But we had come far, and there was so much within him. My knowledge did not distress me. I knew what he was capable of; I knew the purity of his longings, the guilelessness of his ways. I could place my soul into his hands for safekeeping. And, from this point, we would go upward and upward together, toward the ideal.

CHAPTER ELEVEN

We returned. Somehow we forced ourselves to reenter the land of the mundane and ordinary and make for ourselves a place there.

We now had five in our household where before there had been but three. It worked out splendidly, save for the initial embarrassment of entering my old room with Karan and closing the door, or coming out in the morning to encounter one of the girls and catch the look in her eye as she contemplated me. Bit by bit each of us began to accept having a man in the house.

Karan was very mindful of my girls, trying to discover what they liked and doing little things to please them: bringing home a new piece of music for Emma, a book for Grace, indulging both with thick slices of strudel from the German bakery near his shop.

It was a bitter winter that year, and I believe Karan and Sita Beg must have suffered much, though they never complained. "There is no color here in the winter," my mother did remark once. "There is always color in India."

"Yes, the desert is brown and gray, in varying degrees," I agreed, "and the mountains as well."

"Flowers, I miss the colors of flowers most of all," she continued.

"We will plant more in the spring," I promised.

Beneath the stiff coating of January's frost, then, we went our ways, life moving through us swiftly and keenly.

"He is determined to go." Mata's eyes were moist. "Emma did write a letter to my Kishan and persuade him to go."

Emmer! We had written to Emma about the wedding, wishing she could come but knowing the great distance that separated us and the inclement weather of winter would both serve to prevent. She had responded, but a little coolly, I thought; more like the Emma of late and less like the Emma of old. *"Do you intend to give me a run for my money, Lottie?"* She had written flippantly. *"I am on husband number four, and you are on husband number three!"* The sting of her crude carelessness was real; she had been with me after Emma Roselyn was born, and I had been sick nigh unto death. She had witnessed my terrible grieving for Seth; she was there that night when we—just Emmer and I together—heard his jocular whistle through the still stretch of the night. *Oh, how she has changed,* I thought.

"People do not remain static," Karan reminded me when I appealed to him. "Emma has made choices, many small choices during the past years, that have drawn her away from you."

"I do not want that to be true," I bemoaned. "I do not like to see it. What of her offer to Kishan? Do you believe he should go?"

"If he desires to, Charlotte, that, in itself, is an answer. He is young, he has not the assistance I have enjoyed, nor the experience that would help him make a place for himself here."

"But what of Sita Beg?"

"Sita Beg has you now, and the children, and even myself to look after her."

"But they have never been parted."

Karan looked at me out of those serene eyes. "They will be parted now. Both will grow from it, Kishan especially."

The offer was this: Emma had remarried, and her new husband owned a grand hotel where visitors from all over the world stayed. Emma desired Kishan to take over the management of it; his presence would lend an exotic, cosmopolitan air to the establishment; besides, he could speak, or at least get by, in several languages and had the facility to quickly learn more. He was just what she envisioned, just what she wanted—and Emma had grown quite accustomed to getting whatever she wanted these days.

Sita Beg resigned herself; I believe Karan spoke with her privately. We all gave the young man our enthusiasm, as well as our support, and the goods and money he needed to make the journey he planned. "We must wait for the weather to break in the Sierra Nevadas," Arthur reminded him. "But surely, respond to Emma, and tell her you will be there."

Change. The only constant in life, I thought, watching Kishan's eagerness and my mother's resignation. *Karan is right. The boy needs a chance to prove himself, to dig deep and find the gold of his own soul buried there.*

We had been married six weeks. I counted the days, each one like a curled, fragrant petal from a perfect rose. "I want a child," I told Karan one night, late, as I lay in his arms.

"This is my desire also," he murmured. "I want to give you a son to bear."

"I have never borne sons," I laughed. But he could detect the sorrow behind my brave front.

"You will bear my sons." He spoke the words plainly, with no pretense, no pride. And, as with many of the other things he had so quietly pronounced, I felt that these words were but a reflection of future reality that, surely, would come to pass.

Midway through February the weather turned suddenly warm, balmy as April, and we had an unexpected thawing of the snow in the mountains and along the streambeds. I remember wondering if this would affect the farmers, dreading the sight of flooded fields sitting stagnant and useless. I remember thinking, *If it gets warm too early, and stays warm we will not have the water we need for the coming summer.* That was all. Such thoughts are fleeting, idle; they do not portend the future, though it seems to me some things ought to scream through the very air itself to make themselves known.

The second day into the thaw it began to rain, the deluge of warm water loosening the soil and unstable rocks even further. There were reports cropping up everywhere of gullies filled to overflowing and roads washed away by flash floods. Abigail was up north; I had no intimate knowledge of her activities. Of course she would go out, no matter what the weather, if a baby was being born, if a mother required assistance. On that dismal, wet night her husband took the buggy and drove her three miles up the canyon to where a young woman lay, weak and fevered, in danger of losing the child that struggled and pushed but, for some reason, refused to come.

In the dash from buggy to house, Abigail was wet through to the skin, but she had no time for thoughts of herself. Giving instructions to her husband and to the pale young man who hovered helplessly by the bedside, she set to work. The baby was breech. She did not possess the skills needed to operate and take the child; she must attempt to turn it. Otherwise, it had no chance of survival, and the young mother little more.

She sent the husband off in search of a doctor, in hopes of employing his skills. Meantime she did all in her power, from herbal administrations to prayer. "Sometimes, near the very end, they turn of their own accord," she encouraged. Hours passed. The rain beat against the roof, clattering the one small window in its frame. The mother slept fitfully; so did Abigail and Harold. When she roused herself to examine the exhausted woman once more, the quiet miracle had occurred of its own accord—the baby had turned in the womb. Abigail safely delivered him minutes before the husband returned, empty-handed. "It is God's will," she told the young mother. "Your son is whole and healthy. We have been blessed tonight."

It was a fitting benediction of her life, this last scene, those last words. Driving home, slashed by wind and rain, urging the skittish horses forward, they slid and bolted while crossing a narrow bridge. The wagon swayed, teetered on the edge of two wheels, and Abigail was thrown from her seat. Harold righted it somehow and calmed the beasts into stopping once the water was crossed. The sickening fear in his stomach abated as he saw Abigail's still form spread facedown in the roadway, for he feared the burgeoning river had claimed her. He lifted her into his arms. He saw the bump on her forehead, with a small cut above it. He laid her in the back of the wagon and covered her the best that he could. Then he drove on to the next house he came to, not far, less than a mile away. The folk opened their door to him. He carried his unconscious wife in and laid her on the narrow mattress which had been placed on the floor for her—only to see the red stain of her blood spread along its surface.

Frantically they searched for another wound and found a long slash in her forearm, where a major vein had been cut; during the precious moments since her fall her life had been draining away. It was too much—the chill of working in wet clothing for hours, the concussion, the immense loss of blood. She never opened her eyes again; she was not given the gracious chance to depart knowingly, to say any kind of good-bye. Before morning dawned, sodden and colorless, Abigail had stopped breathing.

So quickly, so simply. One moment she was here—full of knowledge and vitality, her strong fingers working tirelessly, her eyes passionate with the desire to heal, to succeed—then on a breath, in a passing moment, taken from us for good.

Harold found Winston at the mill, and they came at once to me. The news was like a cruel blow to me. I had to lean against Winston while a terrible wave of weakness passed through me. "How will we ever tell Abbey?" I breathed.

Winston's face was gray. "Will you come with me?" I nodded. We sent Harold on to Merin's and walked the short half mile from the mill to the sweet little hollow of land where Abbey's house lay. A wet sun shone weakly and intermittently, and the soaked earth around us steamed. We walked in silence, each footstep heavier than the last. As we approached the door Winston said simply, "Will you mind the children, Mother? I should like to go in to her alone, at least at first."

We found her making bread, Charlotte Elizabeth helping, both up to their elbows in flour.

"Grandmama," the child cried. "Look what we are doing! See how plump and even my loaf is."

I bent my head, admiring her handiwork. Abbey lifted beseeching eyes to her husband. I watched Winston nod to her, his misery almost palpable. She wiped her hands along her apron, turned, and followed him out of the room.

My throat felt too tight to speak as I tried to entertain the little ones; but they sensed that something was wrong. After a few moments Winston came out of the back room alone; I had not heard a sound. "Will you go to her?" he asked, his face ashen.

I rose. The muscles in my legs were trembling as I walked past him and into Abbey's bedroom. All I could see was the vision of Abigail's face, strong and compassionate, willing her own strength into me, *giving, giving, never judging, never withholding.*

Abbey lay facedown on the bed, as crumpled and spiritless as a rag doll. I sat beside her and reached out to touch her hair. She remained motionless. I leaned over and kissed her; there was not the slightest response. "Abbey, please," I murmured, "please let me hold you. I need your comfort, too."

She did not stir. "Abbey?" I sat by her side a bit longer, then rose and left the room.

None of us had a fair time of it; Abigail's death pierced every heart to the core. But Abbey did not rally. It was as though an eerie spell possessed her. She looked out at us from a face that was too calm, with eyes that were clear, yet somehow sightless. When it became absolutely necessary she responded to others, but her voice was colorless, wooden, devoid of expression. She performed her daily chores, she took care of her children, she baked and cooked, and even read bedtime stories—but she was not really there.

For the first time in years I saw my son really frightened; he was more uncertain than he had been upon returning from his mission to find his wife at death's door. Then the power of his calling was strong upon him; his own spiritual conviction that it was God's will that he heal her had sustained him through the most difficult days. Now she had shut him out, he could find no way to reach her; he too, in his own way, was lost.

On the day of the funeral Sita Beg offered to remain with the children, and we accepted gratefully. Despite the rigorous demands funerals make on the living, the occasion ought to have extended some comfort to the grieving, as funerals embodying the healing knowledge of the gospel are wont to do. This retained a sense of the miserable, despite the cleansing strains of music and the tender, lofty praise justly spoken of Abigail. Worse than the funeral pall was the pall of concern Abbey's insensate state placed over us all.

The day's events sat heavily upon all hearts, and when Winston took Abbey back to her home and her children, there was no change in her—no awareness, no tears, no response to anyone around her— only the empty screen she had pulled down to conceal her frightened, suffering soul.

Chapter Twelve

A letter came. It had the feel of something that had traveled long distances; I pressed it to my face and smelled the damp mustiness of England, and a wave of longing, bitter and sweet, swept over me.

I had written to Sita at the time of our marriage. I tore open the envelope, anxious to see if she had received my letter, and was responding.

> *Dearest Mother, I want you to know that the news you sent was most pleasing to me. I do feel left out, not to be there when you first saw one another, when you and grandmother met. Reading your letter and thinking of all of you brought me to tears.*

I stifled the feelings which rose up in me at her words. If she felt sorry—if she longed to be with us—why had she chosen to go with Marion at all? I dared not allow myself to dwell upon that, to know that she preferred something other than home and family, other than me; that my daughter felt the world I had rejected could hold more for her than the world I had given her.

She went on, with details of their journey, their arrival in England, their welcome by neighbors and friends, her relief at being someplace civilized and predictable, her feeling loved again, her Aunt Marion's exhaustion; on and on with things which, though interesting, were painful as well. Then she added:

> *I regret to tell you that Ernest is failing. We arrived to find him in a weakened state from a bout with pneumonia. He appears ten years older and so frail, Mother; it would break your heart. Marion is distraught, of course, and relies heavily upon me for services Ernest for*

years provided. I believe change terrifies her—change in essential ways, at least. She had allowed herself to long for the India trip and plan for it; but, in reality, it proved a disappointment to her. Now she is ready to dig in deep, hold on tight to those things which speak security to her.

I arose in agitation. Sita truly expected me to experience sympathy for the ills of a selfish and narrow old woman whose main intent in life now was to woo my daughter away! My heart felt sick within me as I picked up the letter again.

You understand that I could not leave her now, Mother. That would be too cruel. Besides, it is good to be needed. Even Ernest enjoys my ministrations. I feel as though I have some good use here, at least for the time being . . .

The remainder of the letter was a series of pleasantries and endearments that were vague and meaningless, as far as I was concerned. A sense of sadness clung about me all day, like the tatters of a gray, loathsome garment I would fain tear from off my weary limbs, but could not. Would my Sita ever come home to me?

Abigail was buried, and the horrible scar in the earth covered over with the first flowers that spring provided. Abbey did not go near. She followed the routine of her days and performed her duties, but she did not grieve. Sita Beg and I visited her; Merin and I visited her; Susie coaxed her out for an afternoon of diversion in the city. Abbey was gently kind, gently grateful, but she behaved like a puppet, doing all things by rote. The emptiness in her eyes had a terrifying effect upon me; the anguish in Winston's tore at my heart. I knew how deeply he anguished at the suffering of those he loved.

We had three weeks of wet snow and bracing temperatures before spring put her foot down and pushed the messiness of winter into the past with both hands. March went out like a lamb. And Sita Beg's son, Kishan, prepared for his journey to San Francisco and the adventures that awaited him there.

I sent a letter along for Emma, as well as little gifts, pushing back all mean thoughts of her, all sense of being unjustly wronged at her hands. We went back too far; I had loved her for too long, and must be content to accept her as she was, not as my expectations desired.

We sent him off with a great hullaballoo of advice and well-wishing. But his last day in the valley he drew me timidly aside.

"You do not hold me foolish or disrespectful to Mata to do this, do you, Charlotte?" His dark face was so pinched, so earnest that I fought back an impulse to draw him into my arms.

"Not at all. Go in peace, Kishan. Mata understands why you are going, but she is a mother; it is impossible for mothers not to grieve at being parted from their children." He attempted a smile, but failed miserably. Then I put my arm out and encircled his narrow shoulders—this youngest son, rejected by the burly men of his tribe as inferior, though he possessed a finely tuned mind, and a dreamer's sweet spirit. "Go in peace," I repeated. "We will see to Sita Beg; we will care for her tenderly. You are young; you have much to give and much to glean from the years of your life."

A timorous expression of pleasure and relief crept over his features. "You sound like Karan; Karan might have spoken those words."

I could not help laughing. "His presence is too all-pervasive, too powerful for me to resist." I held my arms out, palms upward, in a gesture of resignation. "If I am not careful, I will become merely his shadow, his echo . . ."

Kishan's eyes grew serious. "Charlotte, you are a powerful person in your own right; do not ever doubt it. I find you fascinating. I can see why you took such a deep hold on Karan's heart."

I was touched. "Those are dear words for you to utter," I said, "and I shall treasure them always."

So, this stranger, my half-brother, began to become a person of depth and dimension to me. Then he left.

The day following his departure I worked several hours for Julian at the shop. When I returned, Emma informed me that Sita Beg had gone out to Abbey's house, riding in Susie's carriage and carrying a bag that looked as though it held more than the usual offerings of a pie or freshly baked bread.

I too thought it singular and went about preparing the evening meal. A little after five Karan came home, tied an apron over his clothes, and began to assist me. Half an hour later I looked up to see Winston enter the house. "Have you enough for one more?" he asked sheepishly, and I saw confusion written all over his face.

While we ate he explained to us what had happened. He had arrived home from work at the mill a bit early, as was his habit since the funeral. To his surprise he saw Sita Beg cooking an Indian meal, five-year-old Charlotte Elizabeth on a stool beside her helping to cut and stir, baby Seth happily playing with blocks at their feet. When she saw him she took him by the shoulders and walked back outside with him. "Will you, for love of your wife, entrust her to my care for a week?" she asked.

"Just like that," Winston told us, "her dark eyes so deep and tender that I could not think to refuse."

"What has she in mind?" I asked.

"I was hoping that you might tell me." Winston knit his brow and glanced at Karan, who shrugged in reply.

"She is a woman of depth," Karan replied, "and where she dwells, none of us here has been. If anyone at all can help Abbey, it will be her."

It was a pronouncement of hope and encouragement, but it did not feel that way to us who wondered and waited and had no understanding of what might be taking place.

Thus, for a brief season, my son spent his evenings and his nights in my home again. It was good to experience this intimacy with him once more. His second night home he picked up Sita's letter, postmarked England. "May I read it?" he asked.

I nodded, curious to watch his reactions, reproaching myself for not realizing that Sita's news of Ernest would distress him. "The old man is dying," he said, looking up, and his face was as stricken as it had been when he was a boy yet in London, and his father had died.

"Why don't you write him a letter?" I suggested. Ernest's affection for Winston meant more to him than it might have, because the lad was so bereft of male approval or companionship at the time. Ernest may be a servant, but he possessed a keen mind, a noble, generous spirit, and a store of wisdom gleaned through years of observing human nature—and of patching up the broken and misused pieces of the same.

"I shall," Winston determined. "His goodness to me—I should like him to realize how much it meant."

"I believe he does," I said gently. "But hearing it from you would mean everything to him."

Gracie came into the room and our conversation was interrupted, and thus never got round to the topic of Sita. Though I longed to know what Winston thought, I realized that he was preoccupied with his own perplexities at present. To no one else was Sarah's absence an anguish, her choice of living a wound. A mother's heart cherishes her offspring like no none else can; it is both curse and blessing, and a frightening vulnerability, this price we pay for giving and nurturing life.

Nearly a week passed. Winston had not returned home, and we had received no word from the little house in the Jordan farmlands where Sita Beg held her mysterious sway. Midweek, Winston brought a guest for dinner, a young man he had converted while on his mission in Italy, who had left home and loved ones, a prosperous family farm and vineyard, to follow the conviction of his own soul.

Dante Goldoni was, I suppose, characteristically Italian in his looks: short of stature, compact of build, a high forehead and a long, aquiline nose set above full, sensitive lips. His hair was a mane of thick auburn locks that curled at his forehead and neckline and along the curve of his cheeks. His eyes were black, black as any I had ever seen before, but not a brittle, glittering black, rather soft and dreamy, with the look of brushed velvet. I fear that, altogether, he appeared very much the image of a young god stepped out of the pages of some old mythology. Watching my daughters' faces I could surmise that their reactions to the handsome stranger were very similar to mine.

"I served less than six years after Brother Toronto and Elder Lorenzo Snow opened the Italian mission," Winston reminded us. "Now we have merged with the Swiss mission and have nearly a hundred members."

"That does not seem like many," Emma said off-handedly.

The young convert, far from offended, smiled at her. "Nearly half that number have already come to Zion," he informed us.

"I did not know that. Fifty of your countrymen," I remarked.

He shrugged his shoulders. "Most have gone up north, to the Ogden area."

"But they are friends of yours?"

He shook his head. "I met a few Italians coming over on the ship. But I have no comrades among the emigrants who have come here."

"Dante comes from the south, you see," Winston explained. "Most of our missionary labors have thus far been in the north. But he had a favorite cousin near Milan who met with a serious accident and nearly lost his life. Dante traveled up to see him about the time we began teaching the family." He smiled, his eyes resting tenderly upon his young convert. "He joined the Church, though they did not."

Dante returned the smile. "When I returned to my family, I was afraid to tell what had happened, to admit to them what I had done. When at last I did, my mother wept and my father raged like a madman, denouncing and disowning me ten times over." A long sigh escaped him, and his large eyes grew so vulnerable with sadness that I had to turn mine away. "He did not relent. He considered what I had done to be an act of boyish foolishness. He demanded that I beg forgiveness of himself and the local priest and return to the ways of my fathers." He shook his head slowly. "I prayed much. I faced the sad realization that there was no way I could live the life of a Latter-day Saint there, alone, amidst those who would relentlessly try to dissuade me." He attempted a smile, which sat tragically along the finely molded lines of his face. "So I left the home of my boyhood, the village where my ancestors for a dozen generations have lived their lives."

"And your mother?"

Dante furrowed his fine, penciled eyebrows. "She does not understand. I believe her heart is broken. But she is a magnificent woman, my mother. When I left she embraced me, she gave me her parting blessing." His expressive mouth began to quiver.

"But his father did not relent." Winston took up the strain for him. "Neither he nor Dante's two brothers, Lorenzo and Alfonso, would speak to him, or even come out to bid him good-bye."

I leaned toward our young visitor and pressed my fingers against his hand, which sat outstretched on the table. "I know something of that kind of sorrow," I murmured. "I am sorry you have had to suffer it. I admire your courage and resolution."

His silken eyes, glistening now with unshed tears, sought mine, and I read his soul's gratitude in them. But my thoughts were also with the far-away mother whose beloved son had rejected her way of life, all she held dear, and deserted her—going forever beyond the reach of her aching arms, for reasons and desires she could not understand.

Ten days after Sita Beg moved in with Abbey she appeared at my door in the late afternoon, satchel in hand. Her eyes smiled at the blatant curiosity in my face.

"Susie came for me," she said matter-of-factly, settling into her favorite chair by the window and taking the cup of cardamon tea I offered her. "She has returned to tell Winston that he may this evening go home to his wife."

"What happened?" I asked.

She considered a moment. "It is not easy to speak, to make words for. Each heart has its own rhythms, its own way of reaching understanding. Abbey was, what do you say? smothered by your love and expectations. She needed freedom to grieve where no eyes could watch her—"

"And judge her?" I piped, precipitating the end of the sentence. "We would never do that."

"Exactly." My mata spoke with her usual patience. "Your love, your expectations are what bound her. She could not give in to grief in all its bitterness, its distortion and unsightliness with your anguished eyes watching her, suffering with her."

"Go on," I urged. She had all my attention now.

"She was too bound to all of you." Sita Beg sighed, and the sound was a contented one. "The child needed most of all to discover herself; she needed time for that, and quiet, and the freedom of aloneness."

I nodded, my heart constricted, yet beating a bit wildly.

"I was part of nothing in her life—unattached from all that reminded her of her mother. In turning to me, leaning upon me, she risked nothing. She could find her way, she could build her shattered strength up before she must face life again."

"How is it you understand this so perfectly, Mata?" My heart trembled as I asked her. She turned her soft eyes upon me; I could feel the love that warmed and lit them.

"I cannot say," she replied. "My own life's sufferings have taught me, my own life's joys." She leaned back against the chair, relaxed, contented. But I looked on, amazed. Her expression was hallowed as, in my opinion, her entire life must have been.

CHAPTER THIRTEEN

I am patient, Charlotte, I try, as well, to be understanding, but it is not easy for me."

Karan seldom complained; I let my sewing sit idle in my lap while I listened.

"They simply expect me to think as they do. Is that a characteristic of the white race? They expect me to want to be a Mormon. Yet they ask no questions, offer no help or counsel, show no real interest in what my ways and beliefs at the moment might be."

They meant the men he had started working with at the university; men who were leaders, educated themselves, and ought to know better.

"They respect me," he continued, "because I have worked in far-flung places, well-known and exotic. But they show no personal interest in me whatsoever." He shook his head sadly. "I expected more at their hands."

"As did I," I admitted. "It is easy to grow narrow and a bit complacent in a society where all are the same, all think and feel just as the next person does."

"Is that truly so?" Karan asked. "Are all Latter-day Saints *the same*, as you put it? I can see great diversity in their understanding, performance, commitment—and I am not even looking for these discrepancies."

"It is the respect for agency that we hold so sacred," I reminded him. "We do not drive people to obedience. You, of all men, know that is futile. But in points of doctrine—in hopes of obedience—there is uniformity, oneness."

"In theory. Some care greatly; some not at all; it seems little more than a social order to such as these."

"That goes without saying wherever men congregate together."

He smiled at my words. "I am disappointed. I suppose that is the crux of it; disappointed where I do not wish to be."

He let it drop at that, but I wondered if he knew how his lack of interest in the things I loved wounded me. All had appeared hopeful when he was reading and studying with Winston, but that phase had seemed to cool. Occasionally he and I discussed parts of the Book of Mormon or some particularly interesting or thought-provoking sermon we had heard. There were wards and stakes organized in the city, so we attended meetings with our neighbors, all of whom looked upon the dark, strangely dressed man as an enigma of great fascination. Some pretended to be horrified, others disdainful; I do not think most of them really were. Curious—that most certainly.

And if there was censure in their hearts, then it was directed toward me. Many were aware, even in a vague way, of Maurice's attentions; most knew I was a respectable widow with a dead husband I honored. *Then what sort of nonsense was this?* I could feel them wondering. And, of course, there was my own skin, not as white as theirs. Some had heard of my rather unorthodox wedding—so much to wonder about! But, all that aside, *I* wanted Karan to care; I wanted the principles I loved to draw him the way they had drawn me. I could entreat him or worry him into a serious investigation, perhaps even beyond that; but what good would it do, especially with a man such as Karan. He had to care, from deep within that calm core of his, or it would be as naught in our lives. He had to desire it, in much the same way he had desired me.

Perhaps I was letting it gnaw at me, like a dog with a bone, for I seemed to feel ill and tired, not quite myself during these last days since Kishan had left. One morning in mid-May Merin came to pick wild strawberries, a custom of ours for years now. We would put some into jams, then make a large batch of shortcake and feast on the sweet, ripe berries smothered in cream.

We worked for some time in silence, enjoying the warmth of the sun beating down on our uncovered heads. Then Merin straightened with a sigh, kneading the small of her back with her fingers. "My back bothered me last time." She smiled weakly, almost apologetically. "I may as well tell you, dear Lottie; I believe I am to have a baby again."

As soon as she spoke the words I knew, without questioning. "I believe I am too!" I cried. The pattern of the last few weeks fell suddenly into place for me. I had not been thinking, even hoping, not this soon, not after so long—not at my age. We hugged one another, dancing like girls around the green growth of spring's rebirth, spring's magic that now breathed itself through the joy and wonder of our hearts and the new lives that lay, curled and growing, within us.

We sat in the shade and discussed the amazing matter. She calculated that her child would be born sometime in October, mine perhaps a month later. "I shall be thirty-nine," I breathed, "starting all over again."

"And you will love it!" Merin promised me.

"You still have stars of happiness in your eyes," I teased her.

"It's wonderful, isn't it?" She sighed, leaning her weight against the narrow trunk of a cottonwood and closing her eyes. A wisp of wind, gentle as a fairy's breath, lifted her red tresses like a flaming halo around her head. "At times my past life seems unreal, like something that happened in a dream. I go months on end without thinking about it at all."

I could tell she felt a bit guilty. "Drusilla is all you have left of it," I reminded her. "It is natural and right for your happiness to drive out all the pain and trials of those years. You endured them gracefully, Merin. You have a right to put them behind you now."

"What would I do without you, Lottie?" she asked, biting at her lip and frowning. "You are sister, mother, guardian of my soul—have been from the very beginning. Remember that day in Nauvoo when you found me and invited me to come home with you?"

I nodded. Such memories were painful to think upon. "Now we are sisters in deed," I smiled, "as well as in spirit."

Her eyes narrowed, the frown persisting. "It hurts still to go back to Nauvoo in your thoughts?"

I nodded.

"Is it Seth, then? Has your marriage to Karan made things any better?"

"It should have. His reasonings I know to be true, and I believe what he says: that Seth would want it this way. But I was so happy with Seth, he was so good to me. I cannot help feeling guilty for finding as great a happiness again."

She regarded me for a moment. "I would guess your happiness with Karan, though obviously of a different nature, is the greatest happiness you have ever yet known. And the guilt of this eats away at you because of Seth, and because of the Church."

"Bas! Bas!" I hissed at her. "How can you put into words what I couldn't?"

"Because I love you so well . . . and know you so well." Her voice was as gentle as the spring air, and with the same purpose to it, to cleanse and to delight. "You carry his child now," she continued. "Your spirit must be free to do this. Let go, dearest, as you have often told me I must! To take joy in that which is good and beautiful, to give the best within yourself, this cannot be counted as evil or wrong."

"You are right," I replied, forming the simple words slowly, but meaning them, for their import had settled upon my heart. I had seen too many innocent children hampered, even maimed, by the ignorance and weaknesses of their parents, not to speak of their sins. *I have done what I have done,* I thought, *in full faith. If I do not move forward I will spoil it, and that would be the worst wrong I could do.*

I smiled at Merin. "Have you told Arthur?"

"Not yet. But he will be glad. He would like a girl, you know."

"A daughter would be nice for him. I should like . . . well, you know what I should like."

"Yes," she said thoughtfully. "As I did, you should like a son of your own."

I felt unaccountably shy at the prospect of telling Karan and avoided it for a few days, until one night in our bed when I lay cradled in his arms, gazing out through the drawn curtains to my lawns and gardens, bathed in the cool silver light of the spring moon. So much moved unspoken, soul to soul, between us, that I was not really surprised when he drew me yet closer and whispered against my hair. "There is to be a child, isn't there, Charlotte?"

"Yes, Karan. It does not seem possible, but I know by now that it is truly so."

He smiled, with his eyes, with his face, the joy of his soul pouring over me like a blessing. "You will have your son, dear one."

I put my fingers to his lips. "Do not say so out loud!"

"And tempt the gods? You are superstitious, Lottie," he chided. Then, with his long, graceful fingers he caressed my cheeks, my throat, my unloosened hair. "I dreamed of him last night," he said, "and I believe it was a true dream. I believe this god of yours, who must love you dearly, will give you the long-cherished desire of your heart."

I nestled against him. He was what would be called a visionary amongst his own people; his words and dreams had already been prophetic where I was concerned. I would not doubt him, would not agonize or fret, but accept Karan's love and the love I knew my Heavenly Father felt for me—accept and rejoice in it, today and tomorrow, one precious day at a time.

"Gracie is where? What did you say?" I blinked at Emma a bit stupidly, yet noting the pleasure she took in repeating her information to me.

"She is with that Italian fellow, the one Winston brought home to dinner."

"With him—where, Emma? How?"

"She is helping him with his English, she says. I don't know, Mother."

Emma was irritated, but for my sake only, for the show of it; only the affairs of her own life were of any real concern to Emma. It had been thus for over a year now, and the freedom of working in Julian's shop from time to time did not help any. She was independent; she wanted no opinions, much least controls.

"I'm not like Sita," she kept saying. "I am not going to run off to some godforsaken part of the world just to prove that I can."

"Godforsaken," I would tease lightly, to cover my concern. "That is what most people call this desert out in the middle of nowhere."

She never appreciated my poor attempts at humor, and I wondered, when it got right down to it, what she would do and would not do if there was something she wanted badly enough.

I waited impatiently for Grace to return from her classes; those she was teaching, and the one she was taking from the University of Deseret. Karan arrived before her, which almost never happened.

"Where is our little Grace?" he asked. That was how he always referred to her; his fondness for the child was evident.

I repeated what Emma had told me. He arched the line of one brow thoughtfully.

"Do you think—?" I asked, not really wishing to hear his response.

"Yes, I think anything could happen. How old is Grace now?"

"Nearly sixteen. Hardly old enough to—"

"No, dear one, entirely old enough." He gave me a lopsided grin of sympathy. And I thought achingly, *Does Karan, along with everyone else, think I did wrong by Sita—that I might repeat the same mistakes again?* I tried to return his expression and calm the unreasoned fears that I felt.

When she walked in I knew at once that there was a difference; it shone in her eyes, in the way she carried her head, in the lightness of her step, as though she were treading on air.

"Mother!" she cried, setting her books in a pile on the table near the entrance and running into the kitchen where Mata and I were peeling potatoes and carrots. "You can never imagine the strange thing that happened to me today."

"Tell me, darling."

"All right, but you will not believe it!" I smiled at her innocent fervor, and the blue lights that always lit her gray eyes whenever she was flushed or excited. "That nice young convert Winston invited to dinner—"

"The lad from Italy?"

She gulped, watching for my reactions. "Well, he came into the school today, right near the end of classes. He was so polite, Mother, so hesitant. He wanted help with his English, and he thought that a school was the best place to go."

"That makes sense." Sita Beg's quiet eyes met mine and said much before she turned to set plates and cutlery on the table.

"He was as amazed to see me there as I was to see him." She giggled, then sighed, a little unsure as to how to continue.

"So, have arrangements for the lessons been made?"

Her cheeks turned a lovely shade of rose. "Actually, I have already given him a first lesson, a quick one, of course. He is a great student, and comprehends quickly. Are you too angry, Mother?" Her mind was skipping around a bit, influenced by the erratic state of her emotions. "We stopped in to Julian's on purpose, so that Emma could tell you what I was doing."

I nodded, but a quick stab of pain pierced my heart at the unkind manipulation of my youngest.

"And what is the price of these lessons?" Sita Beg's question startled both of us.

Gracie fidgeted. "That has not yet been determined, not exactly. But the young man can be trusted."

"Be sure this price," Sita Beg continued, "is one you are willing to pay."

We both paused. We knew her words masked a deeper meaning, as they so often did. Grace's cheeks paled now, and her eyes grew wide and thoughtful.

"Every relationship leads somewhere," I ventured.

"Yes, and Dante knows that and is being extremely respectful. *Dante*. Is that not the most remarkable of names, Mother?"

I agreed that it was and sent her out to the garden to snip some chives for the potatoes. "She purposefully misunderstood what I said," I remarked to Mata.

"Perhaps not purposefully. The heart can play many tricks, you know, on the mind."

I smiled. *My mother. My mother working beside me in the kitchen, and a new life growing within me, and a man who loved me, who had wrapped his heart and his honor about me, like a bright burnished shield.* I began to hum and realized the tune was one of Seth's old favorites, and that realization made the moment seem even more perfect, more complete.

"It is good I am not the jealous type." I smiled at Sita Beg. Ever since her ordeal with Abbey she had been returning alone to the little house at least twice a week.

"She still needs me."

"She will always still need you, Mata. My own grandchildren are going to forget what I look like."

"You could always come with us."

"Not with all the hours I have been working for Julian. He is both greedy and selfish, you know, and has no compunction in pushing me."

"Yes, this I know."

I looked up sharply. There was some note in her voice which arrested me. "Do you think I should not be working for Julian? It has been so long, since before we left Nauvoo. It was Winston's idea in the first place. Julian helped to save my life, Mata."

"Those days are in the past. It is this day, and the days to come, you must think of." The calm; always the imperturbable calm, just like Karan. "Think about it," she said.

I did not wish to. "Well, I will be having the baby soon," I mused. "That will play havoc with any schedule I attempt to maintain." I was speaking lightly on purpose, a sense of discomfort growing within me. Sita Beg glanced out the window and then picked up her satchel.

"Susie's carriage is here," she said. She bent close to press her cool lips against my forehead. "Your heart is pakka, my dearest daughter— genuine, good. Do not let the patterns of your life pull you into kachcha—a turmoil of weakness and imperfection. That is not like you, that is not worthy of your good heart."

Her words remained with me all day, echoing in my head, sitting just beneath the surface as I went about my business, as I talked with the people around me. Her words had uncovered things I could no longer be unaware of, no longer put to rest.

CHAPTER FOURTEEN

Summer came, with a breathless, dry heat that made my head go light and dizzy; other than that, I had no time to think about it, perhaps that is why I did not often feel sick. My handsome crow brought a new family for me to admire, their coats as dulled by the desert dust as I felt that mine was.

"He is a saucy fellow," Karan would say, and the phrase from his mouth delighted me, being one of the few things that revealed the British influence on his habits and speech patterns. I believe he had tried consciously to expunge all traces of the hated men of John Company from his life. But he had, after all, been a teacher of the king's own English; in fact, he still was—so much so that the other professors who were confident enough would, with delight, pick out Karan Ranjit's students from the rest. "We teach a down-to-earth, practical, at times almost backwoods English," one of them told him. "But your young men and women come out speaking like stuffed and spoiled little Brits!"

Karan laughed with the others, but he did not like it. "I should have preferred leaving all that behind me, . . ." he said more than once, "be known for myself, not a connection of that sort!"

There came the personal again—so very vital to him. But I understood, and it did little more than distress me on his account.

When I told my daughters of the child that was to come, their reactions surprised me. I had been naive enough to anticipate them responding like the little girls they no longer were, with breathless excitement at the prospect of a younger brother or sister.

"It is embarrassing, Mother," Emma said at once. "Why, if Sita wished, she could easily be married with children of her own now. Think about it!"

"It is not so unusual a thing within Mormondom," I defended. "Look at Aunt Merin."

"Yes, look at Aunt Merin. Her child will be younger than Drusilla's."

"You find that disgusting?"

"I find it a bit ridiculous."

I swallowed the lump in my throat and said nothing. Grace bent over me, her brows furrowed. "I am just a bit worried, Mother, that's all. You are not, well, so young anymore."

"I am not," I agreed, stifling an urge to laugh out loud, which would have wounded her feelings. "But then, I am not really so old." I pulled her slender hand lightly into mine. "Women have babies for a good five to ten years beyond what I am doing."

She considered. "Yes," at last. "But we have never thought of something like this happening with you. All these years without a husband; time and time again refusing Maurice." She shrugged her thin shoulders. "And if you were to have this one and like it, how many more times might you try it again?"

That remark did bring the laughter we were so in need of. But I felt they had shut me out, though neither one of them really meant to. *I have the wonder of what is happening inside me,* I reasoned. *And I have Karan. I do not need anyone else.* But that was not entirely true. One love can never, never supplant another. They were my daughters; for many years they were all I had to cling to, to struggle and fight for. I wanted desperately to be able to share this with them. They were on the verge of their own womanhood; it could have been such a sweet experience.

"Don't push too hard," Merin advised. "Perhaps they sense that."

"Has Emma said anything when she comes over to practice?"

Her eyes grew sad. "No. No, she never discusses it, never brings up things about home at all."

I wished I had not asked. I smiled. But Merin knew the truth she had been forced to speak had hurt me. "We are together in this, anyway," I told her, "and that makes a great difference to me."

"Oh, Lottie, and to me! To me it makes all the difference."

I went away counting my blessings, which, after all, is what one ought to learn to do in this life.

Summer days have a way of slipping past. One feels they ought to be slow and languid, with their bee-lazy hours and daylight extended until past bedtime. But the reality does not seem to work out that way.

July was upon us, then Pioneer Day approaching. We decided to join the hundreds of other Saints—over two thousand, as it turned out—at a picnic celebration to be held at the Silver Lake resort up Cottonwood Canyon. Ten years had passed since Brother Brigham and the first pioneers entered the Valley. *Ten years.* I was convinced we had accomplished more than any other people could have in that time. We had much to be proud of and much to look forward to. And this year, for perhaps the first time in my own life, I truly felt like celebrating.

Such a to-do, such elaborate preparations! When we arrived, there were already three boweries set up for shade while eating and three large plank floors laid out for dancing. Choirs were assembling at different spots, practicing their pieces; I noted half a dozen at first count. Gracie had been singing with the Ensign Peak choir and I found myself looking forward eagerly to hearing her perform. She had a sweet voice, true of pitch, and more powerful than one would expect to hear coming from such a diminutive person.

I glanced around me. *The Saints surely know how to have a good time,* I thought. It appeared as though there were to be brass bands as well. There were nearly five hundred carriages and over one thousand horses and mules, and it would be a safe bet to to say that well over half of the 2,587 people counted that day were children under the age of three! Their happy voices echoed and reechoed into the cavern of air and against the far rocks. I smiled at Karan and realized with a start that he had never been a father, never had children of his own— never held his new infant in the aching circle of his arms. Suddenly I wanted this child for his sake. What a priceless consummation this rare gift would be. *All must go well,* I thought, picking my way carefully over the rough ground. All at once it seemed terribly important to be able to present Karan with his first child.

We had gone through the flag ceremonies. The Nauvoo Legion officiating had joined in a few favorite songs, rousing with spirit and emotion, and President Young had opened the day with a short, splendid speech. Now it was time for food, before the performances of the afternoon would get under way.

High noon. I remember because Arthur took his pocket watch out, looked at the time, and then polished the face lovingly against his shirt sleeve. "This once belonged to my grandfather," he said, and I had leaned close to admire the fine workmanship of the piece. And just then four horsemen rode into the midst of us, dusty and travel-stained, sagging with fatigue in their saddles. The feeling, I believe, must have been instantaneous and universal; the Saints knew the smell and sight of trouble through long experience. I recognized two of the young men who approached the prophet with solemn faces: Porter Rockwell and A. O. Smoot. It took long tense minutes for the message to be delivered and then passed on to us. While the Stars and Stripes fluttered on the breeze we learned that there were Republicans in Congress stirring things to a fevered pitch with their supposedly honorable opposition of what they termed twin relics of barbarism—polygamy and slavery. Our enemies, the infamous Judge Drummond among them, had made wild charges and circulated wicked rumors about the Latter-day Saints. Their word was accepted point blank, with no questions asked, no further thought given. The President of the United States canceled the mail contract which had just been awarded to Hiram Kimball and was appointing a new governor. *A new governor.* The prospect was impossible to entertain. A non-Mormon governor to replace President Young—an outsider, who probably despised us, coming among us and telling us what to do! The outcry was terrible, both that which was spoken and that which was revealed only in the stricken expression of face and eye. But that was not the worst of it. Because of the false abuses that had been reported concerning us, the president was sending an escort to accompany his new appointee—an army force of twenty-five hundred trained soldiers.

The huge assemblage was stunned by the news. No one could think, no one could accept such a reality. *An army in Deseret, which had still been Mexican territory when we first set foot here. Was it to be Missouri, and then Nauvoo all over again?*

It broke my heart to look about me, to see the mixture of justified wrath and of anguished remembrance which made faces and shoulders sag. The brethren rallied us; our celebration must not be spoiled by this. But much of the heart had gone out of us, try as we may. And the music, at least to my ears, had a melancholy sound to it, no matter what the original intent of the tune.

Gracie sang like an angel, her pure heart crying defiance to the unseen enemy in every note. "She knows nothing of trouble and persecution," I said to Karan. "Nor do I want that clutching and fearful shadow to darken her path."

"It may not, even yet."

"You know human nature," I countered. "You, of all men, hold no illusions."

"True, dear heart. But I have been long enough among these people to have learned two things. First, President Young is an imminently wise and powerful man. It will take much to outwit him, especially since he fights for those things most dear to him." He pulled me close, until my head touched his shoulder. "Besides, this god of yours, how can I say it? He is never far from you. His care is a real thing; I have felt it many a time. He did not bring you here to see it all come to naught."

His words brought tears to my eyes, tears of relief and cleansing as well as of fear. Yet I admitted, quietly, for his ears only, "I do not want to have to pay such another price as we have already done so many times over. I know that sounds childish and petty. But it is not as if hacking an existence out of this dry desert wilderness has been easy for the Mormons. No one else wanted this place; no one believed that we could succeed! Why can they not simply leave us alone and get on with their own lives?"

His smile was one of genuine amazement mingled with the kind of tenderness one would show to a willful, unthinking child. "You ask this? You who lived intimately with the abuses of the British in India, who saw the corrupt uses of John Company, their disregard of any life form different from theirs—different, therefore obviously inferior!"

I bowed my head in repentant acknowledgment. "I had not thought of that, impossible as it may seem." I sighed. "I was thinking only of this people. That other life seems like a dream now, far away and hazy. The young man and woman in the cemetery, the anguish of the hospital, the darkness and evil of Dacca, death and ugliness all about me." I shuddered "None of it seems real, only a horrid nightmare I have tried to push from my mind."

"It is well you have," Karan replied soothingly. "Otherwise it would have eaten you up all those years, as it did me."

The shudder turned my skin hot, then cold. But his eyes revealed nothing of that suffering, only a gentle resignation and peace. *How?* I wanted to ask, but I knew he could not begin to answer that question, even if he had wanted to.

"It will be different," I whispered, "it is already." I lifted his hand and placed it against my abdomen where his child was growing within the mystery of that silent protection nature has provided.

He kissed my fingers where they lay intertwined with his own. "Nothing will harm this happiness," I promised him. He smiled, because he believed it; and I smiled with him, because for the first time I believed it myself.

I looked up, my eyes searching for Grace again, but lighting instead upon the lean, raptured face of Winston's Italian convert, Dante Goldoni, as he gazed upon his young teacher. Karan, watching me, glanced to see what it was that had arrested my eye. "Does this displease you?" he asked.

"I am not certain," I replied honestly. "It is not exactly a thing of race and country, not with me, as it would be with most people here. It is every other factor: her age and inexperience, her incredible expectations, his capabilities, his nature; I really know nothing about him!"

"Except that he has made a deep impression upon this very sensitive and intelligent girl."

"That makes it sound too easy," I protested.

"Easy? Hardly. Merely the way God ordained it."

"Well, I do not have to like it," I pouted.

"If you allow yourself to see the beauty in it, the incredible miracle, it will be easier," Karan replied, with his sweet lips pressed against my hair.

When the dancing began they did not even attempt the proprieties. Every time I looked round they had contrived a way to be partners, their faces mirroring that terrible oblivion of all around them.

"Resign yourself," Merin urged gently. "If it were Emma out there, you might have cause to be worried. You can trust Gracie; you know that."

I nodded, trying to do as she said. The coolness of the mountain air caressed my skin, my very pores seemed to breathe it in—clean air, smelling of pinewood and running water and peace. When the music started again I went into Karan's arms gratefully, and it was not difficult to put thoughts of Gracie, of all other things, from my mind.

The days of summer waned, their common routine dampening some of the panic we had felt on the mountain that day. Midway through August we had word from Kishan. He was doing well at his work. Emma was pleased, and the guests of the grand hotel liked him. He had arranged for nightly entertainments, ferreting out interesting people wherever he could find them. He had been delighted to discover a family of Indian performers who danced in the old ways and played the classical *ragas* music of India on their sitars. He had also become acquainted with a group of Japanese performers, among them a young woman of particular grace and beauty.

"We shall hear more of this one," Karan predicted.

Sita Beg smiled faintly, but no words came to her lips to let us know what it was that she thought or felt.

On August 5, at Brigham's call, thousands of the Saints met in the tabernacle to hear what President Young had decided and to pledge our support. From the first his determination came like a thrill spreading over his listeners. He did not intend to submit. He reminded his enemies and detractors that the constitution of America guarantees us all the rights we have ever claimed, and, if granted, these rights would be sufficient to uphold and protect us now—and would be all we would ever ask, "all we have ever asked." With that wonderful warmth of his, somehow both sapient and bold, he declared the Territory of Deseret to be under martial law. "We are invaded by a hostile force," he stated boldly, "who are evidently assailing us to accomplish our overthrow and destruction." He reminded us, and those who wished our destruction, that we had suffered such derision, insult, and betrayal before. That under the pledged faith of a democratic government "our houses have been plundered and then burned, our fields laid waste, our principal men butchered . . . and our families driven from their homes to find that shelter in the barren wilderness and that protection among hostile savages which were denied them in the boasted abodes of Christianity and civilization."

If Karan had been impressed with Brother Brigham before, I believe he stood in real awe of him now. He had never seen this kind of forceful, yet reasonable, show of independence and courage. "Brigham is at the helm," he said to me, admiration showing in every line of his face.

"How will he accomplish what he desires?" I asked.

"Oh, he will find a way, Lottie, be assured of that."

There was a sense of relief in taking a stand, in being united in the direction that the Prophet of God had chosen. *God is with this people,* I remembered, and that knowledge was like a song in me that swept out the ashes of fear. *How could I ever doubt? Ever forget?* I asked myself. "It takes patience more than faith," I observed to Karan. "And—" smiling ruefully, "I was never much good at patience."

"You are a master at patience," he responded. "And are not faith and patience merely two aspects of the selfsame thing?"

A week following the meeting in the tabernacle, a letter arrived from Sita. "Ernest is failing quickly," she wrote. My heart sank a little, remembering his gracious acceptance, his kindness, his fine-tuned perceptions, the deep human qualities that were carefully hidden behind the most proper facade of his serving-class mask. *Mother,* she confided.

> *At times he believes I am Elizabeth. When he looks at me I can tell it is her he is seeing, and not me. He talks to her—I do hope it is not wrong that I answer him as he would wish me to do.*
>
> *I do not feel as though I am play-acting, Mother, or even working to deceive. I feel in a way, as though she is speaking through me—and I know you will not scoff at that. I can, at times, feel her presence in a very real way. And I find it a comfort. I only wish you were here. You should be here. But then, I believe she accepts me as taking your place. Taking your place— something I am not the slightest bit capable of. Mother, I miss you dearly, and at times long for your gentle touch, for your wisdom and strength. Give all my love. Tell Winston that two*

days ago Ernest asked for him; he was lucid at that time, and knew who I was, but a bit confused, thinking, or perhaps only hoping, that Winston was with me. So I talked to him instead, telling him what a good man his little boy has become, recounting some of his adventures and accomplishments. It was wonderful, but caused me such horrors of homesickness for you all.

Sita, I cried *Were you born to tear my heart from its moorings, to catapult me into pain, into awareness everything within me would shun?*

CHAPTER FIFTEEN

The past is always a part of us, no matter what people say; we carry it in our genes as well as our memories.

One day in early September Karan came home from the University with a dark look constricting the lines of his face and a newspaper tucked under one arm—both small matters, but both unusual for him. He sat down in Sita Beg's favorite chair by the window and opened the news sheet on his knees. "Look at this, Lottie," he said, his voice taut with pain, much as it had been those days in the hospital when he had been dragged and mauled by a wild beast.

I read the headlines: *Sepoy Rebellion in India—British East India Company Threatened.* "Is this true?" I asked in my amazement. "Read it out loud to me, please."

He shook his head. "I cannot."

I perused the article quickly. In May the Indian soldiers, named Sepoys from their own Hindi word *sipahi*, meaning soldier, staged an out and out rebellion against the British Army in Bengal. This was not a mere uprising, but was being referred to as an actual mutiny, thoroughly organized and supported throughout most of northern India. The mutineers were attempting to restore the Mogul emperor, now aged, to his rightful throne as emperor of India. The conflict first broke out in Meerut—fierce and ruthless fighting, tooth and nail, for dominance. The Sepoys had captured several cities, including Kanpur and Delhi.

"This does not seem possible," I said to Karan.

"It was inevitable," he answered.

"What will happen now?" I found that the words burned my throat as I spoke them.

"My people will fail, Charlotte. There will be ruthless butchery and killing on both sides. But, as in all things with the British, it is only a matter of time . . ."

"Perhaps not! The Sepoys fight for their homeland, for the old ways of life which are dear to them."

Karan shook his head sadly, but emphatically. "The British will prevail, and it will be worse than before for my people, and the old ways will continue to disappear."

"You are a prophet of gloom!" I cried.

He gave me a sad smile. "I only know what I know." He shrugged his shoulders; it was a hopeless gesture. "I cannot help having such knowledge. It burns in me like the fires of hell; you know that, Lottie."

I knelt down beside him and rested my head against his thin, angular leg. "I am sorry, Karan. I wish I could ease it for you."

"You do, my dear one," he murmured, placing the tips of his fingers against the crown of my head. "You do, every day, every minute."

I turned and stretched, and he bent toward me until our lips met.

Britain and India, I thought, as I nestled in his long arms, quiet and content there. *Both have played such vital parts in my life, formed and shaped what I am, what my children will be. If it were not for the East India Company*, I mused, *might I have been born a native, with no taint of the Englishman's blood in me?* I shuddered to think of how different my life had been then. *Because I was British as well as Indian, I returned to that country. Because I was there when the gospel of Jesus Christ was restored my life, my whole being was transported here.* I sighed. One realization was beginning to rise above the others.

"You said *my people*, Karan, more than once. Is that how you look at it: your people, not mine."

He considered a moment. "I suppose that I do. You know little of them, you have never lived as they lived. For all intents and purposes, you have always been British." The sad smile teased the corners of his mouth still. "The ancient mysteries of the women of your race move through you, fashion your exquisite loveliness . . . but you are British, all the same."

I could not in fairness dispute what he was saying. But I found my own response singular. "I no longer think of myself as either Indian or British, but simply as a Latter-day Saint—in that context, in that one context always."

"Indeed?" His eyes told me he found that intriguing. His eyes told me that he would have to think for a while about that.

Brigham Young called in the missionaries and began to mobilize the Nauvoo Legion, creating what was being called the Army of Zion. He was sending his boys up to the mountains to harass the American soldiers, to get and keep their attention and divert their progress: that was the major thrust of his plan. October was languid, though nights in the high passes this time of year would prove bitter enough. With the long unwinding of the year we held our breaths and waited as autumn's brilliant colors peaked, and then faded.

Before the colors had lost the blaze of their glory, Merin's child, her little girl, made a successful appearance. She possessed a head of red hair like her mother's, and the roundest blue eyes. Arthur was enchanted, *smitten*, as the British would say.

"To think of a creature this beautiful being a part of me!" he said to me, his eyes shining. "It is a miracle, isn't it, Lottie?"

"Indeed," I whispered, kissing his cheek.

They christened her Abigail Esther, Esther for Merin's mother, and Abbey was well-pleased. Susie threw a party, of course. Such occasions were our best chances to take stock of friends and families whose demanding lives prevented the closeness of association we all would have liked. Three "sore spots" in our circle of friends were there: Julian, who appeared wifeless, and wearied, something he'd become accustomed to since his wife took ill six months ago; dear Phyllis, who appeared to grow more thin and more peaked every time I saw her. She had three boarders who had been with her for quite a spell now, and she seemed to be adjusting better than I had dared to expect. But there was no light in her; the spirit seemed dried up, disappointed, peering out at life from a safe distance; and I feared she did not really know how to take part.

The third trouble spot that seemed to be developing was my own daughter, Emma, whose querulousness had been increasing over the past months, irritated I knew by Grace's new romance. As I watched her I felt a tug at my heart. *She is too eager,* I lamented, *rushing out to grab life with both hands when it will rush in to grab and claim her soon enough. She will have none of the moment before her, yet after it has passed, she will never again be able to recapture the innocence and simplicity she has so carelessly thrown away.* I lamented, but I could do nothing about it, which is the greatest source of a mother's grief.

Drusilla, in the end, was adorable with the child; I found it delightful to watch her, dandling her own daughter on her hip and giggling over this baby she did not quite know what to do with. "This is my little sister," she told her wide-eyed little one. "And your Aunt Abigail, so you'd best get on her good side as soon as you can."

All in all it was wonderful to be all together. Grace invited Dante, of course.

"He has no family, Mother. No one at all!" she pleaded. "Can you even imagine how that would be?"

"I can imagine," I replied, my voice a bit grim as I suppressed the impulse to think back, to remember. "But invite him, dearest, by all means."

I grew impatient, wanting my own child, resenting the uncomfortable, confining weeks yet ahead. My birthday came and passed, and I was reminded that I would be thirty-nine when my baby was born.

"It is no matter," Karan assured me. He had taken one of his emeralds and had it put into a gold setting that hung from a fine linked chain. He placed it around my neck, with a kiss against my throat. "To replace that which you wore for so many years," he explained. "To bring out the green lights in your eyes."

Karan could make me feel exotic and beautiful and like the rarest of treasures. I touched the ring on my finger, this ring which had once belonged to the woman who bore him, who was at least in part responsible for the rare, gentle soul of her son. I kissed his fingertips, the prominent line of his cheekbone, the wonderful curve of his mouth.

"You have never been more beautiful, Lottie," he said earnestly. "Do not forget that knowledge. Wear it with the same grace and pride with which you wear your new trinket."

He called the lovely, finely cut gem a trinket because it pleased him to do so. I closed my eyes and prayed inwardly that I would never forget; that I would walk in beauty, the true beauty of spirit which alone could keep that fire of love and pride in his eyes.

"He is leaving you? Whatever do you mean?" I had not seen Merin's eyes so dark with misery for a long, long time.

"Arthur has been invited to join with Brigham's army in driving out the invaders," she said dully. "He wants to go desperately, Lottie, trained for the military as he was."

"Yes," I replied, "I understand what he is feeling." And I did, having been around soldiers during all my childhood, youth, and early womanhood, and having observed their unique manner of looking at life. "You must allow him to do this," I said emphatically.

"The baby is less than two weeks old," she stammered, fumbling with her fingers at the knot on her shawl. "Don't you think that's a little unfair?"

"Yes. A little unfair, but not like Nauvoo, not like crossing the plains." I leaned close and undid the knot for her. "Dear Merin, it is the experience that matters in this case, Arthur's need to prove himself. You know how important that can be to a man."

She smiled weakly. "I have become so spoiled, so complacent," she admitted, "since he came into my life. I suppose you are right."

"It will help things in the long run, make everything better."

She nodded. "But what of the danger?"

"I do not believe there will be much. Brother Brigham is seeing to that. The men are instructed to harass and harry, and even to do that on the run. No out and out confrontations are being courted; that would not suit our purposes, not right now." I leaned back against the bedpost, my thoughts working. "You know, this would be good for Arthur in other ways, too. He has made few close friends since coming here, because of the unusual nature of his business, Susie running him all over the place."

"He deals with dozens of different people every week," she defended. "He has more acquaintances than the rest of us put together."

"Exactly," I said. "He needs the comradeship of good men he can grow close to; he needs to build up real friendships that will influence and enrich his life."

"You are right," Merin agreed, with a deep sigh of resignation. "I can feel that you are."

I reached out for her hand. "We have one another, and you have Abigail to entertain and delight you. It should not be for long. I think Brigham will call them back before winter hits with full force, and the army digs in at Fort Bridger."

"Yes," she mused. "And you will have need of me, yourself, within a matter of weeks."

"Indeed, I shall," I answered, suddenly cringing at the thought of going through labor and birth again. "I wish Abigail were here," I confessed, my voice coming out a bit choked. "Talk about things not being fair."

"I felt much the same. Once, during a particularly difficult moment, I found myself calling out her name."

"Oh, Merin!"

"But I feel she can see us. I believe she is with us sometimes."

"But to share these times with her . . ." I shook my head, needing to clear it of such dark and discouraging thoughts. "I shall return tomorrow," I promised. "Does Emma's playing disturb you when she comes to practice? Would you like her to stop for a week or two?"

"No. Not in the least. She is an accomplished musician and plays so beautifully that it is as though I am enjoying a concert all my own." She smiled a bit sadly. "She is good company for me, Lottie, if the truth be known. I know it does not work that way for you two right now. And I haven't my own girl; I do not believe Drusilla will ever come back from Provo; her husband is too firmly entrenched there."

"Well, I know you are helping Emma, now, when she needs it," I admitted. "If it can also work the other way round, that pleases me well."

I kissed her good-bye and let myself out of the big, quiet house, meeting Arthur on the walk. He jumped at me eagerly. "I have been meaning to come and see you," he began. "There is a little matter . . ." He fidgeted with his hat, taking it off, then putting it back on again, nearly covering his forehead. "Actually, it is not a little matter, not to me, and—"

"Arthur," I shook his arm. "I have spoken with Merin. We have discussed"—I half-smiled—"and settled the matter."

He went a bit pale. I had no inclination to prolong his suffering. "I think you should go with the army, and Merin does too."

He could not believe it. His open, boyish face held such amazement that I wanted to laugh out loud. "It will be a good experience for you, a good way to make friends. And you are well-trained and competent. I believe they could use men like you."

He gathered me into a big bear hug. "You are priceless, Lottie," he sighed. "But then, you always did understand. Remember when Mother sent Hugh and me away to school in England, and Father made you break the news to us?"

I shuddered inwardly. "I most certainly do. You put such a brave face upon the matter; plucky little Englishmen, the both of you. But my heart was near to breaking as I watched and tried to encourage you."

"Strange times," he said, "that seem like something out of another lifetime."

"Yes," I agreed. "It was another lifetime, though it is a part of us still."

We parted. I turned once to look after him. He had reached the porch and was whistling under his breath as he pushed the door to go in.

At the beginning of November Colonel Albert S. Johnston came to join his troops. He bitterly resented the Mormon's interference with the movement and purposes of his men. Earlier President Young had cordially received a Captain Van Vliet who was sent ahead to purchase provisions and assure the leader of the troops' peaceful intent. But even he had not understood our determination to stand by at all costs and protect our own. Arthur left the day following our conversation. The following morning Winston appeared at my door to tell me that he had been asked to work Saturdays for the Church Public Works Department. He had his choice of turning out gunpowder on the site of the old sugar works or going to the little shop on Temple Square where the actual guns were being produced.

"Do you know those men are turning out Colts at the rate of nearly twenty a week?" he told me.

"Do we really need all that for defense?"

"If it ever comes to it we would. I dislike the idea of such work myself, but I will not tell them no." He paused, and I could see a wariness leap into his gaze.

"What is it, Winston?" He had never been one to play games with me.

"Has Karan said anything of all of this to you?"

I shook my head.

"I did not think so," Winston continued. "But I know for a fact that he has been approached, and his assistance been sought."

I could feel Karan's pain, even as my son spoke the words. "It is not their fault," he added, watching my expression. "They know nothing of his background, save that he was an Indian soldier, rendered unfit for action by terrible wounds, and retired to working in government house."

"Nevertheless . . ."

"Nevertheless, I think his decision will be respected. It is not as if every Tom, Dick, and Harry is involved in this. I just thought you ought to know."

I thanked him. As we parted at the door he added, "I can imagine how difficult this must be for Karan, Mother, with his own people fighting right now, tooth and nail, for their rights. All the conflicting feelings and memories that must eat into him daily."

I kissed Winston's cheek. "Pray for him," I said, "that is our best way of helping him."

After he left I went directly to my room, to do as I had admonished my son. When things began to swirl into a dark confusion within me, when I could sense no direction, no peace, the only thing that worked for me was to get down on my knees. It was not always easy to leave the tender affairs of my life in the hands of a Being I could neither touch nor see. But, oh, at times I could feel his presence, feel the strength of his power as he bent down to help and lift me. *Doubt not, fear not*—that had been the sweet, simple counsel the Lord had given Joseph and the earliest Saints. When I did find the faith to cast my burden at his feet, I indeed knew the freedom of walking away with a lightness upon my spirit and a song in my heart.

My child came earlier than I had expected, and I was given scant warning, barely enough to stir my senses into awareness, and then into action; after all, it had been nearly fifteen years since this phenomenon had happened to me!

I was not frightened, but I knew I must act quickly. Just as the thought came into my mind, my mother walked in from her morning visit to Abbey. "Do not let Susie's man drive off!" I cried out to her. "I think this child has decided to come."

After that, matters were out of my hands entirely. I had the most exquisite of care, leaving my own attentions to be turned to the struggle taking place within me. Karan was there in the next room, waiting, though I did not know that. Patty Sessions came to assist—and there is none better—but there was a longing inside me for the comfort of Abigail's strong, capable hands. In the end, it was Dr. Fielding's face that floated above me, long-ago memories of his skill and compassion stirred.

"I want you," Alan Fielding had said, when the tiny child Winston lost his mother and no one else could comfort him. *"Be yourself, Lottie, that's why I sent for you."* The memories swirled and merged in varied patterns, emerging in snatches, that at times made little sense. *"I want you here when my baby is born,"* I remembered telling the doctor. *"You were there with my mother when I first drew in the breath of life."*

I remember struggling to lift my head, my eyes darting back and forth until they found Sita Beg, until their touch made her head raise and her large, luminous eyes smile into mine. She came and stood by my head and smoothed my hair back. "What was it like?" I whispered urgently, "when I was born?"

"I was young. I thought I would never live through it. Then Dr. Fielding put his cool hand on my forehead and said. 'You are fine and strong, Sita. If you are lucky you will have a baby who is half as pretty as you. There is a young man out there wringing his hands, you know, and waiting for you.'" Her eyes misted over. "That made all the difference. After that, eagerness displaced the pain and the fear."

With her words in my mind, her hand clutching my hand, I heard my son's first tentative cry. Pure joy spread through me; the very room seemed to glow in the light of that joy.

But I cannot tell of the moment when Karan walked into the room. I cannot tell of the things that passed when his eyes met mine. I cannot find words to express what it was like when my mother placed my son into my grasp, and Karan wrapped his arms around both of us. Such moments cannot be told in plain, inadequate prose; not even poetry answers the needs of such times.

We named our boy Frances, after my father, and Fielding, rather than Alan, after the man whose integrity and compassion had blessed both our lives. *Frances Fielding Ranjit.* "The words do not go well together," his father complained.

"They go perfectly well together," I assured him, "as their elements do in our son."

Fielding. We thought we would call him Fielding. His dark curls already had a hint of red in them, when touched by the sun, that promised to be brighter than mine. And his eyes were green.

"He is perfect, Charlotte," Karan said. "I believe he will look like you."

"If he is perfect," I replied, "it will be because he inherits the greatness of heart of his father, not his mother's green eyes."

We were complete, the three of us together. And for a very long while nothing else and no one else around us existed at all.

Such times, of necessity, must end. Karan had work he must see to, and as my strength built, so did my desire for action. December had come, and the sounds and smells of Christmas lingered in the crisp city streets: lights and beautiful wares glittering in the windows, sleigh bells sounding over the cobblestones, the excitement of children's laughter, and the overwhelming feeling of love—different from any other time during the year.

Our men were returning from their guerrilla-type warfare. Johnston had nowhere but the burned-out Fort Bridger to take his men. Over a meal of roast duck and Scottish tatties, Arthur told the family gathered round his large dining table some of the details.

"Fort Bridger and Fort Supply were both fired," he said, "a financial loss since the Church owns them, but worth the sacrifice if it serves to humble and hold back these men sent against us. The settlers in Green Valley are deserting and burning their own properties to keep them from falling into the hands of our enemies, and have been heading here to Salt Lake for weeks. We stopped burning supply wagons awhile back, on the President's orders." He took a bite of duck and paused with his fork in midair. "Once the snows set it, it becomes bitterly cold up in those mountain passes. The men will pass a cheerless Christmas there, I can assure you."

That dampened our evening a little, but also made the warm firelight and good food seem even more precious in contrast. "Will they have enough to eat?" someone asked.

"I hope so. President Young will see that they do; that is if Johnston will take anything from his hands."

It was a sad topic of discussion for such a season, for a family gathering of reunion and celebration, and we soon turned from it to other things: to babies and homes, to fields and stock, to weddings and new church callings—and all that meant growth and contentment and progression of life.

It had been a year of abundant harvest, and Brigham urged us to leave all in the Lord's hands and find ways to rejoice. He urged the production of plays, the gathering of friends and neighbors, and the organization of dances, which during hard times, have always uplifted the hearts of the Saints.

It was the brightest Christmas I can remember in the Valley. We were a family united together as we never had been before. It had been a year of miracles as well as tragedies; the good with the bad, the constant thread of opposition to keep our hearts well and alive. As for myself, my blessings had been so abundant that my whole soul was full to overflowing. Learning from the past, I tried to embrace the beauty and happiness I had been granted with a heart that was grateful, but unafraid.

CHAPTER SIXTEEN

It was a dress that began it; or, I should say, brought it all to a head—a most elegant and extraordinary dress, to be certain: a crinoline ball gown with a boned and fitted bodice that swept to a point at the center front waist, trimmed there, as well as at the neckline with flowers set onto ribbon cushions. Its crowning grace was a large bell-shaped skirt, with two layers of elegant lace flounces laid over the green moire fabric. The sumptuous creation belonged to Grace, and she was to wear it to yet one more winter ball.

"Julian has outdone himself this time," Karan exclaimed, quietly admiring the gown and the young girl who wore it so gracefully, and with such a blushed glow.

Emma, entering the room just in time to catch his praise, gave a scoff of derision. "A pity to waste it on Dante. I don't care how dreamy his eyes are, he cannot even speak proper English, and he's poor as a church mouse, and happy to stay that way!" She stood defiantly, hands on hips, regarding her sister, whose expression had fallen at her cutting words, but who returned her no sharp reply.

"Is Arthur sending the carriage around?" I asked. Gracie nodded and turned her head away slightly, but I could see the sheen of tears in her eyes.

"And what would you do without Uncle Arthur to lean on? You can't expect him to take care of the two of you while you sit around daydreaming about music and books."

"That is enough, Emma," I said. "I want to hear nothing more from you until Grace has left for the evening."

"I will settle the matter and leave myself then," Emma threw back at me.

"No, you will not, dear. You will sit right here and wait for me."

She did as she was bid, but she did not do it happily.

I was most relieved to hear the carriage pull up in front of our house, wheels crunching in the half-frozen snow of the roadway. Karan walked Grace out, and we waited his return in silence. When he came in, he paused only slightly, then continued on through the room. As soon as he was gone, Emma turned on me. "All right, Mother. Go ahead. You have me all to yourself now."

I was trembling inside, and praying it did not show; praying, too, that I might be directed in what I should do and say. "What is the matter?" I began.

That took her off guard. "Nothing's the matter. What are you talking about?"

"Much is the matter, Emma." I kept my voice low and persuasive. "You have been very unhappy of late. It is easy to see, it is easy to feel your unhappiness."

"I do not believe that. You're busy every moment with either Karan or the baby. You don't even know what I'm doing."

Or care. That implication was clear enough. "So it must seem to you," I murmured.

"No, so it is, Mother. But, do not concern yourself. I can take care of myself."

"I don't think so, dear. Not altogether, not yet." I gathered my courage. "And, you are right. I have neglected you terribly. A new baby demands attention"—my tone of voice begged her to be reasonable—"and Fielding can be very enchanting."

"Yes, just like Gracie."

"What do you mean, saying that?"

"Face it, Mother. Grace is sweet and gentle, and just pretty enough, and everyone loves her. She never makes trouble or demands things no one else thinks she should be wanting, the way I do. *She* gets the boy—"

"She is two years older than you are, Emma."

"That isn't what makes the difference. She has everyone eating out of her hand; it has been that way from the start."

"The start?"

"Ever since I can remember. She was the adored one, Gracie. I was the one who just came along by mistake after Father died."

I could not answer; I could hardly catch my breath as her words trembled through the still room.

"It is the truth," she sputtered. "She is his daughter, but he never even set eyes on me. I don't remember him! I don't even have an image in my mind when I think of him."

"Gracie doesn't either. She was less than three years old when he died; she has only the vaguest impressions." My mouth was so dry that when I attempted to swallow I had to cough into my hand.

"It doesn't matter, Mother. It is just the way things happen to be." Emma shrugged her shoulders in such a pathetic gesture that I nearly cried out.

Instead I rose slowly and walked to where she sat and dropped down on my knees by her side. "It is cruel and useless for me to argue, to attempt to talk you into feeling secure and loved, Emma, to bully you into seeing you as I see you: rare and brave, gifted and fascinating, with an edge Gracie lacks, with a vital charm, an ability to spot what you want in life and somehow make it come to you."

She was shaking her head. "Don't, please. I know I am not like that—even if you really think you believe that I am."

"How do you think you are?"

"Vain." She shrugged her shoulders again. "Sometimes foolish. Always thinking about what I want, about myself."

"You see nothing beyond that?"

"Not much."

"What of your piano, your music? What of the incredible eye for color and fashion which Julian has seen in you?"

"What of it?" she repeated. "Of what use are those things to me?"

"None at all, if you refuse to let them be." I sighed and reached out with my fingers to touch her, but she drew sharply back. *Have I failed you so much?* But I could not. It was not my pain she was concerned with, but hers alone. *I cannot take her where she will not go,* I thought. *I cannot show her what she will not see. I cannot even draw her into my arms and tell her I love her, because she has chosen not to believe that I do.*

She rose, slipping past me. "I'm sorry if I hurt Gracie's feelings," she said. "That was rude of me, really. I'll tell her so when she gets home tonight."

"Where are you going now?"

"Up to my room. Julian gave me a pattern for a cape, and a piece of damaged goods he said he had no further use for. I believe I'll play around and try to make something of them."

"May I come up later and see what you've done?"

"If you'd like to."

Her frostiness stung me. When Karan came back into the room a few moments later he was cradling a very cross Fielding, who was an hour late for his feeding, and squirming in his father's arms.

"It did not go well," he observed, after a few moments. "I am sorry, Charlotte."

"What can I do?" I half-whispered. "She will not let me come near." Speaking the words aloud did not ease the pain of them, but seemed to release it into a cloud of weakness and tears. "Does she want to be unhappy? It sometimes seems so."

"From the beginning, like a small animal, when she was wounded or frightened she reacted this way. Who knows why? Who knows what went on inside her small mind?"

"*I* should have known."

"Because you are her mother? You loved her, you cared for her; if you could not get past her defenses, only she could alter that." He put his finger gently under my chin and made me raise my eyes to his. "Remember the days in the hospital, those times when you tried to reach me, when your pain was a living thing between us—and I would not. Each human being holds the key to his own soul, Lottie. No one can enter unless he opens the door."

I hid my head on his shoulder, upsetting the baby, but not even minding. From somewhere, silent as a shadow, Sita Beg entered the room, took him from me, and disappeared again, and we were alone, and I could cry, release the burden of tears that burned in my throat.

Later, but before Grace was due to return, I knocked at the door of the room the girls shared. Emma seemed to take a long time in answering. "Well, what have you come up with?" I asked, a bit too brightly, perhaps.

"Nothing, really. The flaws in the material are placed so that I cannot make anything work."

"That's too bad. I hope you are not too disappointed."

"It's all right. I'll make Julian feel guilty and offer me a nice one off the shelves." She flashed an expression that was part smile, part smirk, part a very feminine expression of triumph. "I am very good at getting my way in things like that."

In February Colonel Kane, an old and tried friend of the Mormons, came to the Salt Lake Valley, on his own determination and at his own expense. He was an unofficial emissary from the president, but Brigham stated that it was God who had sent him to do good to this people, and I think we all believed it was true.

President Young stated his policy most clearly in a regular Sunday service in the tabernacle about the middle of March. Boiled down, it was: to remove the grain and women and children from the city, which then, if need required, he and the other brethren would proceed to burn and lay waste.

We knew he meant it. Arthur was sober, Susie fuming. "With one stroke of that mighty will of his he'll destroy all my work of the past ten years."

"It would be worth it, to avoid what we went through in Missouri, and after Joseph was killed in Nauvoo." Merin spoke the words with such quiet conviction that no one gainsaid her; our memories would not allow us.

"Brigham Young will triumph." Karan kept assuring me. "In the end he will beat them, Charlotte, wait and see."

Meanwhile, Fielding bloomed, content and healthy; and so did Grace's romance with the young Italian. Winston took to stopping in often, "just to check on the little lad," he would say with a grin. "It is hard to think of him as being my brother," he once admitted. "You know, anymore, I seldom remember that you and I, Mother, do not share the same blood."

"We may as well," I maintained. "Heavenly Father has somehow got round that. You know, yourself, you could not be more mine."

He liked to hear that; but it was true, we both knew it.

"I believe that is why Elizabeth, my grandmother, came to your aid that night in the mountains. It could have been anyone, Winston, but it was her."

He kissed my cheek. "Yes, yes," he agreed. "It was her."

Before the month ended we had a letter from Sarah Elizabeth giving us the details of Ernest's death.

>He held on until Christmas, tired and weak, but not suffering greatly. He said he liked the prospect of going out with the old year; fit company for such as himself. It was an easy end, but how quiet and melancholy the house seems. He filled up all the cold and hollow spaces, you know, with his spirit and strength. Aunt Marion grieves in her same narrow way, allowing no one to ease her, as though in that very suffering lies her only strength. I am enclosing a letter Ernest wrote to Winston a few days before the end . . .

Winston took the sealed envelope from my hands almost reverently, and read it in private, and for a long time to come, I did not know what it said.

When the wet, blustery winds of March came, Abbey's health began to fail again. The nightmares of coughing and fever and weakness began. Winston tried to hide his fear, but his face began to wear a pinched look. I expected to see my mother pack up her satchel again and be gone most of the time. But there was more, always more to Sita Beg, than I could ever perceive.

One morning, while the baby and I were playing with the crow, cajoling him from his perch on the window ledge, she came into the room.

"Susie's carriage will arrive any minute," she announced in her pleasantly-modulated voice. "I thought I would go in to the shop today."

"The shops?"

"No, Julian's shop," she replied patiently. "I spoke with him Sunday. You still spend far too much time there. You have a nursing infant and a household to run."

"I did not intend to, but you are right," I admitted. "Did he really agree?"

"He likes the idea." The corners of her mouth lifted whimsically. "He likes the novelty of it. Business for him, with the scare your prophet has put into everyone, is slow. It is a good time to, how do you say it? experiment."

She always called Brother Brigham *your prophet*. But the term and the concept were familiar and respected by her.

"I have dinner for tonight planned," she assured me. "You relax and spend time with the baby. Perhaps tomorrow you can arrange to spend the morning with Abbey."

So simple, though it was probably premeditated by my mother for weeks—so smooth, done with the apparent ease of effortlessness, though I surely knew better than that! But, in one stroke, Sita Beg gave me my life back again.

It did not take me long to discover how much I loved this new pattern. I felt that I had my finger on the pulse of my home now that I spent my days here. At first I felt ill at ease, guilty; at first I worried about Mata. That was certainly a waste of my effort and time! Her exotic dress, her musical voice, her gracious manners drew the curious to gawk, and many of them stayed to buy. If he had been delighted with me in Nauvoo, he was enamored of Sita. I should have known; I should have realized that she would be able to do such a thing.

I found myself working mornings with Abbey into my schedule, surprised at the pleasure I found in working beside her, in playing with the children, in getting reacquainted again. We spoke seldom of Sita Beg, but her influence was evident, even in the furnishings of the house and the food Abbey cooked. Certainly this gentle, tried young woman had achieved a mature concept of herself and the purposes of her life.

Charlotte Elizabeth was a winsome girl of nearly six years old now. She saw to adopt Fielding as her personal responsibility. If I had chores to do for Abbey, she took care of the baby with such patience and tenderness that it was a pleasure to simply pause and watch the two of them. Fielding came to adore her—would stretch his chubby arms out, seeming to yearn for her, whenever we came.

"We need one of those around here," Abbey sighed once, after we had watched their abandoned, delightful play.

"A baby, you mean?"

"I know I mustn't think of it," she hastened. "Do not chide me, Lottie, as Winston does."

"I will not, dearest. Winston, grand as he is, has not a woman's heart. He cannot understand the need and hunger within you."

"This is true. His concern for me is so great that he simply cannot see beyond it."

"And he should not be censured for that. I believe it frightens him to realize how dependent he is upon you, Abbey. In his mind all the children in the world could not compare with your worth."

I felt on perpetual holiday. To have time like this with Abbey again; to rise late and play with the baby, still in housecoat and slippers; to linger in my garden, smelling the new roses as they opened and listening to the bird songs; to spend hours making chutneys and jellies; to pause midday with a glass of Mata's iced mint drink and sit with my knees curled under me and a book of poetry on my lap. Such things approached the realm of the heavenly, as far as I was concerned. Besides, I was most often home now whenever Grace or Emma came in from their classes or work. I could observe them more closely, engage in spontaneous conversations, be included in little excursions I had never been part of before. I humored my own pleasure, loath to broach the subject with my mother, by whose good graces my life had come to this state.

With spring came the last of the term at the small school where Gracie taught. "I must find something to do," she had lamented several times. "I must find a new way to earn money."

I longed to ask for what purpose she needed money, and see what she would answer me, though I knew the answer already: she and Dante were both saving toward the day when they could marry.

"Has he ever actually told you that he loves you?" I asked her one evening.

"Yes, Mother," she answered, blushing sweetly. "He has said so many ways, many times."

"You are still young," I protested mildly. "He is the only man you have ever dated, ever thought of seriously, Grace."

"I know, Mother," she admitted. "I think of that myself sometimes. But, there is something about him, something about me when we are together." She shook her golden curls in frustration at her lack of words to express it. "I have prayed much about this matter; you must know that, Mother."

"Yes, Gracie, I know that. Keep praying, then. That is surely the best you can do."

As Spring danced into the garden with her wet emerald slippers, Grace arrived home early one afternoon, dewy-eyed with excitement. "Sister Lucy has asked me to submit articles, to write for the ladies' *Exponent*. And, do you know why, Mother?"

"Tell me."

"Because she remembers the articles you wrote after Father died, back in Nauvoo." I was a bit amazed at that. "Yes. She said, 'if you can write anywhere as good as your mother can, then we will find good use for you.'" She reached for my hands, her young face radiant. "I only hope I can do it, Mother!" She grew suddenly serious. "Dante writes poetry to me, you know. He has a splendid, insightful way of using words, perhaps because English is a new and fresh language to him, one he must struggle with in order to express what he feels in his heart." She paced the room, biting at her fingernails. "I will be humiliated if I cannot succeed at this."

"You will succeed," I assured her. "Concentrate on giving the best within yourself. Forget appraisal and approval and comparison: those are deadly, you know. Concentrate on your love of it. That will make all the difference."

She looked up at me, her eyes filled with astonishment. "You are so wise, Mother. You always give me just what I need when I let myself become muddled or frightened or off the path."

Her tender praise meant much to me; it was one of the things I lived for, more than she knew.

Early in April when the land was drying, dark and fragrant beneath the clean sun, President Young urged that the evacuation of the city go forward full scale. I had seen wagons, piled high with goods, going by the country roads when I drove out to visit with Abbey, but it had somehow not yet seemed real. *Surely*, I kept thinking, *surely something will come along to stop this from happening.* Now the prospect stood stark before us, one we could no longer ignore.

We discussed it as a family. The men, as might be expected, exhibited much more enthusiasm than the women.

"We must try to think about it as Brother Brigham does," Arthur said with a broad wink. "Why, just last week in meeting he said that the prospect of evacuating the city 'gives a spring to our feelings, especially since we for the first time have the privilege of laying waste our improvements, and we are not obliged to leave our inheritances to strangers to enjoy and revel in the fruits of our labors.'"

There was something to that; it was a relief to know that the nightmares of Nauvoo would not happen again. But—to leave!

"We are blessed to have family in Provo," Merin reminded us. "Drusilla's husband has extended an invitation to all of us to fill up the house to the gills, and then spread out over his land."

The question uppermost in my mind, perhaps in all others was: *For how long? Will this be a brief interlude, to prove a point to the invaders? Or might we be turning our backs forever on the homes we have loved, and be forced to start all over again?* If that proved the case, Provo would not be far away enough, though the high point of the mountain separated Utah Valley from that of the Great Salt Lake. Brigham had men out scouting for entirely new places to settle, but I refused to let my thoughts go that far.

In the midst of our confusion, we received a letter from Kishan, telling us that he was to marry his beloved Japanese dancer—Emma taking care of all the festivities and arrangements—and he would bring her here by summer to meet us. My eyes, almost involuntarily, met Sita Beg's. *Will we even be here when summer arrives?* The question flickered between us. I felt a sharp prickling of pain. *Will he find anyone—or anything—here to meet him when he comes?*

One day at a time. I have lived that way before, I told myself. But I did not relish it now. We all did what we must do, with very little discussion about it; Karan said almost nothing at all. For the first time since his coming I felt a thoroughly distressing sensation: a sensation of isolation and insecurity. *There is no Priesthood in my home,* I realized. *Merin has it, and Abbey. But there is none of it here.*

Perhaps it began when we blessed Frances Fielding, and it was my son, not my husband, who held the infant in his arms and pronounced with authority the will of the Lord. Karan had never stood for that kind of thing in my life; I had never needed him to. But now, with nothing but uncertainty ahead of us, perhaps I did. Mortality, with its constant change, had for the first time revealed a small rift in the closely woven web of our oneness. In this we were not united—in this one vital way I could not lean upon my loved husband. And he, lacking the keys and knowledge, could not succor me.

CHAPTER SEVENTEEN

I did what I could to prevent it, but near the end, there seemed nothing but confusion to me.

We were to be a large group that would be traveling together: our family and Winston's, Arthur's, as well as Susie, Phyllis, Julian and his wife, and Dante, of course. But there were complications—complications always arise.

"I dare not move Abbey," Winston said tremulously. "She is too weak for the journey."

"I will help, so will Mata."

He shook his head. "I am afraid for her."

"I know you are, darling. But if things go as feared, it would be far worse to leave her here."

He gave her a blessing, and shortly after that, Susie offered to bring along her best carriage and outfit it for a bed. Then Merin's two came down with the measles, and the trip was postponed a few days, and food and meat—all the perishables—had to be unloaded, consumed, then new supplies gathered again.

Babies can be marvelous creatures at times. Fielding did not seem to mind all the fussing and inconvenience one bit. He looked out with his curious green eyes, watching everything, but remaining as serene as his father was. Out under the sun his red curls turned almost copper, but the darker pigment of his skin did not burn. "He will make the journey well," Sita Beg assured me. "And that is good, because I will not be here to help."

This was an astonishment. "What nonsense are you speaking?" I snapped at her. But she returned me her same patient, still-girlish smile.

"Julian's wife is unfit to travel," she explained. "But he is determined to take her. I should like to go in their wagon. This poor woman needs my help, Charlotte, more than you do."

I acquiesced; how could I do otherwise? I did not know Julian's wife well. She had somehow managed always to stay in the background.

"Travel with us. We were planning upon it."

"She cannot keep up the pace. And you must not be slowed, not with this number of children."

So, it was agreed. We started out on a May morning of lark song and blue skies and fragrant sage . . . though the plowed fields through which we passed lay drying beneath the hot sun, barren of seed.

It was a hot and dusty journey, a trip of frustration and annoyance; when we arrived we would be getting no place, and have, really, nowhere to go.

Provo sits in a pleasant location, alongside the cool lake the Indians love. Drusilla and her husband had prepared for us; hasty sheds had been constructed, tents set up beneath shade trees, and large quantities of food dried or cooked. At first, for a few days, it was like a perpetual picnic, especially for the women and children, who could sew and cook, nurse and watch children while we visited. After a spell of confusion, the men worked out their own pattern. Some helped in the fields, others in mills or blacksmith shops, wherever their talents and experience led. Dante surprised me. He was a skilled shoemaker, something he had learned back in Italy. He spent long hours cutting down and refashioning worn leather, patching and soling heavy work boots that were needed to plant and plow. Evenings were nice. Evenings we ate as a group together and afterward sang and danced. The unspoken agreement was that each helped one another. Abbey, for perhaps the first time, could lie back in a cushioned chair and let the sun pour its healing rays over her; there were hands in plenty to divide her modest portion of work.

After several days, when Julian's wagon failed to arrive, I began to worry. Finally Arthur and Winston agreed to ride back and look for them. As soon as they left, a tight, unhappy feeling constricted my chest, and I waited impatiently. One day, another . . . and on the third day they came: two men on horseback, a man and a woman seated in the front of the wagon, and a new coffin riding in back.

Sita Beg explained to us that night what had happened.

"The movement of the wagon brought excruciating pain to her," she began, "and she kept begging Julian to pull off to the side, to leave her there, or to take her back home. His face was a mask; he dare not acknowledge her anguish, for he knew no way to deal with it. 'We will be in Provo soon where there is a cool lake and trees, and there you can rest.' We went on thus until I could bear it no longer. I eased the reins from Julian's clutched hands and pulled off a ways into a thin grove of cottonwoods where a small spring of water had turned the grass lush and the air cool.

"Clarissa drank the liquid gratefully, and I bathed her hot skin in its coolness. 'I will go back with her and wait,' I told Julian firmly. 'Either that, or we two stay with her, here. The end is not long.'"

"How could you know that?" Merin asked.

"I have seen death come too many times among the wanderers of my own people," she explained, "to have any doubts."

Her simple answer was a pinprick through the dusky veil of my mother's past life—in every way so different from anything I'd ever known. *Death and suffering, and the terrible aloneness of being different,* I shuddered.

"So she died there? Did no one come by? Offer to help you?" Arthur was disgruntled to picture the scene she was drawing.

"During the second night. No, no one stopped, except briefly. And we sent them on their way. There was nothing anyone else could do."

"Julian was frightened, wasn't he?" I knew him too well not to be aware of his weaknesses. I think my mother understood what I was asking: In the end did his fears and weaknesses make it more painful for his wife?

"He held up; I would not allow him to do otherwise." A strange expression curled the corners of Sita Beg's expressive mouth. "Clarissa died holding his hand, feeling what strength he had to give her."

"That was as it ought to have been." This, a bit unexpectedly, from Gracie.

"He has never had a taskmaster," Sita Beg said, rather gently. "A man will, by nature, take the course of least resistance if nothing comes along to prevent him."

No voices raised to contest her statement. "Where is Julian now?"

Winston asked, at length. No one seemed to know. "I will go in search of him," he offered, rising with a stretch of his lean young body.

Yes, I thought, *Winston would be the best one to be with Julian now.* I recalled with such clarity the young boy Winston had been during those last days in Nauvoo, after Seth had died. I remembered him coming to me, saying he and Julian had talked it over and thought I ought to go to work for him. The poor child was so intent upon taking care of the mother for whom he had felt this weight of responsibility since the dark Dacca days. But it piqued my interest, gave me an extraordinary sensation to think of the efficient, somewhat aloof Julian being tutored by the docile Indian woman who had come quietly into our lives from the other side of the world.

I did not see Julian for myself until the following day. He looked drained, both of strength and color; there was a dullness in his eyes I had never seen there, not even back in the difficult days of Nauvoo.

"Julian," I said, "I am so sorry you have had to lose your Clarissa, and in such a manner."

I dislike expressions of sympathy and condolence: they are so formal, so meaningless, nothing but a means of bridging terribly awkward moments between human beings. I know, I have heard them addressed to myself often enough.

"Not as bad a way as you might think," he replied slowly, as if choosing his words carefully. "It was still and private out there, and I had your mother with me." He stared at me, wide-eyed, as though stunned a bit. "She is a remarkable woman, Lottie. Do you realize that?"

"I believe I do. I am so glad she proved to be a blessing to you, Julian."

He gathered me into his arms and held me tenderly for a moment. "I was so frightened, my dear," he muttered. "Couldn't have made it through without Sita Beg, God bless her."

Yes, I thought, after he had left me. *God bless her tender, enigmatic, abundant soul.*

God was with us, as Karan had always claimed he would be. The banishment from our homes was to be neither indefinite nor long. In mid-June President Young came to terms with the army, and agreed that they might enter the Valley—as proof of our peaceful intentions and cooperation. But the conditions were absolute: they must march through the city without pausing at all, without stepping out of line in the slightest manner. Many of the prominent houses and buildings were emptied of people and filled with materials ready for firing. The conditions must be strictly complied with; this was no bluff on Brigham Young's part.

On June 26 Johnston's army marched through our city, the first of the troops arriving about ten o'clock. All day long they filed along the quiet street fronts, heading toward the bivouac eighteen miles west of the city—beyond the Jordan River—where their camp would be made. Strict order and discipline was observed; the rear guard departed near five-thirty in the evening, when the sun was illuminating the mountains they had just passed through and softening the empty wilderness with its soft-hued shades.

Five days later, on July 1, Brigham announced that he was returning, and any of us who wished to begin were also free now to go. We waited and prepared for two days: the streets of Provo were crammed with families in wagons, dragging flocks and herds and children along with them. We arrived home on the Fourth of July, and I thought that most fitting. Here, in the fabled land of religious freedom, we had won a victory of sorts. We had reestablished ourselves, with God's aid, upon the land we had purchased, and others had purchased for us with tears and prayers and their very life's blood. We had triumphed; we were not being molested, we were not being driven away.

Karan thought it a monumental triumph. For, ironically, during this very same time in his country, the Sepoys suffered a devastating defeat. The power of the East India Company was broken, true; but the British Empire itself simply stepped in to take its place, and the Indian people lost even more of what, by every right, ought to be theirs.

Indeed, Karan was thoughtful for many days. I could see that he wished to understand the vast differences in the affairs of mankind. *Is God truly with this people?* I could see the question in his eyes dozens of times every day. I prayed. I prayed that this opening, narrow as it might be, would extend from his mind to the deepest inner recesses of his heart.

We were there and ready when Kishan came with his bride; we felt to rejoice and celebrate, for more reasons than they knew.

Watching the young bridegroom, in his joy and devotion, was touching. I thought he had matured since he left us and looked a confident and competent young man. His bride was as delicate and white as a piece of bone china, with coils of raven-black hair and the mysterious narrow eyes of the Orient, which seemed to be gazing out wisely and mutely from a safe recess. Her name was Michiko Yamamoto, as musical as raindrops, and she looked no more than a child, though Kishan assured us she was a wise and accomplished young woman. She spoke impeccable English, with a sing-song monotone, if such a thing can exist. *Care and propriety, and a stiff mold one never bends or fractures*, I thought, making a rueful comparison between my own daughters and this pale, exotic creature. Then my mata walked up and began to converse with the girl, and I realized with a start how much Sita Beg had changed. It was so quiet and gradual a change that I had failed to observe it; though now that my eyes were looking I saw it everywhere: in voice, movement, facial expression. She had taken unto herself what she desired of our ways and discarded the rest—*as she did with the Crims*, I thought, *as she did with my father's people, the British.* She walked with a relaxed air that was becoming, she smiled so much more often, she asked questions, she tried new foods and new ways, and she read. *Why have I not before noticed the small stack of Karan's books piled on a table in her room?* She seemed to know more than I did about matters of state and business, and how the neighbor's sick cow was faring, or the fact that the hens weren't laying. And then there was the success she had made of herself in Julian's shop.

Mata was a wonder with her new, timid daughter-in-law; they were both strangers in a strange land, and my mother drew her out by the force of her kindness and patience. She listened to the girl, she praised her, not profusely, but sincerely. She drew her into conversations and activities, sought her opinion on various matters, and many times rose an hour early or retired an hour later than others to teach the girl some skill or knowledge which would make her stay among us easier. Kishan noted all this. He had always been devoted to his mother, but now his joy was complete. He respected what she was

144

doing, and his appreciation was all Sita Beg needed to secure her own joy and peace.

With Kishan and his bride, came the corpulent Emma, as loud and brassy as always. If I shied back a bit from encountering her, it was but to be expected, after all that had passed between us. She was uneasy too; I could see it in her eyes when she glanced at me. Karan must have seen it and decided to charm her. He made the first move, going to her, bowing, kissing her fingers, the dark, gentle sumptuousness of his presence irresistible. Nor did he press her and snip the fine thread of his sincerity; there would be time later for Charlotte to come into the picture. First let these two become friends. Then all else would follow.

So that first day of their arrival, I scarcely spoke to my old comrade. Not until the following day when Karan had work to do, and my mother had returned to Julian's, and the young people had all traipsed off to go sightseeing, did I find myself alone with her.

"Things have changed, lovey, haven't they?" she beamed. "Think of them first days in London when you were thin as a rail and scared of your shadow. Then Nauvoo after Seth died, and you were alone with a new babe on your hands. I call those depressing times!"

"Think of all you have done and seen," I cried. "You are a real American, Emma, more than most who come here, pick a safe spot, and stay there."

"Aye, I've had me share of sights and adventures, to be certain," she agreed. "But naught would have brought me to this demented desert kingdom if it had not been for you."

"Do you really look upon it with so much aversion?" I asked. And, perhaps she knew the question was a sincere one so she answered it.

"I never could see these Mormons, lovey; now, you know that." I nodded. I had to agree; I remembered the streets of London too well. "I b'lieve they've cheated you of what life had in store for you, and that's not been easy to watch all these years. I b'lieve, as lovely and clever as you are, Lottie, you'd have made for yourself a grand life somewhere, not groveling and starving out here in the wilderness, your skin wrinkling to sandpaper."

I put my hand instinctively to my hot cheek. "Do I appear that bad?" I cried.

Then she threw her great head back and laughed, with much of the same abandon she used to, and I found those thick arms wrapped around me as they had not been for years.

"I'm right fond of that scrawny little half-brother of yours," she said, once we had settled down again. "Got a good head on his shoulders, and is right respectful. I could trust him with my whole fortune—which is considerable," she added, drawing herself up. "Never had a son, you know. Findin' him was a godsend."

"I am glad to hear that! Strange, isn't it?" I mused. "All the different ways in which our lives have become bound together?"

"You'd claim the good Lord intended it," she teased.

"Of course," I replied evenly. "Intended, and perhaps even arranged it!"

It was all right then. We avoided the subject of Sita and England. I allowed her to fuss over my Emma; I came to her side when she needed me, and stayed in the background when she preferred it that way.

Summer ripened. Their visit extended into a week, and they moved, for convenience sake, into Susie's big house. One week became two, then three. I saw her only every other day or so, and began continuing my visits to Abbey and the children, and the routine of my days seemed to slip into its old, well-liked ways.

Then came an afternoon when I arrived home before anyone else did; a situation, in itself, not unusual. I began preparations for the evening meal, enjoying my solitude, yet looking forward to the happy confusion of everyone gathered together, telling the news of their day. When an hour passed, and then a second, and no one at all appeared, I covered the fruit and pies, and put the curried meat on the back burner to simmer. I fed Fielding and sang him to sleep, then walked out into the lengthening shadows, straining my eyes to watch for them against the low slant of the sun.

The minutes, tedious now that I was holding each in my hand, began to crawl. Half an hour, forty minutes, the tightening in my middle was beginning to hurt. Then I heard Emma's laughter, followed by the higher, lighter note of her namesake's, and there was a definite creaking of carriage springs and the comforting pattern of the horses' hooves striking the dust.

I smiled with relief as they tumbled out of Susie's carriage: my two girls, Merin, Kishan, and Michiko—

"Mother!" Emma rushed up to me. "We have something to show you. You will not believe it! I can hardly wait to see your expression!" she cried.

Gracie smiled in agreement, and I turned toward the house with them.

"Where is Mata?" I asked.

"Nani"—My daughters always used the Indian terms of endearment with my mother—"Nani stayed behind to help Julian clean up," Emma said, giggling at Grace.

"Clean up?"

"You will see, Mother," Grace assured me, as they hurried me into the house.

We crowded into the parlor, food and all else forgotten. Emma glided to the center of the room, cradling a large cotton sack that appeared enticingly full. I looked toward Karan; his eyes met mine with a tender sympathy at my surprise before someone asked him a question, and he turned away.

"I have magic to unveil for you, Mother," Emma began, "magic of my own creating." Then she glanced at the older Emma. "It was Karan and Nani who started it," she admitted. "And Julian, I must not leave out Julian. They are so clever and have been ever so good to me." She laughed in delight. "And, of course, Aunt Emma has come along to finish it all in grand style!" *What in the world is she talking about?*

She drew from the bag a long gown fashioned of watered silk—a gown whose elegant lines hung loose and true from bodice to waist, from waist to ankle. She held it against her own body; it seemed to move and shimmer. It was a marriage between east and west, the graceful, sparse attire of the Indian woman adapted to the styles and expectations of fashion as it resided in American minds. It was achieved so well that the effect was breathtaking.

"Emma's own design," Grace said, her voice kitten-soft with affection and pride.

"Mother, I drew them myself. Julian helped me with proportions and detail, Nani with adaptations of the form and purpose of the sari."

She held up a second, equally as lovely, though subtly different. Another and another; she seemed to possess a keen eye, an instinct for what would work, and the audacity to attempt it. I sat back in my chair, overcome; and Emma was delighted in that.

"Karan," I asked at last. "Where does Karan come into the picture?"'

"It was his idea in the first place," Emma revealed, and I thought there was almost a reverence in the tone of her voice.

"There are other designs to enhance the clothing," my friend Emma declared, with a clear note of pride in her voice.

Karan drew a small box out from the folds of his long, loose jacket and rose and walked until he stood before me. Then he carefully placed what looked like a miniature carved chest on my lap.

I touched its coolness with the tips of my fingers. All eyes were on me. I lifted the lid—my gaze froze in wonder—then I released a long sigh of amazement.

Inside were rows of rings, delicate bracelets and anklets, fine-spun gold necklaces, and heavy amulets, encrusted with stone. I was stunned to think of the fortune I held in my hands. I lifted my eyes to Karan's. "I had no idea. . . . You said you brought gems with you, you must have shown me some in the beginning." I ran my fingers through my disheveled hair. "I had no idea."

I turned to my expectant daughter, her eyes still shining. I reached for her slender hand and cradled it loosely. "You have a gift, Emma, I truly believe you do. You have created such amazing things here, nothing stale and borrowed." I picked up a thin ring which was twisted into a design like a love knot, in which was set one perfect, lustrous pearl. "I can feel the impress of your spirit on each one of these pieces," I whispered, unconsciously tightening my hold on her hand. She dropped to her knees beside me, so that our eyes were level, and for a moment our clasped hands rested together upon the smooth lid of the box. "Thank you, Mother!" she sighed. "More than anything I wanted you to like all of this and approve."

Her words pierced me with a joy that was also pain. *I had no idea you cared so much!* My heart cried out to her. *I did not realize, or allow myself to believe, that your love went so deep.*

It was somewhat difficult to respond to my friend Emma's loud enthusiasm when she outlined her proposals for marketing her god-child's creations. "This will make both of us rich and famous—I promise you," she boasted, and when my eyes strayed toward Kishan, he solemnly nodded agreement. "This lady," he said under his breath to me, "this lady can do anything she desires; this lady can turn all things to gold."

Gold, I thought. *Cold and unyielding against the supple warmth of young flesh.*

"I own interest in three stores and half a dozen high-class saloons," Emma was boasting, "not to mention the hotel by the harbor, that's where the people with money and class come, right, Kishan?"

Kishan nodded again.

"They'll eat this up, lovey, you wait an' see if they don't." She was high, elated with anticipation, and a sense of power and pride, so cold and so different from the Emma I knew all those years ago in England.

CHAPTER EIGHTEEN

In time our visitors left, and we enjoyed languid Indian meals in the peace of the garden, savoring the spices and fruits Kishan had so thoughtfully brought to us. In August Drusilla told her mother she was expecting another child. In September Winston was called to be bishop. That overwhelmed me a little, and I tried to increase my support of the two young people in every way I could think. Fielding was growing. His green eyes gave him a mischievous, at times even mysterious, air. He was docile and good-natured, yet he loved to laugh, he loved to sing with the girls while Emma played the piano. Indeed, she often took him along when she went to Merin's to practice, for he was no bother at all. From before his first birthday he could speak a string of words, many of them Hindi, for his father thought it best to teach him both languages hand in hand. The child never ceased to be a miracle in Karan's eyes. He nurtured him sometimes so painstakingly that it was impossible not to be drawn to the both of them, watching the scene.

But Karan was busier than usual of late. The presence of the army had boosted his business, and he realized quite suddenly that he was not keeping up with demand. My Emma worked with him, creating settings for the pieces he cut and prepared with a caring eye. They were all bound up in the creative venture, and Grace had her writing and her Italian suitor; so Merin and I spent our time with the young wives, dandling our babies on our knees, sharing recipes and home remedies, and not minding a bit. Abbey extended herself in order to be one among us, though we accommodated her limitations as much as we could. Two little ones, a boy and a girl, and Charlotte Elizabeth—as precious a little woman as any mother could ask. Yet, the hunger remained in Abbey's eyes, and when we learned that Mary Jane, too, was expecting another, I had to turn away from the pain of it.

As the holiday season approached we saw more and more of Dante, and I found I was becoming sincerely fond of him. Everything Sita Beg cooked he pronounced "magnifico." I was surprised, though I should not have been, when I arrived home one evening to find him teaching my mata how to cook pasta, with olives, tomatoes, and basil, which we found a most succulent dish. He came often to eat with us; for that matter, so did Julian, I began to observe. We made an unusual group for a Mormon family sitting around the board.

"Your family makes me very happy," he told me once, upon parting. "Felice," he repeated, "happy deep down inside where the heart lives."

And he was working to improve his station in life and himself, still taking classes from Grace, and others from any local academy that would admit him. He had begun making shoes, after the finely crafted lines of his country, and Karan had encouraged the lad to bring them to his shop to sell. He was delighted with the success he was having, but I noted that it did not turn his head. He lived simply, tucking away the money he earned for the future.

"My dream is to own a farm one day," he confided to me. "Land of my own. I should like to keep goats, have a little orchard, make fine cheese."

"That is a good dream," I said. "I pray it will come to pass for you."

"I shall make it happen," he said, his handsome eyes glowing. "Otherwise, it will not come to pass."

Wisdom born of suffering and sacrifice, I thought. *The only real wisdom.*

As the Christmas season drew near I felt a sense of excitement more intense than usual. "Something is in the air," I told Karan. "I can feel it disarming me, drawing me."

"It is the force of young love," he replied simply. "Your spirit is in such harmony with our Gracie's that you can feel in part the intensity of what she is experiencing."

Thus I felt no surprise when Dante came to Karan and me and asked for our daughter's hand. Winston was at the house when Dante arrived; I believe they both planned it that way. The boy's eyes were as frightened as a young deer when he sees the approach of the hunter who holds the power of life or death over him. Yet he was willing to reveal the depths of his longing and need, anxious to attempt to explain the extent of his commitment to this wonderful girl.

"In the restored kingdom of God the woman holds a position of honor. In my culture the woman is the heart of the home. I believe that is how it should be. In this household"—His sensitive mouth grinned lopsidedly—"Among this family the women possess power and freedom such as I have never seen before."

"That, too, is how it should be," Karan said solemnly.

Dante nodded vigorously. "Yes, I know this to be true. If the woman is happy, every person in the family is happy. If the woman grieves, the spirits wilt, like the blight on the vines in the vineyard, and all are bowed down."

"It is a pretty sentiment," I said, as gently as I could. "But can you live it, Dante?"

He respected my question and was not offended. "I want to. I possess the desire. With God's help, and Grace's, I believe that I can."

I was well satisfied with the interview. After we sent a relieved and rejoicing Dante to Gracie, we found Winston in the kitchen eating the last of the scones and grinning like a school boy.

"You will not regret this, Mother," he assured me. "Dante can be trusted. He will care for her as tenderly as even you could wish." Then, with a wink above my head he added, "Though you must not expect anyone, and I emphasize anyone, to rise to Karan's standards. That simply cannot be done."

His tone and manner were one of banter, but I knew that, by and large, he was serious.

Gracie had her ring for Christmas, and it was less difficult for Emma than it might have been because it was of her fashioning—the love of so many went into it that I hoped we did not frustrate Dante and detract from its essential purpose in the first place.

Susie hosted a gala party at her new mansion, which sat just a little higher up the hill than the last. Everyone came, even my Emma and her new beau, dressed smartly in army blue.

I was not prepared for the shock of it. She had simply asked, in an off-hand manner, if she might bring a guest to the party, and of course I said yes. This poor lad stuck out like the sore thumb that he was—being not only a gentile among us, but representing *the enemy*. I was proud of my menfolk. Arthur was the first to draw him out with the one thing they had in common: military service. Of course, he was fascinated by the stories Arthur could tell. Karan, too, discussed matters the boy might be familiar with and tried to set him at ease. I could not have; it was all I could manage to keep from getting ill or into such a temper with my daughter that I'd scold her in front of the company and send her packing home to her room.

I had thought she was past this; I had believed she was beginning to find herself. It seemed a cheap, senselessly cruel thing to do to people you loved, and at such a time. If I could have removed the boy from Emma in my mind, my compassion would have flowed to him: a stranger in a strange land . . . at Christmastime. I believe Dante understood that and was considerate toward him too.

But I knew my Emma, and I feared this was more than a gesture. And that is why I was ill with dread. The boy was polite enough in manner and decorum; there was nothing one could find fault with— save that he was what he was!

As soon as I could gracefully and unobtrusively do so, I left the party, and Karan and I spent the remainder of the evening playing with Fielding, attempting to partake of his innocence and undemanding delight. Grace arrived home before Emma.

"I thought your sister would be with you," I said, my voice sounding more tight and worried than I wanted it to.

"I thought she would be, too. Susie has a new driver, a man who takes over when William is sick. Several of us piled into the carriage. Emma was right behind me, Mother, but when I looked back I saw her standing beside her young gentleman, waving her arm at me. 'Michael's carriage will be here any minute,' she called, 'he will see that I get safely home.'"

I could feel how pinched the muscles of my face were; I tried to relax them. "Go ahead and cry, Mother," Gracie said. "That is what I did most of the way home."

"Do you think she went alone with him?"

"I believe there were to be other couples."

"Other officers and their—"

"Companions," Karan offered. "Would you like Arthur and myself to go in search of her, Lottie?"

I shook my head. His knee had been bothering him; it often did in the cold, damp weather. "Let us not give her the satisfaction, or the goad she may be looking for," I decided. "Mother has heated cloths ready for you, Karan. Let's you and I read for a while."

When I heard Emma at the door I realized that Sita Beg had gone out to unlatch it. I wondered very strongly what she might have in her mind to say. Several long minutes passed. When Emma walked into the parlor alone, I felt that Mata had not been given time to succeed; I suppose Emma had already steeled herself against that.

"Sorry if I have worried you, Mother," she began brightly.

"Do not say you are sorry if there is no sincerity behind the statement," Karan replied firmly. "It dishonors a noble sentiment, and it dishonors you, Emma."

She had not expected this. Karan seldom interfered in matters between children and me. He might approach them later, on his own basis, and try to influence them as he desired, but he never set himself up as the authority figure, except for those few times when he deemed it necessary.

"All right, then," she returned with brittle quickness. "I did it because I wanted to, and I suppose I would choose to do it again."

"It?" I repeated.

"Inviting Michael to the party in the first place, riding home with him and his friends, rather than with the family, coming in later than curfew, much later than I know I ought to."

"And for what purpose, Emma? Why do you 'want to do it,' as you say?"

She glowered at me, biting her bottom lip. "Because I like Michael, and I have a right to make friends and meet people, and decide my own life."

"Where did you meet Michael?"

"At Karan's shop," she chirped triumphantly. "He bought one of the pendants I helped to design. He was very impressed."

"Emma—"

"You deride everything that is different from us, Mother!" she cried. "You don't believe he could be impressed with me, that he could be sincere, not trying to trap an unsuspecting Mormon girl."

"You speak unjustly to your mother, Emma," Karan said firmly. "Unjustly, and with a sad lack of respect."

She threw him a black look, but said nothing, and the sudden thick silence in the room gripped us all by the throat.

"I am tired," she pouted. "May I go to my room, Mother?"

"You may wait for me in the kitchen," Karan said. "I believe your mother should go and get ready for bed."

She whirled to face him, ready for open defiance. But his eyes met and held hers. "This has nothing to do with me being your mother's husband, Emma," he said slowly, "nor with me being head of this household. This has to do with me and thee. And, as you well know, I have earned this at your hands."

She quieted immediately and left to do as he bid her. He turned for one moment to squeeze my hand and press his lips to my forehead, then he followed her out of the room. I sat alone beside the cold fire. I could tell nothing; I could not even hear their voices. I rose, awkward with weariness, and groped my way through the dark house.

CHAPTER NINETEEN

Before the year was out, a money order came from Emma in San Francisco, a staggering sum of money to her namesake for the goods she had sold. "People here enchanted," she wrote. "More to follow." Emma immediately went to Julian's and bought the party dress she had been eyeing. She spent the remainder of the season in company with her soldier, Michael Cunningham, and his friends. She was sixteen years old; a number of girls were already married by sixteen, as she ever reminded me. Memories of Sarah at an even younger age haunted me. The letters we received from England grew less frequent and slightly altered in nature. Sarah was seeing an Englishman with a title, the earl of something or other, who was helping Marion find a suitable replacement for the irreplaceable Ernest. Without closing my eyes, without even shifting my senses, I could picture her there. The green land had taken hold of her and worked its tendrils down into her heart. *It is in her blood,* I thought. *It is a direction that was always waiting for her.*

Spring meant renewal and new life, but for me this year it would also mean loss. Gracie's marriage was set for May, when the roads would be dry, and the fields planted, and the first flowers in bloom. Susie found a little house for them and manipulated the owner into a generously low price, then everyone chipped in and came up with the money necessary to secure it. The army was rendering our family affluent.

"Make hay while the sun shines," Winston cautioned us. "The army will not always be here to pave our paths this way."

Even he and Abbey were building an addition to their little home, and he was running a second mill now, a mill that supplied the army camp's never-ceasing needs.

Of course, Gracie's gown had to be the finest. Emma sent china and silver from San Francisco, along with another payment to my

Emma and demands for a new shipment of her gowns that were in such demand. Emma and Sita Beg worked tirelessly, turning out miracles and never complaining. Julian was happy, since the Midas touch was extending to him. But the worldly, almost greedy pace of our lives sat uneasily with Karan and me.

There was too much to do, and that made the time slip through our fingers. The night before the wedding Grace and I walked out together beneath the pale silver of a spring moon, tender with new beginnings, as she was. We talked of many things, and of nothing. Our spirits moved in harmony. *These are the last moments you will belong to me in this way,* I thought, *the very last time for the rest of this life, and the next.*

Dante appeared too elated to be nervous or apprehensive—and he did look the young god Gracie thought him! But preoccupied with my own viewpoint as I was, I had failed to see into his heart.

When Grace and I returned to the house, he was there waiting for her, but when I left them alone and continued around the outside of the house to the back gardens, he followed me.

"I dreamed last night of madre mio, my mother," he said. The loneliness in his voice appalled me. "That would be my one wish," he confided, "That she could be with me, to share in my joy, to know and love this young woman who has transformed my life."

I turned to him, wondering if my shame showed in my eyes or the altering of my facial expression. "We have been heartless," I said, "giving no thought to the terrible pain this must be for you."

He brushed my apology aside, but the sadness in his eyes seemed to go deeper. "Mezzo amara, mezzo dolce," he murmured, and I saw that his black eyes were wet with tears. "Half-bitter, half-sweet, that is the way of mortality. I remember what the Prophet Joseph Smith said of the Saints who suffered in Kirtland."

"What was that?"

"That the Lord provides. Power in proportion to the work to be done, strength according to the race set before us, and grace and help as our needs require."

I could not reply. I reached out for his hand, and he gave it willingly, warm and pulsing with the strong sap of youth. "Do not forget," I entreated him. "Your biggest challenge will be not to forget."

He understood. And I closed my eyes and prayed that his mother, far away, lonely, unknowing, might somehow, though she would not understand it, share in this moment, too.

It happened. It moved from the hazy realm of anticipation into the commonplace of reality. My little Grace became a wife, established her own precious home, and moved on.

Change is the only constant in life; I had known that for a long time. In June Sita Beg came to me, and if I had been observant I would have seen the lights in her eyes—I would have felt that something momentous was impending.

"We have waited," she began. "It is the right and proper order for the old to wait for the young."

"Waited?" I echoed.

"Grace is settled now," she continued in her affectionate, patient manner. "I have already spoken with the bishop and made arrangements. I should like to be baptized, Lottie."

She must have known how entirely unexpected her statement would be, for she gave me time to recover, saying nothing, though reaching over once to pat my hand. "I had no idea. Are you certain, Mata? Why?"

"You had no idea because I am not blessed with the ability to express the things of my heart. I have studied with Abbey, during those early months when we spent so much time in one another's company. From the very beginning there was something that drew me; you must understand what I mean?"

I nodded, listening still.

"Now for this long while, Julian and I have been reading together and discussing our readings." She paused briefly, then continued, "I have prayed, daughter."

I knew she had a small shrine in her own room, harboring one of the deities of her people. But, as in most things, we had never spoken of it openly.

"I have prayed to my gods . . . and to your god. And from both the same answer came."

"What is that answer?" I asked, deeply interested.

"The answer is to follow truth as it is revealed and confirmed to one's own spirit. Thus I know, with what my spirit has experienced, that I do the right thing."

The joy her words released in me was a sensation very akin to pain. "Have you spoken with Karan?"

"Karan's time is not yet," she replied. "I have spoken with Winston. I should like him to baptize me."

On her own Sita Beg found her way to the truth, I thought, *while I did nothing—exercised no faith, extended no assistance.*

"It was not for you to do, daughter," she replied to my thoughts, as she ofttimes did. "The road to truth begins within one's self, and it is a solitary journey."

I was not reconciled. "I might have illuminated that path, cleared it of obstructions, walked beside you—"

"No," she persisted emphatically. "It cannot be done in that way. You have been here, standing in your own place with purpose and beauty. That is all we can do for others: reveal the best within us, and hope that it speaks to their hearts."

She took me no further during that first conversation, but later that night while I was cutting up bits of scraps for my raven's breakfast, she sat down beside me. "There is something else, Charlotte."

I looked up. I remember thinking: *She looks youthful and hopeful, as though she is going to start laughing for no reason. Expectant—* That is the word that stuck with me when she smiled shyly and said, "Julian and I are going to be married."

"You mean this?" I asked, not knowing whether to laugh or cry. "Julian is a wonderful man, Mata, but he is so unlike you," I stammered. "He has a good heart, but he can be such a blunderer! What if he hurt you? What if you became miserable trying to live life as he sees it, what if—"

She placed her thin, girlish hand firmly upon my arm. "Hush such vague and insubstantial fears," she admonished me. "You know not whereof you speak."

I bit my lower lip against my astonishment. "Do you love him, Mother, in—you understand—in that way?"

"Yes," she answered simply. "I am no longer young, and he is not your father." Her eyes took on a far-away expression for a moment, and my heart pounded painfully. "But God has blessed me, my daughter, to again know that most sacred kind of love."

"I will lose you." That thought had not yet occurred to me.

"I will be close."

"It will not be the same."

"No, it will not be the same. But it will be good." She did laugh then, very gently, like the music of water falling through light. "And it will be infinitely more than either you or I dreamed of possessing less than five years ago."

I moaned at my own blind greed and folly. "It will be better," I told her, "because I will know that you are truly happy, that you are growing, that your life is fulfilled."

So it came to pass. Such a rejoicing, such a harvest as the golden summer ripened into autumn. All life, all love seemed intensified in my mind. *Nothing matters but people,* I kept thinking. *Nothing matters beside the expressions, the joys of the heart.* It was enough. If it grieved me to have Sarah Elizabeth missing from my side, if it stung and frightened me to see Emma hanging happily on the arm of a gentile, if my whole being cried out: *would this might happen with Karan!* it was enough. An abundance filled to overflowing. And I would not be ungrateful; rather, I chose to savor the blessing, and give praise to the Lord.

"Has it really been the same bird, all these years, Lottie?" Abbey asked one morning as my hoary fowl strutted over the window ledge and onto the long slab table where his breakfast awaited him.

"It most certainly is. I could pick him out from all other crows," I assured her. "He eats from Fielding's hand now," I boasted, "gentle as a mother cat with her kitten."

"Yes, he has become quite a pet."

The autumn sun has an intensity of its own, different from the shimmering heat of the summer that sucks and dries the very juices of life. Even at its hottest there is a tingling sensation in the autumn sun, a quickening, an anticipation—almost a sharpening of the fine edges of life. I felt it that morning, and basked in it. In a matter of weeks I would turn forty-one. I had an infant to raise, a newlywed mother, and two grandchildren, with more on the way. *What a delight life is,* I marveled, *if we will allow it to be.*

This uncanny sense of wholeness and harmony pervaded the days that followed. I thought little of it beyond a sense of appreciation and quiet joy.

We celebrated my birthday, and Fielding snatched one of the candles from the cake when no one was looking and had eaten two-thirds of it before his father noticed and pried it out of his sticky, stubborn little hand. The first of the Christmas orders came from Emma in San Francisco, and word that Kishan and Michiko were expecting a child. The Prophet spoke from the pulpit warning us, admonishing us not to permit our daughters to have recourse with the soldiery who dwelt among us because of the wicked designs of our enemies—and Emma saw more of her Michael than ever before. Susie announced her intention to fund the production of an opera.

"I cannot bear to see the hunger in that young man's face," she rationalized. "He is sick for the sound of Paganini and Verdi, so he can be in charge of the whole shebang, and our little Gracie can sing the lead."

It would be an undertaking of momentous proportions, but she was up to the task. Dante and Grace retreated into the world of wonder and imagination which her generosity opened for them.

"Susie shall make a tidy profit on this venture, never fear," Arthur chuckled. His hair was turning gray at the sides, which added a distinguishing touch to the handsome, generously molded lines of his face.

Two days following my birthday several of us womenfolk got together to put up stewed peaches and jars of peach jam. We met at my house. The kitchen there was ample, and we were within yards of a small orchard where we could pick the fresh fruit ripe from the trees. The cool day eased the burden of our hot, heavy labor, and the work went forward quickly. When we paused for a break and luncheon at midday, Abbey put Charlotte Elizabeth in charge of the little ones. "Keep them in the garden," she warned her daughter, "and do not open Grandmama's fence."

There was no warning; I had no sense of premonition. We were cooking and chatting and boiling the last batch, anxious to put our feet up and really rest for a spell. Time had passed—half an hour, perhaps a bit more—since any of us had thought to run back and check on Charlotte and the children. It was Merin who pushed her chair back. "I believe I'll go see how young Lottie is holding up."

"There have been no complaints yet," Gracie grinned. "Perhaps we ought to leave well enough alone."

At first Merin noticed nothing out of the way; all appeared to be in order. Lottie was bent down, sitting on her knees, playing with Merin's own little Abigail. She cast her eyes over the sweet scene, then cast her eyes over the remainder of the enclosed space, automatically beginning to count heads. "Where is Fielding?" she asked. "I do not see him anywhere."

"He was over by the cabbages with Seth," Lottie said, "looking at caterpillars."

Merin counted again. She turned her gaze to the gate, which was still closed and latched securely. "I don't see him, honey," she said.

By the time she alerted us, by the time we all searched, by the time someone found the low spot where one of the fence posts had snapped in two and been pushed aside—by that time we had lost many precious moments.

"He surely can't be far," Gracie offered, by way of encouragement.

"Abbey, you stay with the other children," I instructed. "The rest of us will fan out and search for him."

My path led through the backs of several neighboring lots, rising slightly upward toward the foothills . . . and the course of City Creek as it wound its way down from the mountains.

I choked back the panic that rose in my throat and pushed on. Ten minutes, fifteen, my legs were aching now, my voice going hoarse. Nothing. No sound, no movement. Only a calm and terrible silence that made me want to scream.

I could head in half a dozen different directions, I thought, *and waste vital time—risk everything.* I tried to pray. I shaded my eyes with my hand and gazed into the sky.

There came a sudden scattering of birds, loud and startling. My crow rose above them, purple wings glistening. He cried out once, hoarse and urgent, then swept low over the sloping ground, and I followed, watching nothing but his black, graceful form against a patch of pale sky.

Then a head appeared, from a low spot where the ground dipped down to water level—and I put my hand to my throat!

The head belonged to George Davis, and he was calling out to me. "Sister Lottie—" His big voice made scarcely a ripple in the still afternoon. "Over here, Sister Lottie. You'd best come quickly."

I do not know how my trembling legs carried me to the dread spot—how I kept breathing when I looked down to see my little son lying unconscious and motionless at my feet.

"He was in the water all right," Brother Davis explained as I lifted his limp body and rubbed the moisture and mud away with the folds of my apron. "Figure he tumbled in upstream a bit, but then got caught on this snag here." He pointed to the providential limb, forked in the middle, which had stopped and held the small body. "But, lookee here. I believe he must have struck his head, Lottie. Right here, I reckon." He touched a spot on Fielding's forehead where the skin was swollen, and a purple bruise was building.

"He's breathing," Brother Davis noted, "and that's encouraging. I'd not move him too far right now, but we ought to cover him." He took off his own work shirt as he spoke, leaving only his overalls strapped over his garments, and covered the child himself. "My son's up at the house. He's got as fast a horse as any. Would you like me to send him for a doctor?"

"No!" I said. "Have him ride out to the mill for Winston. I can send Gracie on foot a block away to fetch old Dr. Mitchell."

He nodded, approving my logic. Dr. Mitchell was in his seventies and had been retired these several years, but he would know what to do. Somehow, it all happened, without me. I sat beside my son, gently rubbing his cold limbs, unable to think, unable to feel—even unable to pray.

Dimly I remember the arrival of the doctor, the return to the house, the interminable waiting while the old man examined the injuries. As he made his way out of the room I knew that the verdict would not be a good one; although his face was closed to expression, immobile, I had caught a glimpse of his eyes.

"No broken bones I can find, Lottie," he began. "But that bump on the head is a bad one." He ran thick, age-spotted fingers through his thinning hair. "Concussions can be tricky things, very tricky. I wish we could get him awake. And the boy's taken a chill. He's running a dangerously high fever. I must tell you that, Lottie," he apologized.

"The next few hours will tell," he said, "but you must steel yourself, my dear."

I felt Winston behind me; I did not have to turn around. I shook at his touch when I felt his fingers close over my arm.

They led me to a chair—*why do people make you sit at such times, when all within you is in turmoil?* The doctor gave his instructions to Merin. I remember saying out loud, "I wish Abigail were here!" I must have been trembling. Winston bent down on his haunches, his face even with mine, and began rubbing my arms, gently, rhythmically. I tried to smile, but it took so much effort I could not manage it. I could not control the ungainly shape of my mouth.

"It is like that other time," I said. "That other little boy." Even in my own ears, my voice sounded hollow. "When they called me, I did not want to go to him. 'Why me?' I asked Dr. Fielding . . . Why can't Dr. Fielding be here?"

"Bas! Bas! Mata. Please!" Winston's voice was trembling. I blinked my eyes and touched his cheek with the tips of my fingers. "You were so little," I said. "And your big blue eyes were so frightened."

He wrapped his arms around me and cradled his head in my lap. "I cannot lose him, Winston!" I said. And the words were a desperate hiss that sent shudders from my body to his. I sat for long minutes, trying to control the trembling, attempting to gather my powers enough to speak.

"Give Fielding a blessing, Winston," I said, and my voice sounded unexpectedly strong and lucid. "That is why I sent for you. You must use the power God has given you—power you are worthy to hold, Winston—and do this thing for me."

His eyes were miserable. I knew what he wanted to say to me, but he took one look at my face and his protests died in his throat. He rose heavily, then extended his arm, and I clung to it and, with his aid, stood on my feet. "Have you the faith?" he managed.

"I have faith sufficient," I answered.

"Beyond that is in God's hands."

"Beyond that is in your hands." His blue eyes widened at my response. "You must use your powers to entreat. You must call down a blessing from God."

He understood perfectly. He no longer attempted to evade, no longer shrank from that which faced him. "I should like to pray first, Mother," he said.

He went into the small room which was Emma and Gracie's and shut the door behind him. I turned to the kitchen where the others waited in a sad little huddle, noticing dimly that the children had all been "removed" and that my mata had joined the sad group.

"Charlotte, come and drink this," she said, and I remember that I did as she bade me. It was then that Karan—as dark and wild as a thundercloud—entered the room.

He pinned me with his eyes, sending a sharp stab of pain clear through me. He stopped cold as soon as he saw me and would not come closer. The space of the room that separated us seemed immense—seemed to recede along with all that was in it, so that only we two stood facing each other across the dark gulf of pain.

"My son lies at the doors of death," he cried, "and you did not send for me!"

I stared at him, straining, as though I could not grasp his meaning.

"My son," he repeated. "Why did you not send for me, Lottie?" His voice was hard with cruelty, like the cutting edge of a knife. I shrank from it, yet felt an inexorable draw, an almost detached fascination that made me straighten myself and stand taller and continue to meet the bitter flame of his gaze. I had never in my life seen Karan like this before.

"Why, at such a moment, did Winston come first to your mind?" he demanded. "Why did you not send for me?"

His pain shivered through me, like the withering breath of winter, freezing my skin, freezing my heart. I spoke from some source deep within myself—for I could think nothing, feel nothing, nor did I perceive that there were tears in my eyes.

"I did not think. I did not choose. I must have instinctively known, Karan, that there was nothing you could do."

He stood tense and drawn, his eyes like shards of chipped flint. He seemed to be breathing heavily, but his chest did not move.

"It was not a conscious thought, but I sent for Winston because I knew Winston could bless him, that Winston possessed the power within himself to save my son's life."

My words burned into the void, and the black void twisted and sharpened them before they pierced Karan's heart. He stood defenseless, unresisting, as the terrible pain entered his soul.

Then into the void came a voice I recognized. "Come with me, Karan," my son said. And the stiff dark man turned and followed him. The void trembled and fell apart, and the space where it had been became laced with people—bodies moving and voices speaking, and someone putting a hand to my cheek, a cloth to my head.

I have no idea how much time passed away before Winston entered the room. "Come with me, Mata," he said, and I rose and followed him and went in to my son. Fielding lay in his little bed like a thin, insubstantial shadow of a real child. His green eyes were open. He smiled when he saw me and held out his arms.

I sat for an endless time on the edge of his bed, cradling his body in mine, singing lullabies long after he had drifted into a light, easy slumber and could no longer hear. I sat for a long time until someone tugged gently at my hand and said, "You have been sitting here for hours, Lottie. It is well past midnight. Come away for a little spell. The child sleeps peacefully now."

"Where is Karan?" I asked—and even the words of the question threatened to summon the black void back.

It was Mata. Mata was the only one who would meet my wide-open gaze and not shrink.

"Karan and Winston came out of the boy's room together," she said calmly. "That was hours ago. Karan left the house then, my dear, and he has not returned."

The hours wove themselves out into the colorless fabric of darkness—and I thought of the ghosts and shades of Dacca and trembled. Perhaps I slept. Perhaps there were those with whom I held conversation. Perhaps I walked out under the high stars and searched the darkness for him with my own feeble eyes. When daylight came, gray as a mourning dove, I sat in a chair by Fielding's bed with a coverlet over my knees. The house was hollow with the emptiness that engulfed it. I knew without opening my eyes that Karan had not come back. I knew without lifting my head that I was alone.

CHAPTER TWENTY

The early morning hours passed. Sita Beg remained in the house to be with me; there was no other intrusion. The doctor came, but Mata told me he had been there twice since Winston had administered to Fielding; I retained no recollection of his presence at all.

"You are fortunate," he told me. "Without that priesthood blessing I do not think your lad would've pulled through."

There was little to do save to watch him, keep him quiet, feed him only liquids. I went through the motions, but my heart was not in them; my heart had closed some door in upon itself and could not break out.

My crow lingered on the window ledge for me. "You are awaiting your well-deserved praise," I purred to him. He cocked his silken head at what I thought a gracious angle. "He understands me," I said.

"I am certain he does," Mata answered. "Crows have their ways, as you well know. And their wisdom."

I love you so much! I thought. "He led me to Fielding," I said.

"Ah, then all the gods were with you yesterday."

The bird preened his rich feathers with the tip of his long, hooked bill and regarded us serenely. "In truth, Mata," I replied, "I have need of them still."

There was a part of me that felt an anxiety close to the point of agony—a part that remained numb and detached.

Fielding slept, and as he slept the morning wore itself out. And Karan, a tall dark shape against the lighted doorway, walked into the house.

Without moving he spoke to Mata in Hindi, and she replied. Then he approached me, slowly, as if in a dream, and took hold of my hands, and led me outside to where a fine carriage waited, and helped me inside.

He drove up above the city, as far up the mountain as the horses could safely take us, then carefully pulled the vehicle off the road. The buildings and cultivated fields spread below us—small marks on the vast, curved bowl of the valley. Yet there was a beauty still in the work of man's hands.

"Charlotte," Karan said, not raising his eyes to me. "Can you bear to listen to what I am going to try to tell you?"

"Yes, I want to listen," I said.

"I thought I knew myself. I believed life had handled me harshly and taught me much. I believed I had learned and had eyes that were opened . . . but I have been blind."

His voice was measured and strong; its melodic tones thrilled through me, as ever they had. But the pain of his soul—I had never been able to bear hearing that.

"I have loved you, or so I believed—the vain ironies of the blind man who dwells in his own shadow, and calls it light!"

I wanted to cry out at the bitterness of his self-reproach, but I knew I could not.

"You have given all, Lottie, and longed for that wholeness you have a right to. Yet, I denied you, and I do not even know why."

"You could not go where your spirit did not lead you," I attempted.

"It was a terrible rebuke," he shuddered. "But it was a humbling I needed. And why? Why did my spirit remain cold and indifferent, when the truth and beauty you possessed would have nurtured it into flower?"

"A question like that cannot be answered, at least not simply," I said.

"A question like that must be answered," he contended, "or all else is in vain."

He was beyond me. His pain had taken him places I could not follow. At last he lowered his eyes to meet mine. "I have wronged you," he said. "I have wronged your trust and devotion. God brought me to the edge of the precipice again before he could stop me! But this time"—he shuddered and retraced his words— "Back in Barrackpore in the hospital I lost my livelihood, the outward trappings of my manhood, the girl who was life to me! Back then, Charlotte, I thought I had much to lose—" His voice caught on the last word, and he stopped himself, then shook his head and continued in a low, husky tone. "I had no idea, then, Charlotte, no idea of what life can give, and take. If we had lost Fielding . . ." Those words were part of the black void, and they shuddered with pain. He put his fingers out— long, slender fingers that spoke of grace and enlightenment, much like the lines of his face.

"Will you forgive me, Lottie? Will you have me back again? Will you help me?"

I could say nothing; I have never been able to make reply to the eloquence of Karan's soul.

"I am yours," I said, "more than I ever was, Karan. What you offer me I accept and cherish, as ever I have."

In that moment, when he embraced me, all the elements of our lives, past and present, merged into place. The wholeness became something tangible, something eternal, intermingling the best within each of us into something neither one of us could ever have been alone.

Karan was not baptized until he had studied thoroughly and deeply, fasted and prayed, cleansed himself from the world, as he put it. Before the year ended, before the rivers ran bitter cold or froze over, he received the sacred ordinance and entered wholeheartedly the world he embraced.

It is interesting that Julian said the most significant thing of that day to me. "When I first became a Mormon," he told me, "it was because of what the Church, what the kingdom, could do for me. It has taken me a long time to look at things the other way round." He pursed his lips regrettably. "A lot of time, and a lot of help. It isn't that way with Karan. You just watch him, Lottie, and see. He has embraced truth with a burning intention to serve it well."

"You have become both wise and observant," I smiled.

"And, yes, it is about time!" he admitted, then his eyes softened. "What would I be without your mother, my dear?" he sighed.

"We have been blessed far beyond our deserving," I said.

"Indeed. Oh, most surely, Lottie, we have."

As the day drew to a close I walked round the house, burying the coals in the hearths, checking lamps and door latches—alone in the stillness, so that, when the sound came, there could be no mistaking it. I stopped in my progress and listened, and a quick stab of longing for Seth swept over my frame.

"What is it, Lottie?" Karan asked, coming up behind me.

"Do you hear anything?"

He considered. "Something vague, very much like a far-away whistle."

"Yes," I said, "that is it." I turned to him. "With his love, Seth has freed me. This is the final gift."

"No, Charlotte," Karan responded. "Seth will never be far from you. Nor is this the last. His gifts will keep coming, through the remainder of this life, and the next."

Sarah sent a formal, gilt-edged announcement of the union to take place between Edwin Charles Gordon, the young Earl of Corwood and Longbrook, and Miss Sarah Elizabeth Simmons of Baddenwell. There was a newspaper clipping, and a list of the garden parties and ladies' teas and formal fetes to be held in honor of the couple.

"She has changed her name to Simmons!" Emma cried. "How delightful, Mother! What fun it must be."

"If she is to inherit, she must," I responded, but Emma did not note the desolate tone to my voice. *You might have told me beforehand, Sarah!* I thought, a little bitterly. *Must you make it so obviously clear how little need you have of me in your life?*

When we went to Winston and Abbey's with the news, Winston called me over, and took me to the little room at the side of the barn where he kept his records and did his accounts. "I've something here for you," he said, rummaging through a stack of old forms and letters. "It came some time ago," he explained, "but I believe the time for you to read it is now."

I sat in Winston's old horsehair chair and unfolded the sheets. I did not recognize the hand that wrote them, and began to turn the pages, looking for the signature. "This letter is addressed to you, Winston."

"It is from Ernest," he said. "He wrote it before his death."

"That is right." I remembered now the time it had come. *Dear Winston,* I read.

> *I think of you often, and can remember so clearly the days you spent here as a boy, before your mother took you away from this place. I do not fault her, mind you; she is an incredible woman, and she has followed where her heart has led her. But, you know that inexplicable tie that bound you to this spot and you and I to one another. I hear only good things of you and sincerely hope that the life you are living is what you want it to be. Rare is the man who knows what he wants in this old world and then finds a way to achieve it. I have been fortunate in my own lot; I do not regret nor complain.*

He went on for a bit, recalling old memories, giving manly advice. Then a name in the last paragraph leapt out at me.

> *I believe your sister Sarah Elizabeth will stay on and inherit Baddenwell. And, to my way of thinking, that is how it should be. Your mother—as I know and remember her well!—will not reconcile herself easily to such a fate for her daughter, and such a loss for herself. Thus, allow me to say a word here in defense of young Sarah who, by the way, never defends or explains herself. She was born to this station! She has taken to it with all the natural instincts which generations have bred. Hers is the firm, yet gentle hand that all who dwell on the Baddenwell estate or in the extended parish have come to respect and love. She works tirelessly, yet with a grace and patience which engender affection and trust. She is just, yet merciful; she will serve the least among us until she drops in her tracks from fatigue. 'This is a sacred trust,' she often says, 'to keep the traditions of Baddenwell strong, to do nothing to mar the old honor which generations have established.' She believes she shall have to give an accounting to her ancestors who went before her; as, indeed, she will.*

There was a break in the writing here, a little space, then the letters were bolder and darker—either penned with a sure purpose, or with some trepidation and haste.

Charlotte, my dear, your daughter is so like Elizabeth Simmons, the grandmother you love! The resemblance is at times uncanny. I tremble upon observing little similarities: the way she holds her head when she walks; her manner of speaking to someone who is distressed, in order to calm them; the way in which she rubs her temples with the tips of her fingers when she is ill or distressed; the alert, watchful tilt of her chin when she thinks danger or trouble is nigh—I could go on and on, Charlotte. But, believe me, you would be proud of her, and of the work she does here. You recall, I am certain, that most unusual night when you sought me belowstairs, and we retired to the morning room, and I told you of your father and of your grandmother? Will you recall that I said 'Elizabeth was in all ways a lady.' So it is with your Sarah. There have even been times—and I have told this to no one, my dear, save yourself!—I feel Elizabeth's presence. I feel she is watching, and approving.

I looked up. Winston was watching me. "What do you think, Mother?"

"I think Ernest was a rare and incredible man."

"Can you not be comforted? Can you not dwell upon what is good in Sita, and leave the rest in God's hands?"

"I can try, my dear." I smiled thinly. But, in truth, the letter had made a difference. It was just so painful for me to let go—to be without her!—to submit to her heaven-given agency to turn aside from His way. Yet, she was fulfilling much within herself that was good and noble. Winston had said, "leave her in God's hands." "Doubt not, fear not . . ." the Savior's loving admonition ran through my mind. *I can do it sometimes,* I thought, *but not always. My faith is not strong enough yet . . . not yet a power unto my own salvation.* At that moment I was grateful for time. I needed the full measure that God would allow me if I was to overcome myself, and come to be like him through the things which I suffered and learned.

There was a natural slowing of the pace of living in winter, and Karan took good advantage of it, improving every spare moment of time. He took upon himself the teaching of several additional classes, unconcerned with the salary or the number of students he was given.

Somehow he found a way to become acquainted with each of our neighbors, and when we went to ward meetings he would stop to ask personal questions regarding their children or their business endeavors, their flocks and their fields. They were skeptical, taken aback at the least, and seldom responded well. But that was of no matter; he took pleasure from the trying, from the growing, from the carrying on.

He had almost a sixth sense toward those in need; his spirit could mark them, respond to them, and the compassion he felt was real. He made it his business to assist all within his power; yet he required the strictest anonymity as the only prerequisite to his efforts and aid. Soon the bishops and stake presidents in the area began to learn that they could trust him, turn to him in the most delicate of matters, and never be turned away.

"Mother! Karan has taken leave of his senses!" Emma complained perpetually. "He turns down half the business that comes to us, yet I know of a fact that he continually gives things away."

"We have enough, and to spare," I would assure her, but that did not suffice. She was constantly coming home with stories of what she called his foolishness. "Do you know what Karan did now?" she would demand indignantly. "He ordered three dozen pair of boots, had Dante make them in a variety of sizes, paid for them himself, then turned around and gave them to the Perpetual Immigration Fund."

"For . . .?"

She had not anticipated my question. "For . . . well, I suppose for the converts from Great Britain coming across the plains."

"That pleases me well," I said. "I like to think of lessening their suffering."

"I do not understand you!" she cried.

"You could if you wanted to," I urged. "I have known what it is like to be poor and suffering, to go to bed cold at night, wondering how you will manage to feed your little ones when the next day comes."

"Oh, Mother—"

"Emma. Be still. Try to hear what I am saying. I have experienced these things! I have hidden from mobs of men who were bent on cruelty and destruction. I have left behind me home and possessions and all that I loved. Can you not even try to imagine?"

"I don't know, Mother."

"Please, Emma, try! Now we are in a position to help others. It is a blessing, more to us than to them."

She had grown still, she was attempting to listen, but she could not yet see. Her life thus far had not prepared her. And every day the decisions she was making were taking her farther away.

As winter dissipated and the first signs of spring appeared I felt the demands of the days quicken and pick up speed. Gracie and Dante were immersed in the opera, and Merin had been pulled in as well. Susie had attempted to cajole Emma into learning the piano parts; some were difficult, all demanding, but her skills could match the challenge if she desired it; and yet she demurred.

"Here is a chance to put your gift to use," I urged. "All these years of faithful practice have prepared you, Emma."

"I have my hands full with my designing," she said, but it was not true. The months following Christmas were the slowest of the year, and the spring frocks she had designed for Julian were already in the making. What was holding her back?

Our two new babies were safely born: Drusilla's son and Mary Ann's daughter. It was illogical, I knew, for me to long for more of my own. I had a son—Karan's son—given to me twice over. What more could I ask?

I remember, as that spring approached, that there was a fractured sense to our lives, a great diversion that pulled us in dozens of different directions and preoccupied our minds. This is the only poor excuse I can give for remaining so blind.

March in the valleys of the Wasatch can sometimes be mild as a lamb. While Illinois remains locked in ice and whirlwind, the desert soil warms and thaws, flowers push through the thin soil into the welcome warmth of the sun, and Spring comes early, simply because she feels like it. And, with such a coming of spring, restless longings rise to the surface and tantalize the senses and weave their sweet webs.

For several days I had seen little of Emma. We had quarreled over the same old matters: no, she could not go on a picnic to the lake, the wind was too raw, it was too early . . . if it had been a group of young Latter-day Saints? No, not even then. I remember saying, "Emma, what do you hope to prove by this rebellion? What is possibly in it for you?"

"More than you are willing to consider," she had spat back at me. "There is a world beyond this miserable valley, you know."

"I know," I had responded, fixing the wrath of my whole soul upon her in one glance. But she had turned away from my gaze.

March came, and spring seemed to have decided to stay on for good. On a day of sweet wind and blue skies a small train of wagons pulled out of the city heading for the west deserts, the formidable Sierra mountains, and the waiting promise of San Francisco, the golden gateway to all desires and dreams. Among the party were several young officers, newly released from their stint of service at Camp Floyd, and ready to take on the world. One of them went by the name of Michael Cunningham. And accompanying him, was a young Mormon girl by the name of Emma Taylor, who was not quite seventeen years old.

CHAPTER TWENTY-ONE

Emma left only a brief note; but it said all that could be known, dreaded, or imagined. *Dear Mother,* it read. *I have gone with Michael and some of his friends to San Francisco. I shall be meeting Aunt Emma there, and she will take care of us. Worry if you must, but we shall be in good hands.*

How is it a child can contrive to wound and insult in the same breath?

That was all. What remained unexpressed screamed at me, taunted me day and night. I said nothing, but all knew; all felt sorry for me. Finally Karan came to me. "This must end, Lottie," he said simply. "I cannot bear to see you this way."

"I just need a little time," I protested. "I shall be all right, Karan."

"I should like to give you a blessing."

A priesthood blessing. At Karan's hands. "I believe that is a wise idea," I said.

He prepared himself. To his way of thinking it was no light thing to invoke the power of God; the ancient ways of his own people had taught him that. He prayed and fasted for a day. This would be the first time, and he felt the weight of it.

But when I sat with his hands resting on my head, I could feel the power. Winston had joined him, and I can remember thinking: *With these two servants Heavenly Father is pleased.* At first I was awkwardly aware of his presence, his expressions, his words. Then the real Spirit that pronounced the blessing penetrated my heart. I let my own faith flow like a conduit; with my whole soul I listened, with my whole soul I yearned. When the ordinance ended I lifted my head, and it seemed as if the whole room was aglow.

Several days later I was aware that the feeling, the benediction of that blessing remained with me still. Winston, bringing the children over for me to mind, noticed also. "Heavenly Father can work through a man like Karan," he observed. "After all, Mother, he cannot give us more than we desire, more than we are willing, and able, to receive."

I knew he was right. I understood what he was saying, and I rejoiced. And as the weeks progressed, and we did not hear a word from my daughter, it was this alone which sustained me in face of the darkness and the terrible fears that lurked in my mind.

She is with Emma," Merin attempted to reason. "Surely she will exert some influence."

"That is the point, isn't it? Just how much will Emma allow?" The question and its possible ramifications made both of us cringe.

We did not speak of the situation often, for that made the unhappiness of it so much worse.

And then yet another circumstance developed which demanded our care and concern.

I should have guessed it, but Abbey has long been adept at hiding sickness and discomfort, of stoically going on. The lack of color in her face, the fact that she often grew faint and tired quickly and could not stand long on her feet; the fact that Winston brought the children to my house more and more often, leaving Abbey to rest undisturbed; the fact that she had no appetite and often ate little or only picked at her food. Yet, when Winston told me, I was shocked and could not keep the concern from my face.

"She cannot be with child," I moaned. "Winston . . ."

"I know, Mother. I am frightened, too."

"What does the doctor say?"

"The doctor says her heart is weakened, and the strain on it may be too much. Her circulatory system was also affected by the severity of the consumption and the sustained periods of high fever."

I was quiet, considering, trying to second-guess all the possibilities. "Is Abbey—"

"Oh, Abbey is fine. Serene, that is the word I would use for her, with the simple faith of a child."

"That is Abbey," I said, my throat tightening with unshed tears.

"Last night she said, 'We did not do this on purpose, Winston. We have taken the care that reason and wisdom would dictate, despite our own disappointed desires. So, this must have happened because it was meant to be so.'"

"Do you fault her logic?"

"I don't know!" Winston admitted. "She stared at me with those big brown eyes of hers; you know how trusting they are. I tell you, Mother, at that moment she did not look any older, or any less vulnerable than little Charlotte Elizabeth."

"What did she say?"

"She said, 'we are in God's hands, and whatever he disposes, I am content.' You know what she meant, of course?" His voice had risen a notch. "She meant *whatever*, even if the price is her own death."

I wanted to hush him from speaking the dread thing aloud, but I think he needed to unburden his torment to me. Yet, as the day passed, my sense of unease deepened. The first time I found to be alone with Karan I told him the news.

He was sober in his response, as I had felt he would be. "I must pray on this matter," he said, "I must give it some thought."

Three days later the stake president came by and asked if Karan could meet with him and one of the brethren. I wondered what it could be. Had he offended someone with his slightly unorthodox manners, with his zealous precision?

When he returned to the house it was late. Fielding had been asleep for a long time, and I sat alone, uneasy in the stillness, trying to read. I could not get used to the sudden emptiness, with Mata, Grace, and Emma all leaving in quick succession. Only Karan's presence made the rooms come alive again.

I heard him on the walk. He seemed to be coming slowly, almost uncertainly. I rose and went to the door to meet him. As I met his eyes I knew what it was he was going to tell me. "It cannot be!" I said. "What are they thinking?"

He laughed softly, under his breath, and the sound was amazingly warm and content.

"They are doing what the Lord prompted them to do. Without his urgings, I am certain it would never be done."

"They have called you to be bishop."

"Yes."

"You are not surprised?"

"I am humbled and frightened, but no, I am not surprised."

I remembered then how often he prayed and meditated and searched his own soul. I took a deep breath. "Karan, will the people accept you?"

"I wonder, too," he breathed. "With God's help, Lottie, they must!"

With God's help. That became Karan's byword over the next few weeks. Some of the Saints were too stunned to object and acquiesced out of habit. Others regarding him with sullen resentment, almost daring this stranger to prove himself. Many cared nothing, one way or another. A few, who understood and were able, gave him their support.

It was of no matter to him. He served all his people, with no apparent distinctions; he served and went on, and returned when service was needed again. He did not explain or apologize or waver. But he did somehow organize the priesthood. When a man needed help in his fields, when a plow broke, or an ox died, or a cow went dry, there were men there to make up the difference, to achieve together what a dozen men could not do with each man working alone. He went methodically from task to task, from challenge to challenge. He did not listen to the petty complaints, the tall tales and stories; he simply did what the Spirit directed and fulfilled the needs of the moment.

As the busy weeks passed, Abbey grew pale as a paper-skinned orchid and seemed to waste away as we looked helplessly on. Winston had blessed her, but her quiet pronouncement of the Lord's will, hanging over her head as it were, seemed to get in his way.

One evening Karan came home later than usual and found me in tears.

"What is it, Lottie?" he soothed, gathering me to him.

"Abbey saw her doctor today. He fears there may be two babies, Karan. And twins are common in Abigail's family. The pregnancy is farther advanced than she has told us—over four months, and yet she is still so small. The babies are too little, he says. If she cannot find a way to build her own strength, they will have little chance. And, as for Abbey herself . . ." I could feel my whole body trembling. "The babies will drain her system, and the shock of the birth, whether live or stillborn . . ." I could not go on.

Karan sat regarding me. "Do you believe it is God's will to take Abbey from us?"

"I don't know! If he wants her, if he understands things we do not understand."

He held me at arm's length, gently. "Lottie," he said, "we do not know because we do not want to know badly enough." His words were both statement and hypothesis, and he was considering the extent of them intently, with the great depths of his soul. After he had lulled me nearly to sleep with his tenderness he went out under the night sky, close to heaven, to seek heaven's will. *He torments himself,* I thought drowsily. But I knew, even in my half-awake state that he was doing the work of the Spirit for those of us, many of us, who did not care enough to do our part for ourselves.

By the time I arose the following morning, Karan was already gone, leaving a little note propped on the table where I would not fail to see it. "Do not look for me until dark," he wrote, "but I will not tarry, if I can help it. I have gone to find answers. Pray for me, Lottie."

All that day long, I did. I prayed as I churned the butter and fed the crow, as I weeded the vegetable garden and shelled the new peas. I prayed as I sang to Fielding, as I kneaded my bread, as I wrote my weekly letter to Emma in San Francisco—one of nearly a dozen now that had gone unanswered so far. I prayed for Karan in his strength and desire. I prayed for Winston in his fear. I prayed for us in our weakness and blindness. I prayed for the girl whose dying body held the miraculous spark of new life within its womb. I prayed long enough and hard enough that I knew heaven was listening to me. I prayed until the hours seemed hallowed by a sense of the nearness of God.

When Karan returned I was awake and waiting. I did not ask where he had gone. It seemed unimportant. His eyes were clear, the lines of his face set peacefully. "You have been with me," he said, taking my hand up and kissing it. "I have felt your spirit, Lottie, as I have not felt it for years."

Thus does God contrive to bless us, I marveled. Even in obedience he takes our weak efforts and magnifies them, not only glorifying his own name, but filling our souls with his power and light.

I was not surprised the next morning to find Karan dressed and waiting when I walked into the kitchen with Fielding. "I will feed the lad while you dress yourself, Lottie. I rode out early to speak with Winston. He and Abbey are expecting us. We can take Fielding to Merin's on our way out of town."

I moved quickly. But I felt no concern, no sense of worry to goad me on. After riding in silence until we had nearly reached Winston's homestead, Karan turned to me and said quietly, "It is not God's will to take Abbey from us at this time."

"I did not think so. I saw that answer last night in your face," I replied.

"It is his will that we dig deep into our own souls, that we stretch our own powers."

"You have always known that, Karan," I reminded him, "even when you were a lowly soldier in John Company, your soul was free and your own. Your desires have ever yearned upward."

I suppose my voice reflected the love I felt, which mingled a girl's adoration with a wife's quiet faith and respect.

I remember how Abbey looked as the two men placed their hands on her head. Her pale face with its delicate freckles was softened by damp red tendrils that curled round her cheeks. She smiled at me, her own faith and courage lighting her eyes. We closed our eyes, and Karan invoked the powers of heaven on behalf of this girl and her unborn children. He spoke slowly and simply, the conviction of his words lending them eloquence. He spoke lovingly, entreatingly. He spoke as one who knows both himself and the Personage he is addressing, and rejoices in that knowledge.

He had promised if her faith were sufficient she would be healed from that hour, that her body would respond to the care she gave it and hold up under the demands placed upon it. He had promised her freedom from the bondage she had suffered under so patiently; he had promised that her Heavenly Father would grant her the desires of her heart.

A wonderful peace enfolded us. We drank it into our spirits, seeped it in through our pores. *With God, all things are possible,* I thought. Karan believed those words, Karan lived by them. Yet, he did his part too. *Not wholly a gift,* I realized, *but a partnership as our spirits, weak and inadequate as they are, reach toward God.*

The full bloom of June was upon us when the first word from Emma came. It was flippantly written, and my heart constricted every time she used the word "we"; *we* to mean herself and Emma, herself and Michiko . . . herself and that unprincipled man who had taken the bloom and innocence of her girlhood away from her. *We have rooms in Emma's grand hotel, and she charges Michael but a pittance for them . . .*

"We have rooms." Was that to mean each had separate rooms or a suite of rooms shared together? She did not care that her ambiguity tormented us; she had intended it so. *Emma indulges and pampers us. It is so heavenly here, Mother. Everything is so green. And the ocean! Why did you not tell me what the ocean would do to my heart?*

She wrote as a child would write, immersed in sensations. There was nothing beyond that. And no word, not even a reassuring postscript from Emma to soften the blow.

"Is she really as enchanted and contented as she sounds?" I asked the company in general, being at that moment Karan, Arthur, and Merin.

"No," Karan answered. "She is exceedingly unhappy, Lottie. She is only pretending that she likes the terrible trap where she finds herself."

"Karan, what can we do?"

He did not know yet; I could see that in his eyes. So he brooked no answer at all. But from that moment there was hardly an hour of the day that Emma was not on my mind. I dreamed of her. I awoke in the morning with an image of her pinched, unhappy face floating before my mind.

The honey bee days of July descended. We had picnics by the river, warding the flies away with big bamboo fans Kishan had brought from California. I thought of the dog days in India when it is nearly too hot for man to live. There was none of that languid pampering here; here there was work to be done, and every man was his own servant.

Abbey thrived. She gained weight, and the color began to return to her face. The least effort no longer tired her, leaving her weak and trembling. The doctor expressed his amazement; but we who had been there when the change came were not amazed. Babies. *The idea of two babies, perhaps another girl*—I did not let my thoughts go that far. Anticipation can be a dangerous pastime, especially for such as myself. I began trying consciously to enjoy each moment, each day, as it unfolded its unique beauties to me.

The first production in Susie's new opera house was slated for autumn. We saw little of Dante and Grace, but when we did, their eyes were shining and their cheeks flushed with the excitement of living and achieving their dreams.

The summer days fed us of their honeyed nectar and gently passed.

Near the end of July Karan came home in the middle of the day, walking through the gardens to the kitchen entrance, coming in to the big table where I was cutting out pieces for baby clothes for the new infants to wear.

"An opportunity has arisen. I think I should take it, Lottie."

I knew at once what he meant. I put down my scissors. "Do you truly think you should do this?"

"I want to go get her," he said.

"It will mean an absence of many weeks. What of your business? What of the dangers? What if Emma will not come with you?"

"I have believed for a long time that this is what I should do, Lottie. I have been praying that the way might be opened . . . and now it has."

The relief I had expected to feel did not touch me, only a dull sort of pain, as though a heavy burden had been placed on my shoulders, which I knew must remain there for weeks: bowing my back, bowing my head, bowing my spirit.

"I must leave almost at once," Karan continued. "Tomorrow morning. Will you put aside what you are doing, and help me to pack my things and prepare?"

We moved swiftly. It was good to work side by side with him, but I dreaded the moment of parting and the lonely weeks of waiting ahead. "You should not stay here alone, Charlotte," he advised. "Would you like to stay with Merin?"

"Who would take care of my gardens, and feed my crow?"

"Yourself, of course. You can return every day to perform those tasks. But I would feel better knowing you were not alone."

"I will think upon it," I promised. But I had other ideas. The following morning, after he had left, I drove our fine carriage out to Abbey's house. The carriage and the team which pulled it were results of the prosperity we had experienced, enhanced by the presence of the army and the business acumen of Emma, exercised on our behalf. I shuddered at the price we had paid on both counts—the terrible price.

Abbey was gathering eggs. As I helped her I explained what had just happened. "Karan will be gone for weeks. Bring the children and come stay with me," I urged.

"It is tempting," she smiled.

"Then do it! You are able to make it to the city so seldom. Just think of the things we can do. Besides that, I will be able to help with the little ones. And spending time with them will be so wonderful. I do not really know them well enough, Abbey. I should like this chance to remedy that."

So it was settled. Winston understood and consented to pay a neighboring boy to care for the animals and do the chores in Abbey's absence. He agreed to spend his nights with us, too. The long gray vista had suddenly brightened immeasurably.

August cooled almost imperceptibly into September; the last weeks of summer had passed with remarkable speed. Less than two months now until the babies were due. I began to feel an urgency to have Karan return. Since he had reappeared in my life, like a well-loved apparition, we had never been parted for more than a day or two at a time. I was incomplete without him, a portion of my inner spirit deflated, no matter what I was doing or how happy I felt. I could no longer hold at bay thoughts of what might be happening. It was terrible to be so far away, so cut off from communication.

It was my raven who warned me, who seemed to bring the news, like a gleam of light along the plum sheen of his wing as he flew back and forth, back and forth against the square of my window, crying out to me with sharp little, staccato sounds. I saw no one; there was no visible reason to set the heated iron on the stove top, wash my hands, take off my apron, walk out into the empty garden. The time was midday. I looked at the hollyhocks, leaning heavily against the fence line, their bright heads drooping for want of rain. I drew in the scent of my last growth of lavender, slender, spiked bushes bordering my herb garden. With the fragrance I drew into my lungs a sensation of peace.

They are arrived. The words formed themselves in my mind. I heard the wheels of a carriage coming slowly down the wide city street that ran past my house. I turned—slowly too—to watch the dusty horses pull up and stop. But I found myself running down the stone path and out the side gate, gathering the thin, rigid figure of my daughter into my arms, feeling her tremble and go soft as she buried her head against my shoulder and flung her arms round my neck.

CHAPTER TWENTY-TWO

Some can err, even blatantly sin, and come away unscathed; others bend or break and are blasted by the weaknesses they have harbored within themselves, deeming these friends when, in time, they show the sharp, cruel fangs of an enemy.

It was thus with Emma. She came back subdued, her skin and hair lackluster, her body thin, her eyes dull. All *had* been pretense, as Karan had construed. When he had found her, she was indeed living with the young man who had enticed her away. She made only one terrified attempt at defiance before crumpling altogether.

He had entered their room without knocking, having convinced Kishan of the wisdom of giving him the master key. She had glanced up from a vanity table where she sat plaiting her hair. The young man rose to his feet indignantly; Emma turned round on her stool.

"How dare you?" she had shouted at Karan. "I shall have the police on you. People have rights here. How dare you!"

Karan had pushed the young man aside and walked with steady purpose toward Emma, who shrank visibly at his approach. He did not stop until he had come very close. Then he held out his hand. "Come with me, Emma," he entreated.

"How dare you?" she repeated, her shrill voice mingling with the indignant execrations her companion was calling. Karan ignored them. He extended both of his arms, in an entreating gesture. "Come home with me, Emma."

Tears were gathering in her eyes, and she shook her head. "Go away!" The words were a hiss and a whisper.

"I love you," Karan said. "You know that beyond any doubt, Emma. I will not leave you here."

Then he did for her what she was powerless to do for herself. He gathered her hands up in his and pulled her to her feet. He put his arm around her, strongly, protectively. He walked with her out of the room. He did not pause or look back, nor did she. They walked out together, out of the room, out of the building. Karan had a carriage waiting, and he put her inside, climbing in after her, never letting go his touch of her.

"We drove a long way," Karan told me, "as far from the waterfront and your Emma's world as I could take her."

For the remainder of that night he stayed with her, talked to her, listened. When at last she slept he watched by her bedside until his own eyes became heavy. Then he called down to the desk and had the kindly, middle-aged woman he had talked to earlier come into the room.

"Watch the lass," he told her. "I can stave sleep off no longer. But if she stirs, wake me."

Mercifully, they both slept for hours, and he was there when she wakened. No one, gazing into Karan's eyes, could keep up a pretense for long. He sat with his arms round her, and they talked again for hours—and he gave her reason to hope, to know there could be forgiveness in her life, and a reason to begin all over again.

"She never went back," Karan told me. "I never took her near Aunt Emma and her old friends again."

The odd thing was that Emma made no complaint whatsoever; with a pathetic, childlike gratitude, she placed herself entirely in Karan's hands.

"I returned," he explained, "to gather up her poor effects and settle with Kishan, who was much relieved to see Emma safely out of there."

"How does *he* manage with Emma?" I asked.

"He is a man; it is entirely different. Besides, Lottie, she has changed."

"Indeed," I agreed, "to a loathsome and tragic degree."

Young Michael Cunningham had disappeared by the time Karan returned on the following day. There was no trace of him, and no one had any idea where he might have gone.

"It is as well," Karan said. And I knew he had been tempted nearly beyond himself to take the vengeance of the Lord into his own hands.

We let Emma take her time. She was very much like an invalid coming out of a long spell of weakness and illness, not sure of her bearings as yet. She was changed—and that gave me my greatest hope. The softness in her was not all lethargy. She seemed to enjoy having the children around her, listening to their prattle, reading their little books to them, playing simple games. When Gracie told her of the progress of the opera, her eyes warmed, and there was a sincerity in her responses that had not been a visible part of her make-up before. For long spells she would just sit and look out of the window or play with the crow, who seemed to take to her; and that pleased her too. She had never read much; now there was always a book in her lap or near at hand. I had prayed for many of the things I was see-ing. I kept on praying, and giving her time.

Abbey's twins came early, twins often do. Winston and Karan blessed her, and the labor went smoothly. Though the babies were small, looking hardly half the size of a normal newborn, they seemed to possess pluck and spirit as they struggled their way into this life. Two little girls, with red hair and, for the time being, blue eyes. "Daughters," Abbey breathed, gazing up at me.

"The marrow of life," I smiled, kissing her wan cheek. "The very heart of it all."

On the very day Amelia and Emmeline were born, we received word from Sita that the future Earl of Corwood and Longbrook was on his way. *Blood of ours in England again,* I thought, and the thought was strangely pleasing to me.

Fully three weeks after her return Emma looked up from the book she was reading and fixed me with her eye. "Do you hate Aunt Emma?" she asked.

I caught my breath and considered a moment. "I try not to," I answered, "and most times I manage. I feel a great sadness, and a ter-rible compassion for her."

"She is dying, you know."

"Emma!"

"It is some ailment of the blood and liver. She is eaten up with disease. Did Karan not tell you?"

I shook my head.

"He will, in time. It is his way of shielding you just a little." The words were spoken with obvious tenderness. I knew that the bonds between the two of them, forged in pain, as they had been, were sacred to her.

"She must be terrified," I mused.

"That is it, Mother! I think she is. It has made her—ugly. She cares for nothing and no one."

I wanted to weep. Weep for the old Emmer who had saved my life from despair once; weep for the pale daughter before me, whose experiences had been such that she could say, in hollow tones: *It has made her ugly.* I wondered if I would ever know what things she suffered during those days.

The birth of the twins helped to rouse Emma out of her stupor. She volunteered to spend several days with Abbey, caring for her and the children while she got back her strength. It would be a good association; I knew that. And service, service always has a lightening effect upon the heart that gives.

I was encouraged one morning in late October when Emma announced that she was going over to Merin's to practice on the piano. "Susie is begging me to play for her productions," she explained. "And Gracie needs help with the costumes, now that she has become preoccupied with the immigrants."

"Whatever do you mean?" I asked.

"The group of Italians who arrived a few weeks ago. She and Dante have found places nearby for most of them to live. Gracie has them over to dinner every night it seems, tends their babies, takes them shopping. Now she is organizing an English class, free of charge, of course."

"I am glad to hear it," I cried. And I was. The opera was fine, but helping real flesh and blood people—Gracie opening her heart and home to the needy; that pleased me well.

Then suddenly, out of nowhere, an ugly thing happened that wounded us all.

Karan had been asked to serve on one of the university committees that would be formulating curriculum for the next few years. On the same committee was Brother David Tucker who lived in our ward.

When the first meeting was held and he looked up and saw Karan enter with some of the others and take his seat round the board, Brother Tucker pushed back his own chair, gathered up his papers, and walked out of the room. The following day he resigned his position. *I will not sit with that brown-skinned hypocrite,* he said firmly. By the night it was well known that he had put his house up for sale.

"He is one man," I reminded Karan. "He is out of line, out of step with the Spirit, as well as being foolish and cruel. It will pass."

"It will not pass," Karan responded through clenched teeth, "any more than Abbey would have been healed just because we wanted it so."

I was worried, worried and heart-sick. The days passed. Sunday came, and attendance at the meeting was obviously sparse; and Brother Tucker's family was obviously missing from their usual pew.

Why? I asked the silent vault of heaven. *Has not our travail been enough?*

The weather turned. Black clouds and a cold mist poured down from the canyons. We built up the fires and took our heavy sweaters out of moth balls. I felt small and vulnerable; the first real cold of winter does that to me. I prayed and, as with Emma, I tried to wait upon the hand of the Lord.

Two weeks after David Tucker announced that the house he had built with his own hands and boasted of so lovingly was for sale, the wet cold blew into a blizzard. They sky was filled with tiny ice shards and brittle hail. The wind rose and would not be still. When I put the lights out I remember thinking how much the night felt and sounded like Dacca, where the darkest of nightmares abound.

I do not know how long we slept, or what the hour when Karan shook me awake with an urgent hand. "Dress warmly, Lottie," he instructed. "And come with me. Quickly!"

Within minutes we were ready to walk out of the house. When Karan opened the door the entire sky seemed to be lit by a sunset of orange and red—a lurid red, dusky, yet pulsing. My fuzzy mind strained to remember . . . this felt so familiar, smelled so familiar . . . *Nauvoo!* I glanced about wildly. Now I could smell a fire—see flames licking through sightless windows—across the street, on the other corner of the lot. *Heaven help us!* I muttered. *Brother Tucker's house.*

Karan was already moving, dragging me with him. "I have sent Emma to rouse the other neighbors," he told me. "Now, Lottie, you do as I say."

I nodded; I did not have a mind to cause him further distress right now.

"You take Sister Tucker and the children home to our house and *stay there*. We will have plenty of help once the brethren gather. Anyone who is hurt, any women who feel they must do something to help, I will send over to you."

As we approached the house the heat met us, like an invisible wall, filled with stinging bees. "That is the smoke," Karan warned, as I rubbed at my eye. "Here, use this."

He pushed a dampened handkerchief into my hand, bent over and kissed me, then disappeared into the smoke. I stood a moment, suddenly alone, feeling engulfed in the billows of gray, fearful and threatening. Then I caught sight of Sister Tucker and hurried toward her.

"Come with me, Mary," I urged. She drew away from the touch of my hand, but I persisted. "The children," I reminded her. "It is not safe for them here."

That seemed to rouse her. Together we gathered them and headed out of the close, lurid atmosphere to where the stars shone cold in the windy night.

I wish I had been there. The hours I spent, making bread and cheese sandwiches and putting children to bed, left something to be desired. Emma saw part; it was she who first came running, disheveled and wild-eyed, to tell me. "Karan has walked right into the blaze. No one could stop him, Mother."

Those were the longest moments of my life; I do not like to look back on them, I do not like to remember.

It was hours before the fire was controlled, and the men traipsed, soot-blackened and stiff with the cold, back to their various houses. And, during those ragged hours, I died half a dozen deaths.

At last the kitchen was put in order, the children all sleeping. I was in the parlor serving hot cider to Emma and Sister Tucker, so I saw them walk into the house—Brother Tucker and Karan together, Brother Tucker's arm round Karan's shoulder, half-supporting him. I saw the look on his face. I knew *something* had happened and, whatever it was that had happened, things would now be all right.

Karan was burned, but not badly. Old Dr. Mitchell had already treated him. The men were weary to the point of exhaustion; we fed them and put them to bed. The following morning Brother Tucker took his family to his sister's house where they would stay while repairs were made to his own. Karan went with him; Karan had many things to attend to. I played the woman's endless role, and waited, and bided my time.

When he returned at last, I knew the waiting was over. He sank into his favorite chair, and I curled up at his feet. "What was it? What happened in that fire last night to answer your prayer?"

"Only Brother Tucker and two of his sons were in the house," Karan began, "when I first arrived. They were frightened, and it did not please them to see me walk in. 'What brings you here?' David growled. 'I do not remember calling for help.'

'But you did,' I answered, 'when you stood on the landing and looked into the blazing roar of your kitchen you asked God to be merciful and spare your efforts. You were worried about your bad back; you did not see how you could build such a place again.'"

"How did you know this?" I marveled.

"I did not, Lottie. The Spirit put the words into my mouth. After that we went to work, using axes to cut away the charred timbers, trying to contain the blaze, soaking the walls which had not caught yet. Men came one by one or in small groups; I do not remember, except that I called out orders and we all worked in harmony. I could feel that, Lottie, through the fear and confusion."

I reached for his hand and tucked it under my chin, stroking the long warm fingers as he continued.

"We were successful. We managed to isolate the ruined portion of the house and maintain our control of the rest. And at length the fire, further discouraged by the water we dumped on it, began to burn itself out. Then suddenly"—He ran his other hand through his hair— "there is a small back bedroom behind the kitchen; I did not know this, Lottie, but suddenly a picture came to me, clear in my mind. I could see a young man stretched out on a bed. He was sleeping, and the flames began to curl along the edge of the bedclothes, and the black smoke poured out of them. I moved without thinking. As I started into the fire, Brother Tucker caught at my arm.

'What are you doing?' he demanded. 'You can't go back there.'

'A young man is asleep in the bedroom,' I answered. 'If I do not go, he will burn to death.'

His face blanched and he swayed on his feet. 'That is my son,' he moaned. 'He works at a ranch outside of town. Sometimes he comes in late, just crawls into that bed back there—'

'You cannot go,' said another. 'You cannot save him. There is no reason for two men to die.'"

Karan shuddered; the remembering was painful for him. But I could not help urging him.

"Karan, please! What happened then?"

"I am not altogether certain. I remember turning and facing the others. I remember saying something like this: 'the Spirit has shown me the young boy, and I have faith that the Spirit will protect both of us, for God does not touch men's hearts in vain.' Then I walked in. I do not remember feeling anything until I walked out with the boy."

I sat with my head resting against his knees. I could not speak to him, and he understood that. I think he even understood the extent of my love for him. He did not realize how weak and insignificant I felt, how my pride in him was mingled with a terrible sense of inadequacy, an awareness of how far above mine his spirit stood. But then again, perhaps he did. For when he leaned over and kissed my hair and the back of my neck he whispered, "It was not myself; I know that. I was only the vehicle, because I wanted to be. And that desire, would it exist without you, Lottie? without what you lifted me to? without your patience and faith, when I gave you no reason to hope or believe?"

Karan sees with the eyes of the sage. It is a gift of his people, one he has always possessed. "God took what was there," he explained, "and through his blessing magnified it that I might be able to serve."

A simple explanation, as he gave it, yet touched with the solemnities of eternity which, as the wise soul knows, all good things in our mortal lives are.

Emma worked, as though in work she would find absolution. She spoke little of what she was thinking or feeling, of what was happening inside. But I knew she was spending much of her time again with Karan, and that was good. She would turn to him, and he would know how to help her, how to carefully reintroduce the love of her Heavenly Father back into her life.

One day as we were making pies together, she said, "I have decided to begin teaching piano lessons. Aunt Merin said I could use the piano and have the parlor to myself two afternoons a week. I have three students already who are interested."

"I think that is a splendid idea. Your students are fortunate," I said warmly.

"One is a boy from Wales," she continued. "Just come over. When he gets excited, Mother, I cannot understand one word in five that he says."

My heart caught. This was progress, and I knew it. Time was part of the answer, time to heal, time in which the wounded heart could let go and forget.

By Christmas the boy from Wales, Dylan Morgan, was walking Emma home following his weekly lesson. By February he was staying for dinner and often far into the evening. By March Emma took me aside one night after Fielding was sleeping, took me out into the dim sitting room where the lamps had not been lit yet and it would be easy to talk.

"I want to have a testimony," she said. "The way Karan does. I want to know what it is that makes him, and men like him, good."

I knew what my daughter meant by *men like him*. I held my breath and uttered a silent prayer. "Read then," I began, "you cannot love God if you do not know him. Pray. He will come to you in the silences of your soul."

She was shaking her head. "I am not worthy," she whispered.

"Karan is your bishop," I said. "Have you spoken with him of these things?"

"He knows all. He says God has forgiven me, but I have not forgiven myself."

"Ah. He is right, of course." We both said it in the same breath, and both of us smiled. "You are worthy if you want to be, if each day you make yourself a little better than the last."

"Mother!" she cried. "Can there ever be happiness for me?"

"Emma, dearest, how can you ask . . . when you have already looked into its eyes?"

With April, the earth stirred into remembrance and wakefulness. Sita sent a photograph of her new son, and Abbey's twins began learning to crawl. Fielding, who was three and a half, knew a dozen nursery rhymes by heart. He could ride the neighbor boy's pony so well that his father bought him his own. He had three frogs and a little caged canary for pets, and he fed them each day himself. He liked me to sing him to sleep every night, and he could say his own prayers, never forgetting anything of importance, though he had to interrupt himself sometimes and ask, to be sure.

In April Gracie told us she was expecting her first child, and Julian opened another shop. During spring conference Arthur and Merin were called to serve a mission to the Hawaiian islands.

May was approaching when Emma once more cornered me. But this time she was not alone. Dylan Morgan, with his broad Welsh face and his deep-set eyes, stood beside her, holding her hand comfortingly in his own.

"Dylan and I have a problem," she began, but the way in which she said it belied the words.

"My mother, back in Wales, has been ill most of the winter. But I have just received word from my aunt there that her condition improves. She has sent money. She wishes me to return so that I might accompany her back here, to Zion."

"Your mother has such means?"

"My mother's aunt, who is her dead mother's sister."

I glanced at Emma and smiled faintly. "That has a familiar ring."

Dylan cleared his throat. I had not realized that I was making him nervous. Emma leaned forward. "Dylan and I wish to get married, Mother, before he sails for England . . . so that I might go along." There was elation in her voice and hope; and I thrilled to the sound.

"I have already spoken to the bishop, to your husband," Dylan assured me. "He has given us his blessing."

"Good." I smiled. "I am glad of it. For I give you mine, too." That was a moment of joy I had not thought to experience! "Just think," I said, "you and Dylan can travel to Baddenwell and see your new nephew—and see Sita, after all these long years."

"I never dreamed, Mother!" There were tears in Emma's eyes. "I have wanted to travel, I have wanted to experience things. I could never have imagined or dreamed anything better than how it is going to be."

"That is because God's ways are not our ways," I told them. "We walk imperfectly, stumbling and groping. But he has compassion upon us; it is his joy to bless us, to give us full measure, until our cup runs over. It is his desire to lift us to walk with him in the light."

That is the sum of it. The days of my life no longer overwhelm me. Each one is a blessing in its own right. Each small space of hours contains, within its brief span, the heartbeat of the universe. And, when I try to listen, I hear the beating of my own heart too.

All of my days my Father in Heaven has been mindful of me, has guided my path, has placed me and my loved ones where he wants us to be. And I marvel at his power, at his generosity and his love.

With Karan's help I have learned to place each day, like the precious gift that it is, into my Father's hands. I have learned for myself how completely I can trust him. The journey goes on. I walk with joy in my heart. For, as Karan says, love and truth united create an indestructible landscape of joy.

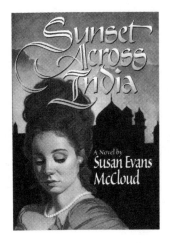

A Novel by
Susan Evans
McCloud

In *Sunset Across India,* Charlotte's chance encounter with a handsome Indian soldier, who helps her after she is bitten by a poisonous scorpion, has forever changed her life. But the social system in 1830s India is rigid and often cruel, and Charlotte—raised in an English household, despite the Indian blood in her veins—is prevented from seeing him further.

Caught between two cultures, Charlotte struggles to understand her situation, those around her, and ultimately herself. Along the way she is confronted by events that test her character in ways she never imagined. The exotic imagery of India lends itself to the drama of this tale as the strong-willed young heroine finds that happiness and despair are often closely intertwined.

Best-selling author Susan Evans McCloud has created fresh characters and a consistently captivating story that charts one woman's harrowing experiences and determined courage. The compelling blend of romance and adventure adds zest to this mesmerizing and moving novel.

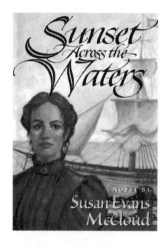

In *Sunset Across the Waters,* the stirring saga that began in *Sunset Across India* continues and shows how one life can be dramatically changed by the events and individuals it encounters. In *Sunset Across the Waters,* the friendship between Charlotte Hillard and Seth Taylor, a gentle, gray-eyed Mormon, has deepened, and Charlotte, despite her reluctance, finds herself increasingly drawn to his religion. Eventually it leads her to gather with the Saints in America, where she discovers the joys of living among those who share her newfound faith.

But as Charlotte experiences the challenges of living in a new land with new ways and new beliefs, she finds that her happiness is not untouched by trial. Sustained by her faith, she learns she must also rely upon the love of those around her.

Readers will be caught up in the romance and drama of this tale about a woman whose courage increases with every test.